Praise for *Ahnwee Days*

While Ahnwee, Minnesota, like many small towns, seemed destined to fade into oblivion, now it is facing extinction, until a group of determined citizens band together to save it. The cast of characters is both bumbling and wily as it fights off the powers that be, including a lascivious politician and one particularly noxious hog farmer. William E Burleson has written a comic novel that will keep you laughing as you root for his quirky characters and Ahnwee's victory.

Lorna Landvik,
author of *Patty Jane's House of Curl*

A story filled with quirky and memorable characters, Burleson tells it with a light-hearted humor that kept me laughing throughout. He paints a vivid and somewhat absurd detailed picture of a small midwestern town with a flavor of storytelling that took me into the lives of his characters and set me down at the table with them. A perfect blend of hapless good-guys and deplorable bad-guys.

R.R. Davis,
author of *The Various Stages of a Garden Well-Kept*
and *Squid Boy Raven Girl*

In this carnival ride of a novel, William E Burleson invokes the nostalgic ghosts of small towns past, the spirit of Garrison Keillor, and a raw and contemporary perspective that urges readers to keep laughing and carry on.

Elisa Sinnett,
author of *Detroit Fairy Tales*

Place: Ahnwee, Minnesota. A very small town.

Population: A full cast of quirky characters.

Problem #1: A-casino rich Indian tribe claim the land on which the town was built belongs to them.

Problem #2: A local pig farmer claims his family inherited the town when the founders grew bored with the place and left.

Problem #3: The state bureaucracy claims the town does not actually exist.

Solution: Read *Ahnwee Days*.

Richard Hartman,
author of *A Night in the Woods*

Ahnwee Days brings us on a humorous and deeply poignant journey into the soul of today's American heartland where a cast of bruised and weary characters, after passively watching their small-town waste away, suddenly jump into action and fight like hell when faced with its extinction. This is a beautifully rendered story of small-town, large-hearted people fighting the complex social and economic forces that swoop down like vultures to destroy today's rural communities. While fiction, the lessons of Ahnwee offer a vivid blueprint for how self-will, self-determination, family and community can overcome all the money and corruption in the world. This all said, fair warning – do not read *Ahnwee Days* while drinking a hot beverage, lest you burn yourself laughing; this may be the most side-splittingly funny book you've ever read.

Frank Haberle,
author of *Downlanders*

Unlike the blades of Ahnwee's errant wind turbine, William Burleson's deviously delightful portrayal of a dying small town comes at you with a facetious wit... like Fargo on steroids...

Vincent Wyckoff, author of *Beware of Cat*

You have no need to be concerned about suffering from ennui while reading William Burleson's *Ahnwee Days*, because this is a witty, comic novel that will keep you laughing from beginning to end. Ahnwee is in (fictional) fact the name of a dying little town on the plains west of the Twin Cities of Minneapolis and St. Paul, where one day over a hundred years ago the town's founder heard a hooker of French descent from the neighboring town of Despar (so easy to misread as Despair) exclaim, "Ah. Oui!" and, apparently very happy with what he heard, named the Town Ahnwee. The novel's modern-day heroine, Sybil, cast by the local media as a "New York dominatrix," has returned home to care for her demented father and, having become mayor, is determined, with her team of supporters, to save the town from the destruction posed by a number of powerful and amusing villains (one of the worst of them being a fellow named Balzac – no relation to the French writer, unless there's a part of the writer's life I know nothing about). Can she succeed? Or will she need some form of divine – or less than divine – intervention?"

Brian Duren,
award winning author of *Whiteout*, *Ivory Black*,
and *The Gravity of Love*

An engaging tale of a speck of a Minnesota town where old arthritic dogs can safely enjoy a nap in the middle of main street and old men living off Social Security can peek a bit of flesh at the local strip club. Ahnwee may sound like Ennui, but that's where the similarities end. Sybil, Ahnwee born-and-raised, is back from the Big Apple and caring for her elderly father who's prone to wandering the town pantless. Now mayor, Sybil's fighting impossible odds to stop Ahnwee from disappearing all together. Hilarious, heartfelt, and humane, Ahnwee grabbed me from page one and kept me reading all night.

Brian Malloy, author of *After Francesco*

Ahnwee Days

WILLIAM E BURLESON

A Blackwater Press book

First published in the United States of America by
Blackwater Press, LLC

Library of Congress Control Number: 2024933262

ISBN: 978-1-963614-00-8

Cover design by Eilidh Muldoon

Blackwater Press
120 Capitol Street
Charleston, WV 25301
United States

blackwaterpress.com

*Dedicated to all the people across the country
who make small towns wonderful.*

The Foreword No One Reads

In the middle of the continent of North America lies the metropolis of the twin cities of Minneapolis and St. Paul, Minnesota. A thriving, vital, prosperous home to three-and-a-half million people, the cities are a veritable Portland, Oregon, of the Midwest, over-supplied with microbrews, wine bars, independent coffee shops, and Green Party politics.

But this is not a story about the Twin Cities.

For our tale, we'll need to take a small plane west from MSP, out over the sprawling shaded suburbs, past the tony lakes of Minnetonka, over the model towns of Hutchinson and Willmar, beyond the last of the trees and over vast, flat golden fields of corn that make up the easternmost Great Plains. Eventually, we will spy a reasonably large casino and a ridiculously huge wind turbine factory near an eerily green lake. Circle around, and you may notice a tiny town, hardly a speck.

This story is about that speck.

Chapter 1: Flounder's Day

The day Sybil's dad walked naked down Broadway was supposed to be a good day. A day for making hay. The day that Sybil finally did something right as mayor. But it didn't turn out that way. That wasn't Dan's fault, or at least not all his fault – the old man's saggy nudity simply added the cherry on top of the shit sundae that was Ahnwee Days.

Shortly before her dad's stroll through town, Sybil had been leaning on the canopy pole in front of Knotty Knits, looking out at a nearly empty main street. Ruby, the proprietor of said store, sat motionless, except for her hands, furiously knitting away on what appeared to be a stocking cap. On the table next to her sat skeins and skeins of brightly colored yarn.

"What are you knitting?" Sybil asked.

The white-haired woman didn't miss a stitch. "I'm thinking it'll be a tractor cozy."

"Wow, no kidding."

Ruby stopped and looked up at her. "Yes, kidding. It's a hat."

Bud, an arthritic yellow lab, lumbered into the middle of Broadway and laid down in middle of the empty street with all the grace of dropping a honey-baked ham. Not for the first time Sybil wondered, whose dog is that? Sybil related to the dog's lethargy. If there were still a bank in downtown Ahnwee, its sign would have said ninety-six degrees. Sybil's New York friends always asked her about Minnesota winters, but they had no concept of how hot it got in the summer. Sure, winter featured below zero temps along with icy roads and the occasional killer blizzard, but summer came with unrelenting heat plus biting flies and mosquitoes. As her dad used to say when he could still use coherent and appropriate clichés, "You can't win for losing."

A light prairie breeze brought an invisible, stifling veil of pig shit to the few occupants of Broadway. When the wind came from any other direction it wasn't so bad, but when the wind came from the south across Björn Björkman's pig manure pond – a shit field nearly the size of the town itself – you could practically shovel it.

"This stinks," Sybil said.

"The air?"

"No – yes, that too – I mean Ahnwee Days."

"It's a beautiful day. Sun's shining. We're alive. What more could we ask for?" Ruby said.

"People. Sales."

Ruby stopped knitting, paused, and said, "Yeah, this sucks."

Ahnwee Days had been Sybil's idea, and she tried everything she could to make it a success. She posted an announcement on the *Hello Minnesota!* tourism website months in advance. She personally went around hanging old-school flyers in not only what remained of Ahnwee but also neighboring towns like Despar, Montevideo, Granite Falls, all the way to Willmar. No grocery store bulletin board missed, no café entrance forgotten.

"Is there anything else you want me to do, Mayor?"

Sybil jumped, startled by the skinny, shaky young man behind her. "No, thanks, G. There's nothing anyone can do here."

G, dressed in western wear, didn't seem to know where to put his arms. "All right, okay, then." He drifted off in no particular direction. Gilbert, or "G," the town tweaker, lived in the abandoned grain elevator. Sybil felt sorry for him, so she gave him some honest work, hiring him to walk around Ahnwee Days dressed as the town's founder, Maximilian Schroeder Junior, an immigrant from Germany who opened a hotel on the lake, the event mistakenly recognized as the beginnings of the town. No one knew what Maximilian Schroeder Junior looked like or what he might have worn, so Sybil set G up with your basic cowboy-type outfit with pointy boots, ten-gallon hat, and bolo tie, all stuff she had around her antique store.

Earlier in the day, Sybil had G stand on a wobbly ladder and hang a big banner across Broadway. That was no small job. Like many small town main streets, the town founders laid it out to be the next Hennepin Avenue in Minneapolis or, for those who dared dream, State Street in Chicago. Sybil had to order a ridiculously long sixty-five-foot banner, which was a big investment for the small town, costing nearly the entire town improvement budget for the year. "Ahnwee Flounder's Day, June 19," it said. Looked good, she thought. Putting the date on it was a mistake, though, as everyone pointed out. If it were more generic, they could use the banner next year and the year after – should they decide to try again, of course – until it finally wore out or blew away. With a date, it was a one-shot wonder. Her bad. The "Flounder's" part, on the other hand, was the fault of the potheads at Let's Go Crazy Printz in Despar. Sybil picked it up on Thursday, far too late to make them redo it. She hoped people wouldn't read it that

5

close – the mind is great for reading what it wants, and no one would expect to see a town celebrating "Flounder's Day."

"Do you think anyone's making money?" Sybil asked Ruby.

"I think it's safe to say no."

In the morning, some of their fellow townspeople left their houses and their TVs and checked out the festival. Not many, but some. The approximately two hundred souls in Ahnwee were nearly all elderly since most younger people – needing amenities such as jobs and places to go and things to do – had long since left for more successful pastures. The remaining seniors didn't get out much, and when they did, they didn't part easily with their meager Social Security.

Sybil and Ruby were two of six vendors out to capitalize on the first annual town celebration. They made for an interesting pair. Sybil Voss, mid-thirties, tall with long, sort of blond hair, imbued the last fizzle of youth and the first capitulation to her coming middle-age. Ruby Berlitz, on the other hand, a mid-sixties, roundish matriarch, maybe five foot tall, would win a Miss Cherubic USA Pageant hands down. Sybil wore yoga pants and a turtleneck. Ruby wore a hand-knit angora sweater (how could she be wearing a sweater in this heat? Sybil in her turtleneck wondered), a peasant skirt, and Birkenstocks (how could she wear a peasant skirt and Birkenstocks in any weather? Sybil wondered as well).

Sybil watched as Bud slowly got up and meandered across the street. The old yellow lab drifted in front of what once had been a grocery, where Sigmund Klein sat under another white tent, shrink-wrapped packages laid out on a table. Sig was a little person, coming in on the ruler by the door of the Stop and Pop in Despar at four foot one. He looked asleep, slouching in a lime-green kid's camp chair.

Down the street from Sig, Augie Flump, his potbelly tent-ing out a dirty white apron, leaned against the wall of his café in the shade by his gas grill, arms crossed, spatula in hand. The sign on his café said, "Flump's Café: Home of the Original Flump Burger." The old dog waddled over and sat in front of Augie, tail wagging. "Hungry, Bud? Here ya go," he said. He picked a burnt bratwurst off the grill, leaned over, and offered it to the hound. The dog sniffed it. Augie wiggled the brat temptingly. The dog turned and ambled down the sidewalk. Augie flung the sausage at him, missing badly.

The lab next drifted by an old couple seated in elaborate camp chairs, the man wearing rainbow suspenders and his wife a t-shirt with a picture of the grandkids (so Sybil assumed). The couple made and sold lawn butts, which are lawn flair in the image of a round butt of a person, generally female, bending over doing something constructive like weeding the garden, revealing frilly bloomers. The husband cut these whimsical pieces of rural Americana out of plywood and his wife painted them. They must have had fifty or more lawn butts to choose from, big and small.

A block away, in front of the Third Lutheran Church, Pastor Farber had his jacket off, but his shirt buttoned to the top as always, stiff white collar just so, as he stood behind a table of baked goods. The good pastor had told Sybil that he hoped to sell a few goodies to raise money for building maintenance. The 1912 Christopher Wren-style building needed a lot of repairs, from roof to foundation; however, the good pastor couldn't even afford candles since the few people who still went to his church, all over seventy, didn't have a nickel.

"You know," Ruby said as if reading Sybil's mind, or at least the direction of her gaze, "He put out a call for baked goods to sell to the hungry mobs, and he didn't get anything but some stale kolaches from Mrs. Andersen. He took it upon himself to bake everything from scratch. He spent all week making cinnamon bread, big sticky rolls, and sugar cookies shaped like Christ the Redeemer."

Right on cue, Pastor Farber reached down, picked up a cookie, and bit the head off Jesus.

Three old fat men, townies, wearing overalls and seed caps, walked past the church. Maybe they are going to look around? Sybil hoped. Instead, they stopped, looked up, and one of the guys pointed at the banner, and they all laughed. They crossed the street and went into Dirty Girls.

Dirty Girls was the shame of Ahnwee: a strip joint, or, as Augie called it, a "titty bar." Technically, Dirty Girls wasn't a bar since it only served non-alcoholic beverages, but there definitely were lots of titties. Sadly, it was the one business that drew people into town on weekends, resulting in no small amount of public urination and other classless insults to poor Ahnwee. At least Jackson, the Dirty Girls owner, and his crew stayed home. Sybil had fully expected Jackson's girls to be offering Flounder's Days lap dances right on Broadway.

"It's two o'clock, Sybil…" Ruby said.

"You're right, you're right, it will probably still pick up. No reason to despair."

"I was going to say maybe it's time to go home."

Right then, as if to save the day, in the prairie distance a GMC Denali crested the hill on the edge of town. Just as the county road turned into Broadway, it screeched to a halt as an enormous pale-blue wind turbine blade swept down across the road just inches off the asphalt. The Denali sat for a moment, as if to say, "What the…" before turning right, onto a side street, avoiding the huge blade altogether.

Hope renewed, Sybil speed-walked back down the street to her own canopy in front of her antique shop, New York 'Tique. In honor of Founder's Day, she had pulled out tables and tables of matchbox cars, Barbie dolls, souvenir plates, doll tea sets, big-eyed children pictures, butter churns, hats, fast-food glasses, broken music boxes, Beanie Babies, Happy Meal toys, unfinished needlepoint, string art, used coloring books, puzzles (guaranteed to be missing pieces), eight-track tapes, broken cameras, lamps without shades, and half of a parachute. Unfortunately, her only sale for the day was to the yard butt couple who bought a wagon wheel, at a discount, to cut in half and put at the entrance of their driveway.

As expected, the Denali reappeared, turning onto Broadway. It slowly rolled by Sybil, tinted windows up. When after two blocks it ran out of business district, the Denali did a U-turn in the middle of the street and made a second pass, this time stopping right in front of New York 'Tique. Loud vintage Dolly Parton music poured out in the second between the passenger door opening and the engine turning off. An older couple got out.

"What's the smell?" The beefy male driver wore cowboy boots and a plaid shirt and wrinkled his nose.

His wife had a beehive and wore a shiny gold top over her oversized breasts. She slapped her cell, using this tried-and-true method to improve an electronic device's performance. "I can't get a signal. I knew I shouldn't have gone with AT&T."

It wouldn't have mattered who she went with, the good mayor thought, since there simply was no service in Ahnwee. She saw no need to provide that detail.

"So, is the lake famous for flounders or something?" the man said, making Sybil flinch. The man pointed across the street, "Look, Dolly," (Really? No kidding? Dolly? Sybil thought.) "jerky." He stared in amazement. "And the guy selling it is a midget. Isn't that something."

Sybil felt compelled to say, "Excuse me, but the term is 'little person.'"

If the man heard Sybil, he didn't show it. "I'm going to go get me some Midget Jerky," he said, crossing the street to Sig.

Dolly the Dolly Parton clone walked under Sybil's tent, switching to shopping mode, head swiveling around, stopping at nothing. "Do you have any Precious Moments?" Sybil detected a bit of an accent but couldn't identify it.

"No, sorry." Dolly's fingernails were amazing. Could she pick anything up?

Yet she could, picking up a rusty beer sign, seemingly just to be doing something. "They're so cute, you know? Those big eyes. I must have a hundred of them by now."

"Yeah, they're different."

Apparently lost on Dolly was that calling something "different" was the biggest insult possible in Minnesota. The woman drifted between the tables of stuff. Sybil surveyed her domain. What brought her to sell this junk? She had always loved antiques: Red Wing Pottery, Russel Wright, Roseville, McCoy, Rookwood, Van Briggle. Nice Danish Modern furniture. High-style fifties lamps. She had done well with this selection in New York. She had had a clientele. When she moved back to Ahnwee, she went into the same business she was in in New York. Now, two years since putting up her shingle, she had all but abandoned these fine examples of mid-century design in favor of selling wagon wheels and rusty beer signs.

"Oh! Lawn butts!" Dolly pointed and yelled. She crossed the street, struggling to walk normally in her ridiculous heels.

Sybil sighed.

Down the street, Dolly's husband finished a transaction with Sig. In the quietude that was Founder's Day Sybil could hear Sig say, "Yeah, that's highly offensive. We prefer to be called 'little people.'"

"What's up with the wind turbine?" the man asked Sig, changing the subject seemingly less out of embarrassment and more out of lack of interest. "I've never seen anything like it. Isn't there a building code or something for those monsters?"

If the smell was Ahnwee's most indelible olfactory sensation, the wind turbine at the end of Broadway was the town's most dramatic sight. Five blocks away on the edge of town, next to a water tower spray-painted "Despar Rules!" the Wind Energy Now wind turbine's blades swooped high over the town. Wind turbines are a common sight in this part of the country, if less common standing alone and not as part of a wind farm. But that's not what made this wind turbine special: The blades were too long and the pedestal too short, and anyone driving into town needed to have good timing. It was like a giant miniature golf course with cars as the ball.

Right on cue, a car came down the hill and through the wind turbine. It had to be a local, because out-of-towners never drove through; they always freaked out and went around on a side street.

As it got closer, she could see it was a convertible '56 Chevy and, top down, who was in it.

Sybil sighed even louder.

The Chevy rolled down Broadway and skidded to a stop on the wrong side of the street, right in front of the GMC Denali and Sybil. "Cindy! How's Flounder's Days going? Bringing in the bacon?" the little rotund man yelled from the passenger seat.

"Flounder's" made Sybil flinch once again. To Sybil, County Commissioner Harry Balzac was a gasbag, both in his self-aggrandizing blathering and in his general physical shape. "It's Sybil, not Cindy. And it's going fine, Commissioner. Things are going fine." Another gust brought the stink of pig shit to a new level, and Sybil tried hard to keep a sincere-looking smile.

Jon Fjord, the mayor of Despar, sat behind the wheel. Sybil had met him once briefly at a mayor's conference. She had not formed an opinion of him at the time, but for sure, joy-riding with Balzac meant he was worthy of suspicion. Sure, he was a handsome man – fit, with dark, bedroom eyes – but Sybil dismissed him immediately as a tanning-bed victim who probably had a punch card at a manicurist. Both men wore suits, an unusual sight in this more jeans-and-seed-cap part of the county.

"What brings you two to our fair city?" Sybil asked, standing next to her table of Coke memorabilia.

Balzac banged his car door against a butter churn. He didn't seem to care. Jon Fjord got out as well, the yellow lab walking over, tail wagging. "Hey, Bud." Fjord patted him on the head and scratched behind his ears. Balzac looked around as if inspecting his property. "The lord gave us a beautiful day for a drive, so we thought we'd see how your Flounder's Day was faring. Plus, I haven't been to your beautiful town in a while, Mayor," he said without looking at Sybil.

"Like I said, it's going fine. How's it going in Despar, Mayor Fjord?"

"Jon. Call me Jon. Great. Great. Have you been to Home Depot?"

"No."

"They opened a couple weeks ago, but today was the grand opening. The commissioner and I cut the ribbon, thus the duds." He waved at his suit. "Had to be a thousand of people there. You wouldn't believe it."

"That must have been rewarding for you," she said, looking at Balzac. "I know how much you like big business." Sybil was trying to be nice, but she knew that sounded snarky. However, if Balzac or Fjord picked up on it, they didn't show it.

"God rewards those who succeed," said Balzac as Jon

Fjord began poking at Sybil's tables of stuff.

Sybil disregarded the Möbius strip of a comment. "How's the hardware store doing?"

"What?" Commissioner Balzac replied, preoccupied, looking across the street at Dolly Parton bending over flipping through the yarn butts, cleavage in full glory.

"The hardware store? How's it doing?"

"Where?"

"In Despar. Norm's Hardware."

"Don't know."

"Do you think Norm will be able to stay in business?"

"I have no idea," Then, coming to his senses, Commissioner Balzac turned back to Sybil, "Norm will be fine. He's a survivor."

"Tough for him to have to compete with Home Depot. He's been on Main Street his whole life. His father opened it, didn't he?"

"Grandfather."

Sybil got distracted momentarily by the thought that that must mean Norm is in fact Norm the Third. "I bet Home Depot will be very appreciative this fall when it comes time for your re-election."

He seemed not to hear her jab. Balzac pulled out a pack of cigarettes from inside his suit jacket, tore off the cellophane and the little area of foil, and threw them to the wind. He lit a smoke with a gold Zippo. Still looking across the street, Balzac took a big drag of his cancer stick and casually flicked it, ash landing on an antique Hamm's Beer bar light.

Fjord waved to Augie and turned to Commissioner Balzac. "Harry, do you want a Flump Burger?"

Harry Balzac said no, and Jon Fjord walked across the street.

Balzac drifted around the tables of junk, pausing occasionally and randomly. Sybil had the distinct feeling he had something on his mind, and it wasn't beer signs.

"Cindy, I heard a rumor. I was wondering if it was true."

"It's 'Sybil,' not 'Cindy.'"

He came in close, as if to whisper, but still talked in a normal voice. "Is it true about that godless man, Björn Björkman?"

Sybil didn't know what Balzac was talking about, and she wished he'd back away.

"I hear he's suing, saying that the town of Ahnwee is his."

Sybil, uncomfortable, wasn't about to show weakness by backing away. "Björn Björkman? The pig farmer?"

"One and the same."

"How could he say that? Ahnwee has been here forever."

"He says he has the deed."

No way. People live here, Sybil thought. People with titles to their houses. Balzac must be wrong. I'm the mayor, wouldn't I know about a lawsuit before anyone?

"If I were you, I'd see what I could do to stop him. Maybe you need a lawyer. Fight that old atheist."

"Look at these lovely yard decorations!" The woman yelled to Sybil as she walked across the street, holding two lawn butts, one in each arm like Moses and the Ten Commandments. "Aren't they wonderful? My book club will howl when they see them." Sybil now knew for sure she wasn't a native Minnesotan, since if "different" is the premier insult, "not bad" is the highest compliment a modest Minnesotan can give. "Wonderful" – now that would be different for someone to say. The husband and Jon Fjord walked back as if they were new old friends, both eating Flump Burgers, while Bud followed slowly but optimistically behind.

Dolly leaned the lawn butts against the back bumper and fiddled with the key fob, while Mr. Dolly tossed his bag of jerky in the SUV through the open window and leaned against the vehicle. The man took a bite of his burger and mid-chew, froze. Dolly froze. Commissioner Balzac dropped the cigarette out of his mouth. Jon Fjord laughed. Bud wagged his tail.

An elderly man walked down the middle of Broadway. All he had on was a cowboy hat: no pants, junk to the wind. He was singing the theme song to *Green Acres*.

"Dad!" Sybil yelled.

Chapter 2: Time For Bars

The screen door slammed behind Sybil as she shooed her father into the house. Dan wore a t-shirt as a bottom, each of his bony legs in an armhole. Back in town that was the best Sybil could do. She had dragged her father into New York 'Tique and asked him to wait as she dug around in a bag of old clothes in back. Sybil found the shirt, but there were no pants anywhere. She decided the shirt-as-a-bottom plan was better than a Dior dress, even though she wasn't sure why and felt guilty for thinking that. By the time she got back to her father he was outside again, halfway down the block with Ruby. Ruby didn't seem flustered a bit, and the casualness of it all made the scene somewhat surreal. Sybil led her father back to the store and somehow got the t-shirt on his bottom half. It should have worked well enough to get him to the car without much more embarrassment, except that her father kept pulling the t-shirt up as far as he could, making his distended old man stuff hang out the neck hole. Sybil would pull it back down, but he would just pull it right back up. There might have been a time Sybil would have felt funny about seeing her father's junk but, for Sybil, modesty was a luxury.

Sybil retrieved a pair of pajama bottoms and brought them to her father in the kitchen. "Please, Dad, put these on," she said, holding them out.

Dan held a piece of white bread. He looked at Sybil; he looked at the bread. He carefully tore the crust off, dropped it on the floor, and rolled the bread into a hard little dough ball. Sybil stood there, left arm getting tired from holding out the pants. Dan took a bite out of the dough ball, looked up, and threw the ball at Sybil, bouncing it off her forehead.

"Please?"

Sybil's father snatched the pajama pants from Sybil and put them over his head, completing his ensemble. On a better day, Sybil might have found this hilarious. Today, it added to her ever-gnawing feeling of hopelessness.

There was a knock at the back door of the Levitt Town-style one-story house. That the knock would be at the back, not front, door was Standard Operating Procedure for Ahnwee – front doors were for company, and if you knew someone, were related to someone, if they were related to someone you know, or if the homeowner had heard of them, then they were no longer company. Needless to say, front doors in Ahnwee didn't get worn out. Most of them didn't even have walks. In this particular case, the knock was more notable for its rarity – not many knocks on the door at the Voss estate.

Sybil opened the door to Ruby holding a tray covered in plastic. "I thought you could use bars."

Ruby followed Sybil in, and, without discussion, Sybil busied herself putting the coffee on. No one in their right mind would have bars without coffee. The kitchen was simple, with asbestos tile floors, a burnt orange stove and an avocado refrigerator, and a great deal of bric-a-brac around the room. That was her mom's legacy, rest her soul. She liked to collect little things, such as saltshakers and toothpick holders, up to items no larger than commemorative plates and cheap plastic snow globes that were mostly half-full, having somehow lost water over the years. The whole house was like that, random collectibles displayed on faux-antique bookcases and curio cabinets. Sybil didn't question it. The tchotchkes were her mother's, and they belonged more than she did. It was like this when she was growing up, and Sybil assumed that's where she got the antique bug. Not that there were any bona fide antiques in the house, but she did seem to inherit the zeal to collect useless things.

"Ruby?" Sybil's dad said, entering the kitchen.

Ruby looked him up and down, still the t-shirt for a bottom and pajama pants for a top – now arms in the leg holes, face where his butt should have been.

"Nice look, Dan."

"Did I hear 'bars'?"

"Sure did."

"All I smell is ass."

"Dad," Sybil said, gesturing with the coffeemaker basket, feeling one step closer to a nervous breakdown.

"Dan, you look like a fool," Ruby said. "Now go put on some normal clothes and come and have a bar. And for your information, they are peanut butter, not ass."

He turned and walked into the doorframe, spun around, and went back into the living room, where there was a crash that sounded like a hundred-and-thirty-pound man falling onto a coffee table.

"You okay, Dad?" Sybil yelled, pouring water into the coffee maker.

"Where's the beef!" wafted in.

"Sounds like he's okay to me," Ruby said.

Sybil shrugged, sighed, and turned the coffeemaker on.

Ruby pulled small plates out of the cabinet, laying two bars on each.

"How's Dan doing, Sybil?"

Sybil put the three small plates on the fifties yellow Formica table and sat down. "I think you and everyone else had a pretty good demonstration of how he's doing."

"Walking around with no pants on? I'm not so sure he wouldn't have done that twenty years ago."

Sybil shrugged. "He has his good days and bad. Recognizing you and talking about bars is the most coherent he's been in a while."

"Have you considered a nursing home?" Ruby sat down and took a sip of coffee. She appeared to try to stifle a sour face. Sybil often forgot there's a difference between Ahnwee coffee and big city coffee.

Sybil leaned back her chair, reached behind her, and fished some napkins from the drawer. "He's spent his whole life in this house, in Ahnwee."

"Yeah, sure, but everyone has a time. Autumn of our lives, and all that crap."

Sybil took a bite out of a bar, and it tasted like comfort.

"And what about you? Obligation is great and all, but I think I'd need a security guard and a lion tamer to take care of Dan."

It felt nice to have it acknowledged that she had a tough situation, not that it changed anything. It was what it was. Her brothers could do something, as in actually help, but she knew that wasn't happening anytime soon. Sybil didn't want to talk about it. Time to change the subject. "Ruby, do you know anything about Björn Björkman saying he owns Ahnwee?" She took another bite of bar.

"No. News to me."

"Commissioner Balzac was starting to tell me about it when Dad came walking down the street."

"Who knows what that big boil is up to."

"Balzac or Björkman?"

"Either." Ruby winced at another sip of coffee.

Sybil looked deep into her cup of black coffee. "Why would Björkman want Ahnwee? How could he have title to the land?"

"Maybe we should go find out."

Chapter 3: Pastor Farber Throws in the Kitchen Towel

Pastor Fabian Farber brought his leftover trays of pastries into the parish house kitchen where he unceremonially threw them all into a big plastic leaf bag. He could have saved himself a step by bringing the bag outside and disposing of it all right there, but he didn't want anyone to see him do it. The failure. The waste. But mostly the failure. He tied up the huge bag and took it out to the trash, and with a slam of the lid he was done. Finished. Kaput. Those weren't just wasted pastries; those were the straws that broke the sheep's back.

Back in the kitchen, he looked at the big metal cookie sheets on the table and considered his options. He could take them to the sink and wash them, dry them, and put them away. Or he could kill himself.

Yes, he thought, definitely the latter.

How to do it? What would Jean-Paul Sartre do? Throw himself off a building? There weren't any buildings tall enough in Ahnwee to do anything but maim, including his church. Hang himself? No rope. Take pills? That seemed attractive. Clean. Not too scary for whoever finds him. Put his head in the oven? Now there was a thought; dramatic and more than a little poetic given that the stove played a role in his fundraising fail. The old parish house had poor insulation, so loose that you could feel a breeze, so there was probably little chance of the building blowing up. And if it did, he seemed to be the only person who cared anyway, and he would be dead.

Pastor Farber lifted the top of the old range and blew out the pilot light. He turned the dial to broil and opened the door of the oven, smelling the sweet, sweet smell of natural gas. He started to get down on his knees in front of the oven, but he didn't want to get his pants dirty, so he found a kitchen towel and laid it neatly on the floor. He knelt, and for the first time in a long time, felt like praying. But he then decided, why bother? He looked in the oven, listening to the hiss of gas. He felt lightheaded. Holding the door open below him, he leaned into the dark oven, banging his head on the oven rack causing him to take the Lord's name in vain. He pulled the rack out and leaned it carefully against the side of the oven. He leaned forward again, holding onto the oven door, but hated the feeling of grease on his palms. He tried lying backwards, looking up at the ceiling, but that didn't work at all. He decided that a little grease never hurt anyone, so he flipped over again. He put his head in the oven and closed his eyes and took a deep breath. He felt high. He liked it and felt glad he had chosen this over pills.

An alarm shrieked, causing Pastor Farber to jump, banging his head against the top of the oven compartment. It was deafening. He got up, looking at the smoke detector, CO_2 detector, and, apparently, gas detector high on the wall. For the second time, he took the Lord's name in vain. He turned the gas off, but the screeching continued. He got the little step stool from the corner and folded it open in front of the wailing piece of plastic. On the top step, he got up on his tiptoes and reached up, hitting the big button in the middle. Nothing.

Why do they put buttons on these things if they don't do anything? He struggled with the white skeet, feeling around for another switch or any clue as to what to do. The sound was unbearable. He pounded on it with his soft fists. He grabbed hold of it on each side and tugged and tugged. It let go without warning, and he fell backwards off the stool knocking his head on the table.

The good pastor laid in that spot until the next day. When he finally woke up, he felt his head and said aloud, "So this is what a concussion feels like." He stood up, looked at the clock, and walked to Flump's Café for a late breakfast.

Chapter 4: Bar Harbor Ahnwee Is Not

After Ruby left, Sybil quietly picked up her father's plate from the end table and brought it to the kitchen. Dan was fast asleep in his recliner, *Adam 12* on TV. She filled the sink, squirting in some dish soap. They never had a dishwasher, unless you call Sybil or her mother the dishwasher. She didn't mind it, really; she could look out the window into her shady yard. When did the maple tree get so big? Amazing how time slips by and, every once in a while, it catches your attention. She remembered helping plant it as a kid. There used to be an oak there before, but it got taken out by straight-line winds, peeling off a few shingles with it. Dan went on the roof and fixed it himself. Her father was still her father then.

She changed her mind about the dishes, leaving them to soak. She needed a dose of Drew.

She went in her bedroom and closed the door. Sitting cross-legged on the bed, she opened her laptop. Looking around as her miserable old computer booted up, she was struck, not for the first time, how around her everything looked the same. Dolls on the top shelf of a bookcase full of books she read in high school. Posters of Jennifer Lopez and the Black Eyed Peas. One could think nothing had changed, yet everything had. To Sybil, the same yellow curtains, the same paint-chipped dresser, the same end table with a cigarette burn from experimenting when she was sixteen, wasn't comforting, it was haunting.

She clicked on the icon and felt joy. "Hey, girl," the head on the screen said. Big shock of curly sort of red hair, light black complexion with freckles, Sybil felt instantly relaxed at the sight of her bestie. Drew filled Sybil in on the latest Drew dramas – dating the wrong men, and who was sleeping with whom. It was all strangely reassuring. At the same time, Sybil could see their apartment behind Drew, and it made Sybil miss her old life more than ever. Sybil noted how fit she looked – strong jaw, shoulders, the look obtained only from lots of yoga. Since moving back to Ahnwee, Sybil, in her own opinion, needed to drop a few pounds. Being in Ahnwee and taking care of her dad meant that her own health was on the back burner.

Suffice it to say that moving back home was never part of Sybil's master plan. Her plan from when she was old enough to choose her own TV shows was to live in New York: *Friends* and *Sex in the City*, subways and Times Square, the center of the civilized world, where apparently a girl can work at a coffee shop and get a huge SoHo loft for cheap.

After college she moved to the big city, where she found herself living on her own in a miserable little apartment in Queens. It sucked. She decided her mistake was settling for a borough – she had to live in Manhattan. Thus, she needed a roommate, so Sybil connected with Drew though a Craig's List ad. Drew was from Boston, and her situation was that she had to get out of her downtown apartment because her roomie was addicted to opioids. Sybil and Drew could not have been more different, and they hit it off immediately. They got a reasonably priced and convenient to the subway walk-up in Washington Heights. Sybil hoped to find a place to belong, but she quickly found that no one in their right mind wanted to belong in Washington Heights. No, New York was not the New York of sitcoms. Real life wasn't a Seinfeld-esque Upper West Side apartment with kooky neighbors; real life was men in rags sleeping on your apartment building doorstep. Still, while not a nice neighborhood, it was technically Manhattan and that was good enough.

Sybil felt like an oddball in New York, with her politeness and punctuality and her *Fargo* the movie accent. Drew was much more worldly, and she took the little Midwestern girl under her wing. They made lots of friends. Sybil found that in the big city it's extra credit if you are an oddball. Drew, who was a trainer at a fitness club downtown and bankrolled by her surgeon mother, managed to find a circle of new-money Beacon Hill expats who threw great parties, and Sybil came along for the ride. Her economics improved as well. After working for peanuts in a couple antique stores in the Village, she started her own store selling mid-century modern, Prairie 'Tique, just a few blocks away from their apartment. It was very popular among her new circle of upper-crust Bostonian friends. She dated, mostly men but a few women, something she had never imagined as a possibility in Ahnwee. All of which only increased her social stock, and soon she fit right in. True, you can't take the small town out of the girl, but you can take the girl out of the small town and dress her in black.

Through all the ups and downs of living in Manhattan, she could never have imagined living in Ahnwee again, as she said over and over to anyone who would listen.

"How'd Ahnwee Days go?" Drew Asked.

"Don't ask," Sybil said, even though Drew already had. Sybil told Drew about the shitty business, Dolly Parton, and her dad.

"Yikes, that's an epic fail," Drew said. "Seems like there's not much hope, is there?"

"What do you mean?"

"For Ahnwee. For small towns."

"Drew, have you ever been to a small town?" Sybil felt defensive.

"Yeah, Bar Harbor."

"Bar Harbor doesn't count."

Drew looked like she was feeling picked on. "I read."

Sybil reflected how she had never seen Drew read anything deeper than *Elle*.

"Small towns are suffering. Everyone knows that. Farms suffer, old industries fail, big box retail siphons off business from main street, young people move away to New York – some becoming my roommate, you might recall – and there you have it."

"How do you know all that?"

"I read it in *Elle*."

Drew was right, and the good mayor knew it. Downtown Ahnwee, three blocks long, was an assortment of mostly two-story buildings floating among a large number of vacant lots. A treeless expanse of concrete and asphalt, the building stock that remained was classic small-town Minnesota: brick façades, arched windows, stone lintels – buildings that an architect might comment about as having "great bones" – plus two or three lower, detail-less buildings born of rare and random investment in the sixties and seventies. A far cry from its heyday, when Broadway included a bank that worked on a handshake, a grocery store that charged outrageous sums for their sausages, a hardware store whose proprietor knew just which parts were needed for each house in town without the homeowner saying a thing, a department store where all the kids got their new if unfashionable school clothes, Ruby and her husband's drugstore where Ruby's husband the pharmacist knew what you were taking without having to look, several diners including Flump's Café, a couple bars, the town newspaper, a post office, and every other necessity expected of an actual community.

That was when Sybil was a kid. Now only Flump's Café remained from those earlier, more prosperous days. Other than the previously mentioned newer, less practical businesses of New York 'Tique and Ruby's Knotty Knits, all the rest of the storefront windows were boarded over with plywood, not even a "For Rent" sign to add an air of hope. Plus there was the new strip club where the VFW had been. No, hard for a town to be more depressed than that.

"Sybil, when are you moving home?"

After two years, she felt both pleasure and pain from hearing New York referred to as "home." "Not soon enough."

They chatted a bit more about Broadway shows Sybil had no access to, and a social circle that was fast becoming a distant memory. After they signed off and Sybil settled back with a fresh cup of coffee, she thought more about the Ahnwee Days bust specifically and small towns in general. She knew, as Drew had said, that part of the reason for this post-apocalyptic landscape could be chalked up to small town economic woes, and that Ahnwee had good company across much of farm territory. But there was no denying that Ahnwee seemed to exist under a cloud. One just needed to breathe the brown air to understand "cloud of misfortune" in a new way.

CHAPTER 5: NOT GOOD FOR ONE'S COMPLEXION

The next day, Sybil and Ruby sat on Björn Björkman's deck in front of his pink seventies' rambler. The pink house was maybe ten yards in front of an old rotting farmhouse, making for a strange juxtaposition of buildings. A short distance away, along the dirt road, three enormous metal buildings with no windows loomed, huge fans on their sides. What had been a blue sky on the way there was now somewhat brown, as if you could see the stink. Sybil wondered if the shit haze could damage her Prius' paint job.

"Who's deaf?"

"What are you talking about, Björkman?" Ruby said.

He pointed at Sybil and said to Ruby, "Why did you bring a sign language interpreter?"

Sybil had to think about that one, but she finally realized it was in reference to her being dressed in black.

"Would you like some coffee?" Mrs. Björkman interrupted, coming out the kitchen door. Sybil didn't know her name; she had never seen her in town, and Björn didn't introduce her. Sybil guessed she was maybe fifty, maybe more – hard to judge, since she was too big for wrinkles. Mrs. Björkman was pear shaped and wore stretch pants, which made the front of her hips look like a butt.

Sybil wondered if coffee would increase or decrease her chances of vomiting from the smell, and she decided on what she thought was the conservative course. "No, thank you." Ruby also declined, perhaps for the same reason.

"Mother, this ain't no social call."

At what stage of life do women become happy with being called "mother" by their husbands? Sybil thought. They made an odd sight next to each other – "Mother" Björkman dwarfing Björn Björkman, who was no more than five foot two and maybe one hundred and thirty pounds. He was quite possibly the ugliest man Sybil had ever seen. Björn had some sort of skin condition, with erupting boils all over his face. Sybil wondered if a person hung around this pig farm long enough, is that what they'd eventually look like?

"I have bars. Would you like some bars?" Mrs. Björn held out a plate.

A light breeze off the manure pond increased the overwhelming stench, causing Sybil to throw up a little in the back of her throat. She was sure the bars would send her into a vomit fit, so she said no to bars as well, as did Ruby once again.

"Mother, please. This is business." Björn picked up one of the bars and took a ridiculously huge bite out of it.

"Björn, what's this about your having a claim to Ahnwee?" Ruby said, knitting something small and green.

"Yup. Got the title to the property. All of it."

None of this made sense to Sybil. The boil-covered man must have finally succumbed to some sort of sewage-induced madness. But he seemed so certain, so confident.

"How on earth could that be?" Sybil asked.

How that could be can only be answered with a trip back in time to the founding of Ahnwee.

It all started in 1893, when one Maximilian Schroeder, Junior was sent by his father, Maximilian Senior, to the New World from their home in Wiesbaden, Germany. Maximilian Senior was a wealthy railroad man who made his fortune in iron horses and developing tourist destinations for Germans going on holidays. This was a relatively new concept, to go on holiday, brought on by the increased wealth amassed under Otto von Bismarck from their collection of new colonies. Maximilian Senior decided the gravy train (so to speak) was only just beginning for Germans and vacationing, so he began to look off the continent for new locations. He sent his youngest of three sons to the New World to scout out new opportunities and secure a place for good Germans to go and rest and have a good time.

Actually, that was just the reason given. In fact, it was more that Maximilian Senior needed junior to go somewhere and make himself useful. Junior had gotten into the habit of hanging around Strasbourg drinking absinthe and generally giving the family a black eye. Maximilian Senior sent him on his way with the mission of finding a site somewhere in the Wild West, just like in the little pulp novels that Maximilian Senior read: full of horses and buffalo, cowboys and Indians. If during his excursion junior got scalped by Indians, well, these things happen.

Maximilian Junior, or Max, a dandy who wouldn't have been caught dead in western wear, made his way to New York and then – when he heard there was a spectacular World's Fair going on – to Chicago. The World's Columbian Exposition was indeed splendid, with its fake Beaux Arts architecture, electric lights, and the world's first Ferris wheel. Maximilian, however, never saw any of that, spending his time outside of the event grounds where there was a veritable city of delights temporarily set up and doing business catering to the throngs of tourists. Needless to say, Max went broke in short order with nothing to show for it, not even the fond memories of all the prostitutes, since absinthe played hell with the brain cells.

Needing cash like now, Max wired home. Maximilian Senior said something in German that would be best translated as "too bad, so sad." Max again wired that he had a really good lead on the perfect property, but he needed walking around money to keep afloat. Maximilian Senior wired back something like, "Tell me when you find it, and we can talk." Max wired Maximilian Senior again. "I found it! It's perfect! Send money now!" and went on to describe a paradise that would make Adam and Eve feel like they were in Gary, Indiana. Amazingly, Maximilian Senior fell for it and wired his youngest the money.

In fact, Max did indeed have a lead on some property. Not from trying, but from a conversation over cards. Playing poker one night in a tent outside the fair, he met a Swedish man who said he owned a good-sized parcel of land on a lake west of Chicago, and he needed to get rid of it. He said he had to sell because his dear old mother was sick and needed her medicine. Of course, that wasn't true. His actual reasons were that he owed even more people money than Max did, including to some serious, serious men, and that he hated it. He had traveled there from Chicago just once, and that was enough. He complained to everyone who would listen – except Max – that the goddamned mosquitoes will pick you up and carry you away, and the winters were long and unbearable. Plus, there wasn't anything to do for more than a day's ride, other than the brothels in Despar, and everyone knew those girls had syphilis.

So Max bought it from the Swede, sight unseen, for what

appeared to be a song. The song turned out to be the blues. Max took two trains, getting off in Willmar, before riding a full day to his new Eden. There he did not find oak trees, white sand beaches, and rainbows as described; he found untilled prairie, swampland, and Indigenous people for neighbors who seemed to be holding a grudge.

Still, Max, always a trouper, made the best of it. Never mind the winter; Germans love the snow. Sure, the site was nearly inaccessible, but the train would be coming soon, he could just feel it. Max was right about that: by 1895, it ran to the new town of Despar, just a few miles west of his property. He set about to build Maximilian Senior's resort, bringing in all the lumber on the new train and locating it on the lake to the west of what would one day become downtown. The West Glacier Lodge it was not, but it was a hotel with a restaurant and twenty rooms. It opened in June 1896, the date since used as the founding of the town – however inaccurately – and the date Sybil would choose over a century later for the first "Ahnwee Days."

They started advertising for visitors in Germany, calling the place the "Ahnwee Lodge," after a beautiful Indian princess who was supposedly had been rescued from a crocodile by a handsome brave. Max made that up of course, given the nearest crocodile was in Florida. The name actually came from a Despar hooker of French descent who said, "Ah. *Oui!*" and Max thought it sounded vaguely Indian.

Tourists came. The Ahnwee Lodge attracted Germans looking for cut-rate bargains in their Wild West experience, and that's pretty much what they got: no buffalos, no cowboys, no smiling Indians selling belts and dancing (however, lots of resentful ones just to the east who were routinely spotted urinating in the hotel cistern). Soon, fewer and fewer Germans came as word spread about the Ahnwee Lodge. Max went broke in short order and in 1900, in a desperate display of insurance fraud, set fire to the hotel.

Sixteen people were staying there at the time, all part of a religious cult from Hof. That was the biggest group Max had had in quite a while, and they had paid in advance. Ironically, the cult's focus was the belief that God loves round numbers; therefore, surely the world would come to an end before 1900 was up. They went to the Ahnwee Lodge to await the rapture and to be as far away from Europe and big cities as possible, since cities burned a lot those days, and they believed the world would be consumed in fire. When the hotel blazed, they ran outside to catch a ride to heaven on golden chariots or whatever transportation option God had invested in. They were disappointed.

Good news: no one was killed. Bad news: the guests lost most of their stuff, and they were stranded with winter on the way.

Max, too, lost his home in the fire, something he had failed to plan for, so he, too, had nowhere to go. In Despar, he owed money to everyone – namely the brothels and bars, which, in those days, was nearly everyone – so instead, he turned to his neighbor to the southeast, a cantankerous Swedish farmer named Jan Björkman. Björkman was quite the opposite of Max, never gambling, drinking, or carousing with ladies of ill repute, never parting with a dime if he could possibly help it. His wife made all their clothes and grew all their food, while Björkman worked his land like a one-man army.

There was only one thing Jan Björkman did spend money on: land. Eventually, he and the missus would have four boys, and the patriarch Björkman would tell them, "Land is the only thing you can count on." Starting with his quarter section (the standard plot when the Indigenous people's land was ~~stole~~ opened for white settlement), by 1900 he had amassed eight times that, twelve-hundred and eighty acres.

What happened next, or, more specifically, in what order events happened next, would forever remain unclear.

For sure, Max went to Björkman, offering him fire-sale prices for his land. Jan Björkman offered him no mercy (he couldn't stand Max) and took him to the cleaners. Max got a lousy four thousand dollars, half what he paid for the land alone just seven years earlier. Björkman got the paperwork and everything, all very official.

On that very same day, Max sold his land to the German cult for five thousand dollars, featuring equally official documents. Who bought what first was a mystery. Regardless, with nine thousand dollars now in hand, he took off for Buffalo, New York, where the Pan American Exposition was planned for the following year. That was the last anyone ever heard from Max. Presumably, the man who one day would be erroneously celebrated as the founder of Ahnwee landed in a shallow grave somewhere, but no one every bothered to find out.

Of course, the now seventeen German cult members (a woman gave birth to a screaming baby boy shortly after the fire) had no idea that Max had sold the same land to Björkman. They just knew Max had left, and that was just fine since he was a morally reprehensible ne'er-do-well who had given two of the cult women syphilis. They set up a half-mile east from the old lodge and commenced to work like crazy to get buildings up and supplies in before the snow, going into Despar by wagon for lumber (the cultists had cash because they were a frugal bunch, and they saved their money despite its presumed uselessness after the much-anticipated rapture).

In November, Björkman finally rode over to what he thought was his property to survey the burned down lodge. He was pleased. He was also wet, since it was raining pretty hard. Unfortunately, the rain meant he couldn't see very far, and as a result, he had no idea the Germans were building a settlement not far away.

Björkman wouldn't live to see the town. The first snows came early, and, in the spring, he went to the pig farm in the sky when technology got the best of him. Björkman believed that progress would make for an easier life and more profits, which was all true, of course, at least in the long view. He had proudly bought a newfangled tractor, the first tractor in that and several surrounding counties. He didn't have it long. If a person didn't adjust one of these early steam engines just right, the pressure could cause an explosion. And so it was with Björkman's tractor: on its second day, he forgot to open a valve, and the thing exploded with a boom heard seven miles away in Despar, atomizing Björkman. All they found of Jan Björkman was his left thumb.

Björkman had neglected his family for years, and they put on their best heartbroken faces for the poorly attended funeral, his thumb interred in a tiny casket. He also neglected to tell his family in the months between striking a deal with Max and his obliteration that he had bought Max's land. While this would seem hard to believe, it was not if one knew Björkman, who was not a big conversationalist or big on family time. Then, he neglected to file the paperwork with the county registrar, partly because the registrar was a position of authority he didn't recognize, but mostly because he never got around to it. Back then, it was a long ride to Willmar, especially in the winter. As a result, his heirs had no idea about the transaction, and continued to live as usual, with two of the four brothers working the farm (for the other two, one had moved to Despar and opened a horseless carriage dealership, and the other moved to Minneapolis and joined the ballet).

Flash ahead over a hundred years, and the farm had

evolved into a factory hog operation, the very same hog operation featuring the enormous shit field that on a warm day
brought Ahnweeians to their knees. Jan's great-great-grand-
son, Björn Björkman, couldn't care less that the smell hurt
the town and its people, since, first, he was making money,
and, second, he hated the town ever since the town sued to get
Björkman to do something about the stench.

They had lost.

Then, one day, Mother Björkman got inspired by the show
Clean House, and she decided to throw out all that old junk
and boxes that had been cluttering the attic as long as she
could remember. In a metal lockbox was old man Björkman's
deed to what had been Max's land. Björn Björkman had no
clue as to all the history that went into this deed being in the
attic, nor did he spend a lot of time worrying about it. What
he did do was get his lawyer on it (he had one on retainer),
who, after some brief research, said the deed was legitimate.

All of which meant that finally Björn Björkman would get
his vengeance on Ahnwee.

"I inherited it from my great-great-grandfather, with everything else you see. Now I'd appreciate it if you'd pack up and
leave. I need to expand the manure pond."

"You want to build a manure pond where Ahnwee is?"
Sybil said.

"No, I want to expand the one I have. I need to go north,
to keep it away from my house, and that means into your shithole town." He chortled. "Ha! I made a funny: 'shithole'!"

"Mr. Björkman," Sybil said, "Ahnwee has been around a
long time. You'll need to show us this title."

"My attorney has it. It doesn't matter what you think, Mayor," he said using air quotes around "mayor," "My mouthpiece is worth his weight in gold, and he says we own the entire town. We'll just let the court sort this out, won't we?"

"Oh, Björn, is that nice? Maybe we can work something out," Mrs. Björn said, standing next to her seated husband, looking down at him with a strange, and somehow inappropriate, smile. Her hair was in a bun, and Sybil wondered how she avoided headaches from her hair being stretched so tight.

"Be quiet, Mother. There's nothing to work out," he said up to her. Turning back to his company, "You bozos sued me for running an old-fashioned, fourth-generation family farm. You sow what you reap."

"You mean 'reap what you sow,'" Sybil said.

"So YOU say, New York."

Sybil wondered if he knew that she had lived in New York – knowing such details about others would be situation normal in small town life – or if he was just referring to her appearance again.

"You environmental fascists have nothing on me. I even did it your way, following the oppressor's rules and got a license after your useless attempt on me through the courts. My CAFO is one hundred percent on the up and up."

"CAFO? What's a CAFO?" Sybil asked.

"This, Frenchie: a Concentrated Animal Feedlot Operation. That's what a highly-sophisticated business like this is called. A CAFO."

Frenchie? "I thought you said it was an old-fashioned family farm."

"Same thing."

"Björn, your manure pond smells up the town," Ruby said. "No, it smells up the county. It's a blight on everyone living here."

"Tough shit." Björn laughed. "No pun intended! Ha!" Björn took a bite of his bar, leaned back, still snickering. He stopped suddenly, leaned forward, and, spraying Sybil with bits of peanut butter bar, said, "You shouldn't be worrying about me, anyway. I'm a good American. You should be focusing your meager efforts on stopping that no good Injun, Malcolm Moose."

"Malcolm Moose?" Sybil asked, not knowing what he could possibly be talking about.

"Björkman, what could you possibly be talking about now?" Ruby asked.

He looked at Ruby, and then Sybil, and then back and back again. Then he laughed. "You don't know about Malcolm Moose? Malcolm Moose and the Big Moose Casino? They want your land. They say they have a treaty. Let me tell you this: that Injun Big Moose doesn't have a chance. He can't win. If he did, all of us good Americans would have to move back to Europe. Of course, he used to own the land, but we stole it from them fair and square."

"The Big Moose Casino wants Ahnwee as well?" Sybil said, mostly to herself.

"That's right. So stop fighting with me, give me my land, and let me expand my manure pond."

"Not going to happen, Björkman," Ruby said.

"If you people weren't a bunch of city slickers, you'd understand about real Americans and their God given right to do what they please."

"'City slickers'?" Ruby said. "You know I've spent nearly my whole life in Ahnwee, Björn. We went to school together, that is, as long as you went to school."

"That's what I mean. All you townies up in airs about your junior high school diplomas. Living in your highfalutin'

'Ahnwee.' 'Ahnwee this,' 'Ahnwee that.' You all think you are better than us."

Sybil was dumbfounded that anyone would consider Ahnwee 'highfalutin' or anyone living there would be a "city slicker."

"Ruby, why don't you take New York here and get the hell off my sovereign property, namely this deck and then that dump of a town of yours." Björn looked up at his wife. "The only use for Ahnwee is that titty bar. We may be country folk, but we are not squares, right, Mother?" He reached up and squeezed her butt. She giggled. "Mother and I have an understanding." He looked at Sybil. "You know, Mayor, if you didn't wear all those black clothes, got a decent haircut, and lost twenty pounds, maybe we'd invite you up some evening."

Sybil threw up.

With Sybil's Cocoa Puffs all over the patio furniture, the meeting was over. They got back in the Prius and set off back to Ahnwee as Björn hosed his deck off, cursing them at the top of his lungs.

Back at Flump's Café, Sybil and Ruby found Augie leaning on the old Formica counter across from Sig Klein, the two of them doing a crossword. The diner looked like it hadn't been remodeled in thirty years, featuring yellowed ceiling panels and worn black and white floor tiles. Pictures of people holding up fish and the occasional taxidermy fish itself decorated much of the walls. The place smelled unmistakably of grease and vaguely of roach spray.

Ruby sat next to Sig, and Sybil next to Ruby, on the round

stools, vinyl torn from age. Sig's stature didn't change the fact
that he was a handsome, forty-something with dark eyes and
hair. Sig ran a roadside stand selling jerky to the west, halfway
to Despar seven miles away. He had on a t-shirt with a hula
girl and the words, "South Pacific Jerky." Sybil felt bad that
she had never stopped at Sig's business, not even once, even
though she drove by it all the time. She had known Sig from
a distance for practically her whole life. She remembered him
because, frankly, he stuck out.

Augie poured both Sybil and Ruby coffees without their
asking. They proceeded to tell everyone about the likely fate
of Ahnwee.

"Now let me get this straight," Sig said. "Björn Björkman
wants to tear down Ahnwee and make it a shit pool?"

Sybil and Ruby nodded to the affirmative, then looked
down, despondent.

"Ahnwee is going to be torn down?" Pastor Farber said.

Sybil hadn't noticed him, sitting on the other side of Sig,
even though he was the only other customer in the place. In
front of the pastor was a paperback: *The Metamorphosis*. Sybil
thought that weird, but she wasn't sure why.

"Not if we can help it," Ruby replied.

"God does work in mysterious ways," he said. The comment made no sense to Sybil, nor did the fact that he looked
happy about it.

"What happened to your melon, Farber?" Ruby asked. He
sported a big bandage on the back of his head.

"Banged it cleaning the oven."

Ruby looked at him, head cocked as if deciding whether
to believe him, but soon seemed to opt for letting it go. Sybil
considered that maybe a concussion explained his behavior.

"Oh, give me a break," Augie said. "Old Björkman doesn't
have squat. I have the abstract to my property, title free and

clear."

"I'm just saying what he said," Sybil replied, but she understood the disbelief. How could a whole town be torn down? But she had to admit to herself, who but the two hundred townspeople would notice? It was not like things were going well for Ahnwee.

"Björkman having title to our property is weird enough; weirder still is what Björkman said about the Big Moose," Ruby said.

"What's that?" Sig asked.

"Mr. Björkman said Malcolm Moose had a claim to our land as well," Sybil replied.

Augie reached behind himself with a spatula and scratched his back. "I mean, yeah, all this was once theirs, but I'm sure there's some treaty or something."

Sig pushed his crossword book away. "Well, I guess we should find out."

Chapter 6: They Try Their Luck at the Big Moose Casino

Sybil, Ruby, and Sig got out of the Prius on the vast asphalt plain in front of the modern, nearly windowless building with a vaguely Native motif. The Big Moose Casino was huge, an almost Las Vegas scale with a new hotel, convention center, and auditorium.

The casino was something of a sore spot for the people of Ahnwee. In the past, the highway ran through town, becoming Broadway as it passed through, then proceeding around the north side of the lake. When the state built the freeway, it went south of the lake, effectively bypassing Ahnwee. There was an expectation in Ahnwee that an exit would be added heading north into town. Instead, the Big Moose Casino opened, with the exit going right into their parking lot. Ahnwee was effectively cut off. When the then-mayor went to the department of transportation asking for a town exit, they told him that by regulation, exits cannot be that close together, and the next exit was Despar, seven miles ahead. Ahnwee was out of luck. You could still get to town, if you got off the freeway at Despar, passed through town to Old Highway Seven, and continued around the lake to the north for seven miles, like the old days. Possible to do, but not easy.

Plus, in a clear case of Minnesotan passive-aggression, there were no signs telling drivers how to get to Ahnwee in Despar. There wasn't a direct route between Ahnwee and the casino either, even though the casino was practically in Ahnwee's backyard. In fact, from her deck, Sybil could see the backside of the casino.

Therefore, after she had picked up Ruby, they drove in a huge clockwise circle – through the wind turbine, up the hill past the shit field – stopping to pick up Sig at South Pacific Jerky – continuing six miles west to Despar, down Main Street, onto the freeway, past the strip of big-boxes – Walmart, Dollar General, Target, Pick and Save, Sam's Club, and the new Home Depot – and on east through the flat, nearly treeless countryside for six more miles to get to, well, Ahnwee's backyard.

Sybil, Ruby, and Sig stood looking at the building. They wondered where to go before deciding that the front door seemed the only choice, where, upon asking to see someone in charge, they endured intensive screening by admin assistants, assistant managers, assistant to the assistant managers, and the sous chef before they found out they were in the wrong place. The office was in a separate building behind and to the east, hidden by the bulk of the casino. There they were greeted by a uniformed guard with long black hair, who, to Sybil, looked like the big Juicy Fruit guy in *One Flew Over the Cuckoo's Nest*, a thought she considered racist and tried to banish from her head but could not.

"What are you, a mime?" the guard said to Sybil, who was dressed in her usual all black. "Shouldn't you have a beret and a white striped shirt?"

"We're here to see Chief Malcolm Moose," Sybil said, wondering if she had said that right. Chief? President? She wished she had left off the title all together.

"Malcom isn't a chief. I mean, he wishes he was, but he's not."

"Sorry, I didn't…"

"No one sees Malcom. Why would the boss want to see a mime? And aren't you guys supposed to not talk? Hey! Do that box thing. I love the box thing."

"She's not a mime," Sig said.

"Looks like a mime," he said, looking her up and down. "So, what do you want, then? Are you selling beads?"

"We are from Ahnwee," said Sybil.

The guard let out a little laugh. "Ahnwee. Really, you guys still there? I thought your town fell in the shit pond a long time ago."

"Listen, we are here to see Malcolm Moose," Ruby persisted. "This is Sybil Voss, the mayor of Ahnwee."

The guard looked at the odd trio, leaning back, one eyebrow raised. "The Mayor of Ahnwee is a mime? You white people are nuts."

"I'm not a…"

"And what do we have here? Are you a Hobbit?"

"Hey, screw you, Juicy Fruit," Sig said through his teeth. Which freaked out Sybil; it was as if Sig had read her mind. Plus, the guy was four times the size of Sig.

The big man just laughed. "Man, if I had a nickel for every time I've been called that."

"Tulip," Sig said under his breath, so quietly that Sybil wondered if he really said it.

"We insist on seeing Malcolm Moose. There's some story about a deed we need to clear up," Sybil said.

"Why didn't you say so? Ah, it's about the rent you owe on our property. Of course. Come this way." He opened the door with a flourish. "By the way, just so you know, because of the glow stick lake you're not getting your damage deposit back."

The guard led them down a short hall where he stood up straight and announced to the young female admin assistant, "Her lord highness, the Mayor of Ahnwee, her mother, and a strange Hobbit!"

Neither Sybil nor Ruby bothered to correct him. Sig's head turned red, and he let out a little growl.

The admin assistant shrugged. "Ignore him; he's been streaming *Downton Abbey*." She looked at Sig. "And sorry about the Hobbit thing."

Sybil said she wanted to meet with Malcolm Moose, and the assistant told them to go away. Ruby persisted. The assistant still told them to go away. Sig said "Daisies," apropos of nothing, and was ignored. Finally, while standing in the outer office trying to decide what to do, a husky, saggy-faced man in a suit walked out of the office. "Malcolm Moose?" Ruby said. He said yes. They said they had to talk to him. He said he just wanted to get himself cannoli from across the parking lot at the casino deli. They were persuasive, especially Ruby who wouldn't let him get by her to make a break for the door, so eventually he agreed to give them five minutes of his time.

Sitting at his oak desk in a high-backed leather office chair, surrounded by framed plaques and citations, Big Moose looked every bit the statesman. Sybil, Ruby, and Sig, sitting in small, uncomfortable folding chairs, looked every bit the losers.

"Yeah, sure, we want what's ours," Big Moose said in a perfect Minnesota accent.

"How is Ahnwee yours?" Sybil asked.

"You mean besides the usual, that all this," he spread his arms wide, "from sea to shining sea, is ours and you stole it?"

"Well, yeah, I guess," Sybil said, realizing as soon as she said it that she just admitted that the land was stolen. She wondered if she was in over her head.

Sybil was, of course, in over her head. And Ahnwee, like all of the United States, did in fact sit on land owned by others, others who never left. Therefore, all tribes from coast to coast had a legitimate beef about how their land was taken. But Big Moose had an unusually strong case, built not just on what was right, but on white people's law.

To understand how it worked, once again we travel back in time, before Maximilian Schroeder Junior won the land that would be Ahnwee in the card game, before Max was even born.

Ahnwee achieved its land grab not so much at the end of a gun – although, there was that – but at the end of a pen. The gun part was the war of 1862. The U.S. government signed a treaty with the Dakota living around the Minnesota River to give up nearly all their land. That sucked on the face of it, but the Dakota weren't stupid, and they could see things weren't going their way. They knew that in the east whole tribes were wiped out and marched thousands of miles to live in places no one should live. Putting up with self-righteous farmers plowing up their land and having to live in a ridiculously small area was horrible, but it was probably the least of the horrible options available. Making the treaty a bit more tolerable was that the great white chief's soldiers were to give them grain – ironically grown by those self-righteous farmers – so at least the tribe wouldn't starve. It was right in the contract, right there in black and white.

That was the theory, anyway.

Soon enough they were starving. This, even though the soldiers had full coffers of grain at the Lower Sioux Agency. At a meeting to remedy the situation, one white trader said,

"So far as I am concerned, if they are hungry, let them eat grass."

Two days later, braves took the grain and killed forty-four men. The trader who made the culinary suggestion was found with his mouth stuffed with grass.

The war went on over August and September. The braves did well for themselves under the leadership of Chief Little Crow, driving the Europeans east and killing dozens of soldiers and hundreds of farmers and laying siege to Mankato and St. Peter. Finally, Colonel Henry Sibley led fourteen hundred soldiers into the fight, defeating the outgunned Dakota. The end result was one of the worst atrocities perpetrated against Indigenous people in history, and that's really saying something: Chief Little Crow shot in cold blood; thirty-eight braves imprisoned, tried, and hanged; and everyone else – mostly women, children, and the elderly – sent off to a place far away where no one should live. The result was the same as everywhere else in the country: the Dakota lost their land.

Most of them, anyway. Some Dakota didn't participate in the war. To a reasonable person there were lots of reasons to have stayed out of the fight, the inevitability of losing, for one. One man who steered clear was John Big Moose. Big Moose was a sketchy character who was part Dakota and part French, a popular combination of the day. Now, Big Moose didn't get his name from having seen a Big Moose or anything stereotypical as all that. It was a mistranslation of a slang term the Dakota kids used for him that the white translators didn't understand. His name would more accurately be translated as John Big Dong. Big Moose – or Dong – not only did his name proud, he also was quite successful with it. He managed to father eighteen children with three different Dakota women, including the daughter of a chief.

While a coveted lover among the women of the tribe, the

men didn't have much time for him, since he had a nasty habit of turning up in the wrong teepee. But the soldiers liked him: he had a good still, and he hardly used any lead in it. So, when Big Moose's relatives went to war, he hid in a root cellar. Seems he was more of a lover than a fighter, and besides, he made a lot of money off the soldiers. When some braves came looking for him to join the fight, his wife and his two girlfriends told them he ran off with a teenaged Ojibwe girl. They laughed and said, "Same old Big Dong."

After the war, when the time came for everyone to be forced marched away, he fortunately had enough good will with the soldiers – plus liquor for bribes – to stay. In fact, when the Europeans began their land rush to take over the Dakota land, he not only stayed put, he also managed to carve out a full section (a section being a one mile by one mile square) and then some for himself and his family, just to the east of a beautiful lake.

John Big Moose became something of a local fixture for the new, paler people in the area, making a lot of money selling liquor and souvenirs. Soon he was old. He decided to divide his land among his eight sons (his ten daughters, in the tradition of white people, got nothing). He died in 1892 at the ripe old age of seventy-two, leaving behind his wives, two girlfriends, sixteen surviving children (two daughters died young – one in childbirth and the other in a balloon accident), eighty grandchildren, and fifteen great-grandchildren.

The portion of the land that would host Big Moose Casino a century later managed to stay in the family. Generations of Big Moose's heirs made a living with a classic roadside tourist trap on the state highway to Despar selling all kinds of stuff made in China to families seeing the USA in their Chevrolets. Then, when casinos started to open on tribal lands across the country, the savvy great-great-grandsons and daughters of

John Big Moose were able to get a casino of their own – with the help of a state legislator with a blackjack problem – even though the land wasn't technically a reservation.

As for the rest of Big Moose's land, within just a few years of his death that section-plus shrank considerably. Back then, across the country white con men were like Russian hackers, lurking in the shadows looking to screw over some poor dude. They would approach Native people who couldn't read or write English and offer them a deal of some kind, for example, renting their land for a season to plant corn. There'd be an official contract and everything, and the native guy would give his mark, trusting what the colonizer told him. Hell, what's up with white people and paper, anyway? A man's word is what mattered, right?

Four of Big Moose's sons couldn't read, and sure enough they found themselves in this oh-so-common jackpot. Big Moose couldn't read either, but he had been a good judge of character or lack thereof; unfortunately, you can't teach that. While Big Moose's sons were told they were renting their land for balloon races, the contract – surprise, surprise – in fact said that they had sold their land for next to nothing.

The main swindler was a rotund man and former soldier from the 1862 war who saw it as his duty – not to mention in his self-interest – to take Indian lands. He had some success with that, amassing quite a bit of land all over the state. However, besides not having a moral compass, he also didn't have a great attention to detail. In short, he didn't even bother to get a witness to sign the transactions, never mind a notary. More on that in a moment.

The former Big Moose land bordering the north and west side of a beautiful lake would change hands several times, first "owned" by the swindler himself, who, when the land wasn't as profitable as he hoped, traded it to an Irish merchant for the merchant's fifteen-year-old red-haired daughter. That merchant went broke after investing everything in his new business of selling stock tips via Morse code. He ended up hocking the land to a Swede at a fire sale price to get some money to keep his mistress in the style to which she wanted to become accustomed. That Swede was the very same Swede who met Maximilian Schroeder Junior outside the World's Fair in Chicago and sold it to him to get some cash to pay off his gambling debts.

But about that original lack of attention to detail. That the land wasn't obtained in the first place with even a half-decent contract had come to the attention to the great-great-great-grandson of John Big Moose when looking through old documents. Now Malcolm Moose was determined to put his Doctor of Jurisprudence to good use suing to get his family's land back.

This was the land that made up all of Ahnwee.

Of course, Sybil and Ruby sat in front of the chairman not knowing any of this.

"Simply, four of my great uncles were defrauded of their land. The so-called 'contracts' they signed – that we've kept safe and passed down all these years just for this moment – aren't worth the horse shit they were printed on. By the way, you're the Mayor of Ahnwee, you say?"

Sybil nodded.

"How long have you been the mayor?"

"A little over a year."

"How is it you've never paid me a courtesy call before?"

"Well…"

"I mean, your so-called town is right outside my loading dock."

"Yeah, I…"

"You'd think you'd have dropped by before this."

"Ah, see…"

"Bring some bars or something? What kind of neighbor or are you?"

"Sorry, see…"

He let out a big belly laugh. "I'm just shitting you. Of course you didn't come for a visit. We're Indians. We're happy you didn't since you'd probably have brought smallpox-infected blankets with you."

Ruby looked up from her knitting. "Cut the crap, Moose. You can't have our town."

He leaned back, looking officious. "Well, we'll see about that. I believe the courts will see it our way. Not only do I have the swindler contracts," he said making air quotes around the word "contracts," "when my great-grandfather negotiated for this land – his own land – with the Great White Asshole in the East, he was smart enough to get iron-clad contracts, not the usual wampum and beads treaties." Air quoting "treaties." "I have those documents, too. I didn't go to William Mitchell College of Law to get dicked with. Capiche?"

"Why do you want to take Ahnwee now?" Sig asked. "The town's been there for a hundred years. Why now?"

"First of all, we always wanted our land back, just no one ever paid attention to us. Amazing what a paradigm shift it is to have a successful casino and an army of lawyers. Second, we are planning to offer an RV court, bring in some more of that retired colonizer, nickel-slot action. Third, with Björn Björkman planning to go to court to take over the town for his hog operation, we have to act now, or we'll be out of luck forever."

"But we live there. It's our land," Sybil said, sounding far whinier than she wanted to.

"Ironic, isn't it?" He laughed. "But hey, as much as I'd like to spend my time chatting with you colonizers, I have stuff to do. I know, hard to believe a lazy Indian wants to get something done, but there ya go."

As they filed out of the office, Malcolm Moose yelled, "And mayor, don't think I didn't hear you admit having stolen our land!"

They drove their way back through Despar and around the lake, through the wind turbine and down the hill, and back to Flump's Café, which, as usual, was nearly empty, but for Pastor Farber at the counter and Augie Flump reading his newspaper.

"So, what you are saying is," Augie asked, struggling to fold up his paper neatly. "Big Moose Casino, who wants to use Ahnwee for an RV park, is fighting that pig shit farmer for the land?"

"Yeah," Sybil said between fork-loads of pie. "That's about it."

"How can he have title to our land? Third Lutheran alone has been here over a hundred years," Pastor Farber said, sliding a bookmark in his paperback, *The Myth of Sisyphus*. Sybil noted this as she noted *The Metamorphosis* two days earlier. She thought it added to the weird.

"Jerry and I had our store for over forty years, and his father had it before him," Ruby said. "I'm not giving up my store, and I'm sure as hell not giving it to either that Morlock, Björkman, or that smartass, Malcolm Moose."

"It's not right," said Sig. "That blowhard was this close," Sig said, holding up his index and thumb in the traditional way, "to getting a four-foot-one can of whoop-ass."

"See, now I would have guessed you'd be madder at the big guy who called you a Hobbit," Ruby said.

He looked like he was thinking about it, then, "Well, that piss-wad, too."

"As satisfying as watching you administering a beating would be, especially to the big guy, I think what we need is a lawyer," Sybil said. "Both Björn Björkman and Malcolm Moose said they had lawyers, so two − or three in the case − can play that game."

"Amen," Pastor Farber said.

"Déjà vu," Ruby said.

Augie nodded, apparently reminded of the epic lawsuit four years prior, the one Björkman had referred to. According to Ruby and the nodding Augie, the last time Björn decided to expand, six residents of Ahnwee sued him saying his farm would ruin their use and enjoyment of their property. A bitter court fight ensued with Björn's side arguing that manure is a part of nature and as such, belonged. The townspeople argued that fifty thousand pigs in way too small buildings is not "nature," but an environmental nightmare. That many pigs leave lots of crap − twenty-million gallons a year to be exact − and it has to go somewhere. The standard practice was to build a giant, open-air manure pond. That he did, resulting in three thousand acres of unholy goo. Björn pointed to his license from the state and made an "I have a right to do what-ever I want on MY property" argument. It worked.

"I don't know. Heck, maybe we could do better this time," Sybil said to blank stares.

"Sybil is right. We lost that time, but that doesn't mean we shouldn't try again," Sig said. "Maybe this judge won't be a crook."

"He wasn't so much a crook as a suck-up and moron," Ruby added.

"Crook, moron, whatever," Sig said. "I say we try the legal system. If that fails, it's the can of whoop ass," pounding his index finger on the counter.

Sybil scraped the last of cherry pie off the glass plate with her fork, making a terrible chalkboard sound. She said to no one in particular, but more addressing the room in general, "It doesn't make sense. Dang, how can this be?"

They stared despondently ahead.

"Dang?" Sig said.

They all looked up.

Sig looked at Sybil. "Mayor, what does Björkman keep in his smelly pond?"

"Manure," Sybil said.

"How would you describe Malcolm Moose?"

Sybil looked back and forth at people, not understanding the line of questioning. "I don't know. A meany?"

"What are we?" Sig asked, smile creeping in.

She shrugged.

"We're fucked, right?"

"I wouldn't say that," she replied.

"Wouldn't or won't? Mayor, do you ever swear?"

She straightened up. "Sure I do. When I'm mad enough." But she looked away, knowing that she was lying. She never swore. Something her mother drilled into her, that had stuck for good.

Sig laughed.

"Oh, don't tease her," Ruby said.

"I think it's refreshing," Pastor Farber said. "Not that any of it matters."

Sybil flashed back to New York, where people would make

fun of her, assigning this very non-New York behavior to her Midwestern-ness, and she was desperate to change the subject. "Let's call Schreiber."

Chapter 7: Alfonse Schreiber, Esquire

Sybil, Ruby, and Sig sat at an Arts and Crafts oak table with matching chairs in New York 'Tique, holding unmatched souvenir coffee mugs.

"Okay, let's try again," Sig said. "What's the opposite of 'he'?"

"She," Sybil said, rolling her eyes.

"And the hairy little guy in the *Addams Family*: Cousin… what?"

"It."

"Now put it together. What do you have?"

"Sig," Ruby said, "Really, give it a rest."

He laughed a laugh too big.

Sybil turned a shade red too bright.

They were waiting for the lawyer, Alfonse Schreiber. After their discussion at Flump's Café the day before, Sybil made the appointment with his receptionist, a girl who sounded like she was on helium. They were to meet at 10:00 a.m. at New York 'Tique with Ruby and Sig there to help.

Sybil thought how "help" was a gross understatement for what she needed at that moment. First her dad, then the casino, and now the pig farm. No, she didn't need help; she needed to be put out of her misery. Why couldn't the universe just let her go broke with her crummy business, spend her best years propping up a man who only knows TV shows prior to 1980, and grow into a shut-in old lady with eight cats like she planned?

Regardless of how she felt, there they were, looking determined and all business-like despite the not very business-y atmosphere of an antique store – stuff everywhere, shelves all the way up the walls and counters saved from the old hardware store. It was difficult to get around in, but Sybil kept an area toward the back to do business. That's where Schreiber found them when he arrived half an hour late.

He laid a leather bag on the table and pulled some papers out. He looked at one, and then another. "In my professional opinion, you guys are fucked."

"That's not helpful, Schreiber," Ruby said.

Alfonse Schreiber, Esquire, had "helped" Ahnwee with the failed lawsuit against Björn Björkman and the might-as-well-have-failed lawsuit against Wind Energy Now. He was a town kid, now fifty and living in Hutchinson, newly divorced, sporting a lifelike toupee and a soul patch, a Joseph Abboud sport jacket, jeans, and flip-flops.

Sig took a sip of coffee and winced. "Yeah, be specific, will you?" He said, adding whitener to his mug. Sybil kept a pot of coffee on, theoretically for customers, but since she had about three flesh-and-blood customers a week it was really for her, making it – shall we say – a robust brew.

"Well, after we talked yesterday," Schreiber replied, "I did some checking. Seems the wheels are well in motion on this, and frankly, maybe impossible to stop. There were hearings in May…"

"Hearings in May? What hearings?" Ruby said, taking a sip of coffee and making a face like she bit into a lemon.

"I didn't hear anything about hearings," Sybil said, holding tight to her "Polebridge Mercantile" mug.

"Mayor, you should have gotten a letter. Plus, the notice was probably posted in the back of the Willmar West Central Tribune. That's customary, anyway." Schreiber blew on his coffee and took a sip. He recoiled.

"What happened at the hearings?" Ruby asked.

"The minutes show that a number of people testified that Ahnwee was blighted, and no one spoke up against it, so it moved forward." A small trickle of brown sweat began to run down Schreiber's cheek. Very Rudy Giuliani, and Sybil couldn't take her eyes off it.

"I don't understand," Ruby said. "'Moved forward'? To where? What's the next step? Isn't there going to be a trial?"

Sybil felt admiration for Ruby for being a strong woman who knew how to speak up.

"Trial? No. It's all up to the county board now."

Ruby worked furiously on a pink baby blanket. "The county board? Since when do they settle title disputes?"

Schreiber looked around the table. "Title dispute? No, you don't understand. This is to get your town declared a blighted area to qualify for tax-increment financing and redevelopment."

Sig pointed a finger at Schreiber. "Are you drunk?" He looked at the others, throwing his hands skyward in exasperation. "Christ on a bike, this guy's drunk at ten in the morning."

Sybil once again thought of Rudy Giuliani.

"Alfonse, Björn Björkman is trying to say he has title to the entire town," Sybil said.

"Not to mention the Big Moose Casino looking to grab it up before Björn Björkman gets his hands on it," Ruby added, looking up from her blanket.

Schreiber looked at each in turn, then, "Man, you guys

truly are fucked." The trickle of sweat almost reached Schreiber's chin.

"Schreiber," Sig said, "that's that can-do attitude that cost us last time."

"Just for the record, that shit trial judge was a whacko." Schreiber said, leaning forward.

"Focus, people," Ruby said. "Alfonse, what's going on?"

"Look, I got a message that Ahnwee might be taken over and torn down, and to look into it. So, I did. I don't know anything about Björn Björkman or the Big Moose Casino, but I do know your town is doomed. I googled 'Ahnwee' and 'doomed' and the first hit was the county site with all the papers filed and the minutes from the board meeting. Wind Energy Now testified that the lake was toxic and unfit for people to live near, and the town is closed and in ruins. They declared it a blighted area, making it available for government bonds. At the July meeting, they will vote to approve issuing bonds for redevelopment, to pay for clearing it, cleaning it up, and burning the soil. That's when they are giving it to Wind Energy Now for a dollar. That's all public record."

No one said anything. No one moved. The trickle of sweat reached Schreiber's chin, hung on desperately, before dropping into his coffee cup.

Sig broke the silence. "Are you shitting me? Really, if you're shitting me, I'm going to go Sin City on you."

"Let me understand, Alfonse," Sybil said, trying not to let the meeting get out of control. "We have Malcolm Moose saying they are the victims of fraud a hundred-plus years old and he can prove it. We have Björkman saying he has title to the town. Now Wind Energy Now got the town condemned?"

Schreiber seemed to ignore Sig's hands planted firmly on the table as if he was about to launch across after him, instead focusing on Sybil. "Yeah, if what you are telling me is true.

Do you want me to look into Big Moose and Björkman, too?"

"I would guess that would be a good idea," Sig said, not trying to hide his sarcasm.

Chapter 8: It's All About the Core

Sybil, Ruby, and Sig set out to pay a visit to Wind Energy Now.

Like Big Moose Casino, Wind Energy Now abutted the town. Also like the Big Moose Casino, no road ran between fair Ahnwee and the vast Wind Energy Now facility. Unlike Big Moose Casino, it was not the result of passive-aggression; simply that no one had thought to build a road between the two.

After sending Schreiber off to do something useful, they set out in Sybil's Prius. Up the hill through the wind turbine they drove, then across the flatlands, past Sig's South Pacific Jerky, across more miles of flat, and then, as they approached Despar, the fields yielded to junk yards and trailer parks, before becoming Main Street with classic Minnesota brick small town architecture. They drove along at twenty-five, angle parking on either side, through five blocks of businesses: a craft store, a bar, another bar, Norm's Hardware, model trains, comic books, another bar, and Let's Go Crazy Printz, sporting a banner exclaiming, "Big Sail!" But no longer the Woolworth and Sears, places Sybil remembered well from her youth, nor the grocery that was bigger than the one in Ahnwee, nor the movie theater where she got her first kiss.

"Who's hungry?" Sig said.

Instead of getting on the highway, they went to Applebee's on the service road, between the Sam's Club and Office Max. They didn't like giving a corporate chain business, but a person can't eat at Flump's Café every day. Sybil thought about this moral dilemma: choosing between giant corporate conveniences and what remained of their main street. Ahnwee's assassins lined the highway calling to them with their cheap stuff, carefully crafted marketing, and air of casual inevitability. Like small towns across the American heartland, Ahnwee simply could no longer compete against this.

Like small towns everywhere, Ahnwee was once a center of commerce for the region, a town filled with hope and immigrant optimism.

To understand the rise and fall of Ahnwee, we need to go back once again to its founding. The doomsday cult members had made it through their first winter, given their work ethic and abundance of cooperation, both qualities of any good cult. They believed that they had received a reprieve from the end of the world and were thankful unto the Lord, and they were determined to make the most of it until the next time the world was about to end. They had a meeting and decided they liked the name, Ahnwee, for their town since it was imbued with authentic American Indian culture. They set about to build themselves sturdy frame houses, shops, and all the other accoutrements of a real town. They were happy. They planted gardens. They sired children. Soon, relatives from the Old World started moving in and building houses. More businesses opened on the newly plotted Broadway, the street they laid out to be nearly as wide as Berlin's *Unter den Linden*.

Soon, Ahnwee became a popular destination for German immigrants, happy to find people speaking the mother tongue in the New World. The population grew from seventeen in 1901 to fifty-five by 1905, and an incredible three hundred and fifty by 1910. In 1915 they built a glorious Lutheran church (they named it "Third Lutheran" because they felt "First Lutheran" would be bragging and "Second Lutheran" not much better than "First"). These were heady days for Ahnwee, with businesses booming as a minor agricultural center for the German farmers in the area, competing with Despar those seven miles away. While agriculture was a mainstay of any Minnesota prairie town, Ahnwee's claim to fame was as a tourist destination. Max Schroeder could never have imagined it, but he did, ultimately, succeed in that Germans liked to go to Ahnwee. Several hotels and resorts did brisk business along the lake as visitors looking to relax arrived by train from the Twin Cities. Even more businesses opened and thrived. A school opened. They built an opera house, which was the pride of town, bringing to Ahnwee not operas, but musical acts, plays, and comedy shows from all over the country. The tourists loved it, as did the locals. Abe Lyman and his band played there in 1938 to three hundred happy visitors, residents and farmers alike, an event still talked about in some circles.

By 1940, the census recorded twelve hundred residents.

Unfortunately, that was about it. The war came, and German tourism never recovered. By the fifties, the resorts were closed and torn down. More and more young people left Ahnwee, moving to Willmar or even the Twin Cities. The population began to decline. Farms grew in size, meaning there were fewer farmers farther apart to buy goods from the hardware store and drugstore. The farm crisis of the late 1970s and early 1980s didn't help, driving not only farmers under, but also a number of the town's businesses. When the railroad decided to drop its spur to Ahnwee in 1985, it was the end of agribusiness.

By the time of Sybil's formative years in the 1990s, much of the old remained, running on momentum and denial. She remembered shopping for clothes on Broadway at a one-floor department store, getting groceries at a perfectly fine little market next to the old, abandoned opera house, and buying cheap perfume for her mother at Berlitz Drugs. As business slowly but unrelentingly eroded, people went about their lives, generally oblivious to the town's impending doom. What else was there to do? A highlight for town history during Sybil's youth was in 2000 when an elderly drunk guy, who swore Abe Lyman was his real father, torched the opera house, taking the grocery next door with it, making for a particularly photogenic blaze on the evening news. But the biggest blow came when Sybil was a teen and they "improved" the highway into a freeway, bypassing town. As a result, big box retailers were built along the freeway in Despar, dooming the last of Ahnwee's businesses.

Ahnwee went down not in a blaze of glory but in a whimper of cheap prices.

Insult to injury? That was the wind turbine.

A couple years before Sybil moved back from New York, Wind Energy Now was found to be dumping chemicals on their property. Not chemicals that they themselves used, mind you, but chemicals brought in from elsewhere and dumped on Wind Energy Now' property. It cost companies with noxious chemical waste pennies on the dollar to pay Wind Energy Now to let them come at night and empty their blue plastic barrels, and Wind Energy Now figured they had the land, so what the hell. It worked for a few years, but then one day on Lake Ahnwee, which Wind Energy Now and the town of Ahnwee both bordered, all the fish simply floated to the top, including some impressive sturgeons. From then on, the lake was dead. Now not even milfoil, an invasive seaweed and scourge of many Minnesota lakes for fouling propellers, could live in Lake Ahnwee. Boaters might have been happy about the propeller thing if anyone would be willing to boat there, but no one in their right mind would go out on that lake. Due to the particular mixture of the dozens of chemicals that washed into it, the water soon glowed a florescent green. In fact, if a person were willing to sit close to it, they could read a book at midnight during a new moon.

To make up for their criminal malfeasance, Wind Energy Now offered Ahnwee a free wind turbine, promising them enough power for the entire town for as long as there was a Wind Energy Now. The residents of Ahnwee, all two hundred and sixty-two of them, gathered in the church to decide what to do. It was a difficult meeting. Some thought they should clean it up, but others thought it was a land rights thing, that Wind Energy Now had the right to dump whatever they wanted on their property. They asserted that if you don't want to get cancer, boils, or gruesome lesions, then you don't have to go near the lake. Eventually, the reality that Wind Energy Now had thirty lawyers with Italian suits and all the town of Ahnwee had was Alfonse Schreiber, a sweaty, middle-aged ambulance chaser, they agreed the free power sounded good if Wind Energy Now would throw in broadband.

They built the wind turbine on top of the only thing that could be called a hill anywhere nearby, at the very end of Broadway on the west side, just as it ceases to be a street and becomes a county road. Right away, two problems arose: the least of them was that most times of the year in the last half hour before sunset there was a strobe effect all over town. Two residents who were epileptic had to move after the first week. But the biggest problem was that they made a huge mistake: they used the UDF150 tower with GTF 148 blades. They should have used a UDF212 tower. This meant the tower was too short, so that cars driving down Broadway heading out of town had to drive through the blades swooping around almost touching the road. At first there were a couple accidents, but no one was killed, and the townspeople grew used to it.

But used to it or not, every sweep of the blade, every strobe effect in the evening, every evening green glow off the lake, reminded the remaining residents of Ahnwee that the best days for Ahnwee were far, far behind them.

After lunch, and after Sig won a huge superball from the claw machine in the entrance of Applebee's, they continued east on the freeway. The rest of the five-mile drive was prairie: flat and mostly treeless, except for the occasional unnatural bunches of oak and cottonwoods in the distance where a farmhouse used to be. When farmers had settled on the Dakota land, they of course built houses, which meant planting trees around them in an attempt to mitigate the brutal winter winds. Then, one by one over the last century or so, most of them sold their land and moved someplace else, leaving abandoned farmhouses and tufts of trees every half-mile. The remaining farmers now had huge farms, perfect for efficient corn production to satisfy America's thirst for gasoline and sugar.

Wind Energy Now' enormous parking lot teemed with what looked like a thousand cars. In front of the enormous, green-painted concrete building was perched an enormous metal abstract sculpture and prairie grass landscaping, and across the lot, seven enormous semis idled, waiting to get their enormous loads from rows of enormous wind turbine parts.

In the lobby, a male receptionist wearing all Columbia and a headset, leaning on a standing workstation, greeted them. The office appeared right out of some *Architectural Digest* magazine, black Wassily chairs as guest seating around kidney-shaped glass tables, giving both a modern and retro feel at the same time. Tiny LED lights hung from a grid of wires overhead, the floor made of cork. After Sybil identified herself as the Mayor of Ahnwee, the receptionist touched a button on his headset, announcing the guests. He said, "Ms. Hoffman will be pleased to see you immediately."

After saying how sorry she was for keeping them waiting, even though they had been there less than a minute, Ms. Hoffman said, "I'm so sorry about your town," shaking Sybil's hand. Ms. Hoffman wore a floor-length hemp skirt and a "Life is Good" fuchsia sweatshirt. She looked to be in her forties with a full head of gray hair, and her frame the kind of thin that says not eating enough protein. "If there's anything I can do, please call me any time."

"Yeah, okay, right, see, that's what we are doing right now," Sig said.

Ms. Hoffman walked behind her desk and sat down awkwardly. The desk dominated the office, and along the walls were a rack of Swiss exercise balls, a fica tree, and a huge flat screen playing CNBC. "Let me get you some refreshments." She touched her headset and said, "Ted, please bring us some kale juice." She turned back to her visitors. "We juice our own kale as part of our worksite wellness program." Then, "Please! Sit down!" She gasped in embarrassment for not having offered.

Sybil, Ruby, and Sig looked around the chairless room. Then Sybil noticed Ms. Hoffman bouncing slightly, and Sybil saw through the top of the glass desk that she was sitting on one of the balls. Sybil pulled a red ball off the rack, set it on the floor, and sat down. Her colleagues observed her, and each took a ball from the rack. Ruby sat down. Sig did not. Not much taller than the ball, he stood behind the red globe. "Really?" he said.

Ms. Hoffman saw the problem with horror. "I am so, so sorry. How insensitive of me." She touched her headset. "Ted, please find me a small ball immediately. IMMEDIATELY." She turned back to Sig. "At Wind Energy Now, we take great pride in running a truly accessible business, celebrating those people who are differently-abled. I don't know how we missed this; it seems so obvious now. I pledge to you we will remove all these ridiculously large balls and replace them with ones more accessible to all in our society."

Sig appeared to be trying to maintain control. "Yeah, well, that's not necessary. But something to sit on would be nice."

"Ted," Ms. Hoffman said into her headset, hand on one ear. "We need something for our new friend, Sig, to sit on NOW."

Sybil bounced slightly, trying to get a handle on it. She heard Sig mutter, "Tulips."

"Mayor, you look like someone who enjoys yoga. We offer mandatory noon yoga classes for all our comrades."

"Comrades?"

"Our staff. That's what we call our staff. You are welcome to join us any time."

What made Ms. Hoffman think she liked yoga? Sybil wondered. Even though she lived with Drew the yoga instructor in New York, she really didn't like yoga all that much. Too much pseudo-spirituality. Then she remembered: she had on

74

black yoga pants and a black shirt, looking every bit like a charter member of a yoga studio.

"As Sig was saying, we are here to talk about Ahnwee," Ruby said.

"Yes, yes, of course you are. Like I said, we here at Wind Energy Now are so sorry to hear that your town is going to be torn down."

"The hell it is, lady!" Sig said. He closed his eyes and said through clenched teeth, "Daisies."

"Oh, am I mistaken? I'm sorry, do I have the wrong town?"

"No," Ruby said, now knitting away on the ever-growing pink baby blanket, exercise ball or no exercise ball. "You have the right town. We came to see what we need to do to stop you from taking our homes."

"You are misinformed." Ms. Hoffman laughed slightly, an insincere sort of laugh. "Wind Energy Now isn't going to tear down your town."

"It's not?" Sybil said.

"No. What right would we have to do that?"

"Exactly," Sig said. "But wait a minute, if you're not tearing the town down, why are you sorry?"

"WE are not tearing down your town: the county is. I understand – now, I wasn't there, but from the meeting minutes – that Ahnwee is in the process of being declared a blighted area and thus eligible for tax increment financing."

"What does that mean?" Ruby said.

"It means the county will sell bonds to tear down the buildings and then subsidize a business to come in and make something of it. To improve it."

"And that business would be?" Ruby said.

"Wind Energy Now," Ms. Hoffman said with that same smile. "We plan to build a parts storage facility there."

Sig stepped forward, "Lady, I ought to – " He stopped,

closed his eyes, and said slowly, "Marigolds."

"How is it Ahnwee is 'blighted'?" Sybil asked, hoping to keep the lid on things while not falling off the ball.

"Well, all I know is what I read, but I recall they talked about how all the businesses are closed and there are many abandoned houses. Plus, the lake is polluted."

"Yes, we know," Sig said, "You polluted it!" He took a deep breath. "Pansies."

"A really unfortunate incident. Really."

"Really," Ruby said.

"Really," Ms. Hoffman said.

"And not *all* the businesses are closed. There's mine, and Ruby's, and the café," Sybil said.

"Sad, isn't it?" Ms. Hoffman said, still with the smile that was really beginning to creep Sybil out. "Say, how is the wind turbine working out?"

"No one has been hit in the last month," Sybil said.

"Good. And hopefully the broadband is still a benefit."

Sybil thought about Zooming Drew. Broadband was nice.

"Ms. Hoffman," Ruby said, calmly knitting away. "You can't have our town. Those are our homes. Sure, most of the businesses are gone, but we're still there and we're not moving."

"Good for you! Stand up to the man!" she said.

No one knew what to say, jaws slack. Sybil wasn't certain if Ms. Hoffman was simply passive-aggressive, or a full-on psychopath.

Ted the receptionist brought in a case of printer paper and set it down next to Sig. "I'm sorry, but this was all I could find."

Sig looked up at Ted. "You want me to sit on this box?"

Ted said nothing.

Sig closed his eyes. "Petunias – oh, fuck it! I'm going to

mess you up!" Sig said, taking off after him. Ted screamed, running around the room, staying ahead of an out-for-blood Sig only by virtue of his long legs. Sybil was so startled that she bounced off her ball and into the fica tree.

It was late afternoon and rather than drive all the way back to Ahnwee, they went to Sig's store halfway between Ahnwee and Despar. The small, bright mango-colored cement block building was right off the county road with a dirt parking lot in front and a house in back, with cornfields on both sides. The sun was at its most prairie summer intense, and Sybil went to the pop machine by the door and asked Ruby if she wanted one. RC, she said, so Sybil dropped the coins in for Ruby and an Orange Crush for herself, the change box echoing with near emptiness. She joined Ruby on the blue retro metal lawn chairs.

"Let me make sure I understand all this," Sig said, opening the machine with a key and getting a can of Dad's Root Beer for himself, before sitting down. "The county says the town is blighted, so they'll issue bonds to tear it down and subsidize Wind Fucking Energy to store wind turbine parts there, the very same peckers who polluted the lake in the first place making the town blighted."

"Yup," Sybil bounced, admiring the classic chairs.

"So does old boil-face Björn Björkman know that? Or Malcolm Moose?" Sig said.

"Beats me," Sybil said. "Maybe they do, and they are trying to cut Wind Energy Now off at the pass." Sybil wiped her forehead with her palm, which she wiped on her black yoga pants. She continued, "What do you guys think we should do?"

They sat, saying nothing, light breeze from the west chasing the stink away. Sybil thought about how she hadn't spent time at anyone else's house in a long time. Sig had it good out here, she decided. While not a mansion – just a cement-block store and a doublewide in back – Sig had landscaped it with trees, walks, a water feature, and several raised garden beds of all kinds of flowers, bright and colorful in the sun. "Great garden, Sig," she said.

He told her about his life-long interest in gardening and landscaping. "It relaxes me."

"What's up with your saying flower names back there?" Ruby asked.

He looked embarrassed. "It's something I try to do to stay in control."

"Well, it sure didn't work."

"You know, Sig, you'll probably be fine here. They shouldn't tear this down," Sybil said.

Sig scratched his head. "I spent my whole life going to Ahnwee. It's not right. What are we supposed to do? Hang around goddamn Walmart?"

No one said anything, all bouncing slightly in the metal chairs, Ruby's hands in constant action as always. "I hate going to Walmart. That place and all the others like it wrecked this town." Ruby said.

"I go to Walmart. I admit it," Sybil said, rubbing her shoulder where she landed on the fica tree. "If not there, then Target or Dollar General, but it's all the same. What else is there? Everyone who sold anything useful went out of business a long time ago."

"Knitters would beg to differ," Ruby said without a hint of anger.

"Sorry."

"No, you're right. And I go to the big boxes, too."

"It's the world we live in," Sig added.

"I miss my drugstore," said Ruby. "I miss the store, but I miss my Jerry a lot more."

It was the first time Sybil heard Ruby refer to her late husband. She couldn't imagine losing someone after a lifetime together. "It was a good store, Ruby. What a store should be."

"I remember going in there when I was a little," Sig said.

Sybil wanted to laugh, but she felt guilty and controlled herself.

"I don't know if anyone will have fond memories of going to those humongous stores on the highway in Ahnwee," said Ruby.

"Have you ever been to Disney World?" Sybil asked.

Both Sig and Ruby shook their heads no.

"I went there with college friends on spring break. The first thing you find is a fake main street. It's like a three-quarter scale make-believe small town. Every year a few million tourists file down the spotless street buying useless souvenirs in fake barbershops and fake hardware stores so they can roll in nostalgia for a time they never saw and a community they never had. Yet they go home, and instead of building a real one for themselves, they shop at Shopco. You know what I wish? I wish we could have a real town with a real main street again."

Sig and Ruby nodded.

Sybil thought, is that really what I want? Yes, but something else, something a real main street represents to her: a community. Connectedness. Maybe other residents of Ahnwee already felt like they had that, but Sybil spent scant time with anyone but her father, as if a virtual shut-in herself. Oh, she attended the occasional mayor-type meeting, and of course she Zoomed with Drew, but still, until all this craziness brought her, Ruby, and Sig together, she hadn't realized how starved for human contact she was. She wanted to feel like she belonged. She longed for friends. She needed conversations with neighbors.

Yes, she had to admit it, if only to herself; she was sort of enjoying that part of the crisis: being around other people.

"Our town," Ruby said.

Sybil asked what she meant.

"You asked what we had. We have our town, and we have each other."

Chapter 9: Those Songs *Are* Catchy

After sitting around South Pacific Jerky and drinking enough pop to get a good sugar high going, Sybil, Ruby, and Sig hit on a plan: Commissioner Harry Balzac. Balzac could save the day; after all, he was their representative on the county board. He was the one person who had the pull to make it happen. If he said Ahnwee wasn't blighted, the other commissioners would shrug and go long, they were sure of it. They decided they needed to have a meeting with the old hippo and get him on board.

But enough for one day. They each had a business to attend to; it would wait until tomorrow.

Sybil went back to New York 'Tique in hopes of getting some work done, even though she was hardly in the mood. It was all too much. When she ran for mayor a year ago, she did it partly out of a belief that she could breathe some life into the old town, and partly because Augie and Ruby and a couple others suggested it and she was honored to be asked. How many times in your life will you be asked to run for mayor? That she ran unopposed only made it sweeter. She figured that being mayor wouldn't be much work considering the size of dear Ahnwee, and that it would be good for the ego. It was in fact not much work – answering junk mail, signing stuff, going to a conference or two on her own dime. But it wasn't good for the ego at all. Most days or even weeks, she could forget she was the mayor for lack of anything to do, and when she was reminded, it wasn't good. On those days, being mayor was like running a highly dysfunctional committee, populated with people who had loud opinions and didn't do anything, people who did stuff but the wrong stuff, and people who immediately set about to tear you off your high horse. Sometimes she felt alone, exposed, thrown under the bus.

And now all this.

After an hour, and in the middle of packing a vintage Hot Wheels case for a regular customer in Phoenix, she decided to go home. Granted, it was only two o'clock, but she had had enough for one day. Shipping junk could wait.

Given that the wind was out of the south and the usual smell was livable, she decided to walk. Her car was right there in front of Flump's Café on Broadway, but her house was only three blocks away. In her old New York neighborhood if you got a parking spot within three blocks you were doing well, so she didn't think anything about leaving her car and stretching her legs. She did sometimes sense that people in Ahnwee thought she was a goofball for walking so much; she could see the looks, the pointing, practically mouthing the words, "who walks?"

Off Broadway, she walked in the street (no sidewalks) past houses, most dating to the teens and twenties, of random styles and upkeep, some with paved driveways, some not, a few idyllic with porches and lawn furniture, most with rusty clothes washers and couches on an uncut lawn. No one was outside. Many of the houses were abandoned, and the ones that weren't were nearly all occupied by the elderly. If she wanted to see the people of Ahnwee, all she needed to do was walk in the back door, where they'd likely be watching *The*

Price is Right.

It wasn't always like this. She remembered how when she was a kid, she and her friends were outside all summer, especially on such a gorgeous afternoon, biking and playing games they made up on the spot, chasing littler kids and being chased by dogs. It was all very Dick and Jane. Not anymore. When her friends grew up, they left at the first opportunity. That's what Sybil did as well; she was eighteen years old when she went away to college hoping never to return. Nothing about Ahnwee was attractive for young people. There was more to look forward to in life than watching a town die; the TV said so every night. There was the promise of the world of *Friends* and *Cheers*, a world of coffee shops, attractive people, and guaranteed social success. Never mind most never found it, but once a young metaphorical immigrant sees the allegorical Statue of Liberty, there's no going back. Eventually they got jobs and significant others and kids of their own. Still, Ahnwee offered nothing more for a young family than it did for a young single. Plus, what could those families do for a living? Bottom line, there was no good reason to move back to Ahnwee for anyone under sixty, so no one did.

Except for Sybil.

On the corner of Second Street North, Sybil was heartened to see a gray-haired Mrs. Schmidt working in the garden in front of a small white house with peeling paint. The woman's posture reminded her of a yard butt. The woman stood up, wiped her hands on her apron, and waved. Sybil waved back. She had waved at Mrs. Schmidt for as long as she had been alive. All the time she was in New York only one person waved at her walking down the street, and he was dressed as a plush toy. She knew everyone in town. In New York, she didn't know the guy across the hall who she would see but never speak with, who wore an electronic ankle bracelet the entire time she lived there. These are good people, she thought. She planned to escape back to New York someday, but these people deserve better than having their houses unceremoniously torn down.

She remembered the time that Mrs. Schmidt called her father because Sybil had parked on the street steaming up the windows with her high school love, who later turned out to be gay. Sybil smiled. You couldn't prove it that night. Anyway, her father didn't do anything dramatic like go outside and bang on the windshield. Instead, when Sybil got in the house, he was waiting for her with his best stern look. He didn't seem mad, really. More serious. He stood there, straight backed, authoritative, everything she looked up to, and he said, "Be careful. A small town like Ahnwee never forgets."

Those were good days. She wasn't really popular, but she tried by participating in the school paper and lettering in cross country skiing – an activity she hasn't pursued in years – and got through school with minimal psychological damage and a reasonable share of optimism. Nothing but upside as far as she could see. Off to college, get married when she was good and ready, be a professional.

She did go off to college, to the University of Iowa, and earned a degree in public policy. Why public policy? She was never sure, other than there was a promise of intrigue and influence. It didn't turn out to do a thing for her career-wise, but she thought it did look good when she ran for mayor. Since then, she had come to realize that it made no difference in the world, that to be Mayor of Ahnwee the mirror test was the relevant criteria. And intrigue and influence? Negatory on the influence, she was finding out. And intrigue? Be careful what you wish for.

She arrived at her and her father's house, a simple white box of a fifties vintage on the outskirts of Ahnwee, two blocks from Broadway. Everywhere she looked were ghosts. The weeds were taking over the petunias she had planted along the walk that spring. Sybil was never much for gardening. Back when her mother was alive, these flowerbeds would have been filled with carefully curated annuals such as mums and zinnias, plus her mom's prize rose bushes along the foundation. The rose bushes were still there, but due to lack of care, it was hard to imagine their former glory. Yes, Sybil thought, Mom would be spinning in her grave to know how her lovely yard had gone to pot. When Sybil was a girl, she always thought it was too perfect, too frou-frou. Her mom would start plants from seeds in the basement under lights to get a jump on the short Minnesota growing season. As soon as it looked feasible, usually around the second week of May, Sybil would help her get them in the ground. When she was a teen Sybil would complain about having to do it.

What she wouldn't give now to be tending flowers with her mom.

Going in the back door and into the kitchen, she yelled, "Hi, Dad! I'm home!" She could hear the television blasting *Petticoat Junction* in the living room.

"Sybil?" Dan said. He stood in the doorway wearing only his tighty-whiteys.

His coherence gave Sybil pause. "Yes, Dad?"

"Do you feel like a nut?"

"What?"

"Do you feel like a nut? Sometimes you feel like a nut, sometimes you don't."

Sybil relaxed. "Yeah, I guess I do. Do you want anything to eat?"

"Almond Joy."

"Yeah, well, we don't have any of those. Let me fix you a grilled cheese." Dan drifted back into the living room as Sybil pulled the Kraft slices out of the fridge and opened up a new package of Wonder Bread, both Dan's favorites. She put the sandwich in the George Foreman grill.

Lately, Dan had been paying more attention to the old commercials showing on TV Land than the sitcoms that he had been focused on for so long. Either way, Sybil considered TV Land a blessing – it meant she could still go to work, knowing exactly where Dan would be when she got home. That is, until Ahnwee Days. Happily, since then things had returned to normal, with no more streaking Broadway. Sybil laughed a tiny bit under her breath at the idea that any of this was "normal."

Of course, it wasn't always like that for Sybil's father. He had had an amazingly normal life, for most of it.

Dan was born and raised in Ahnwee, and he went to school at the long-closed Our Lady of Eternal Judgment until eighth grade, before heading off to Despar High. After Dan graduated, he went off to the Army like most boys. He was lucky and didn't go to Vietnam; instead, the Army assigned him to the 9th Infantry and the defense of Fairbanks, Alaska. Apparently, the thought was that so goes Fairbanks, goes the nation. Dan had the heady responsibility of counting stuff – shells, bullets, nuclear warheads, that sort of thing. It was good work and generally warm, which made Dan's morale infinitely better than most Alaska grunts who were out on the tundra. While there he met Margaret, or Maggie, Placnick. He met her as many young soldiers met their future brides – on leave in town at a dance club she had snuck away to. Maggie was a long-haired beauty and the middle child of seven. She sold bear claws by day – the pastry kind – at a little bakery sporting bottomless cups of nearly clear coffee. Soon Dan was spending all his free time drinking weak coffee and gaining weight.

After four years of defending that beautiful if godforsaken piece of real estate, he got his honorable discharge and moved back to Ahnwee with his new bride. As the only son, Dan and Maggie moved into the family home and Dan's two older sisters moved to Minneapolis where they met young men of their own and lived good lives, if short – one dying from breast cancer at forty and the other from a shark attack at twenty-nine.

Dan and his wife had lived a reasonable life in Ahnwee. In addition to raising two boys and one girl, Maggie looked after Dan's mother in her later years, having been widowed early when Dan's father had died of alcohol poisoning after drinking too many Smirnoffs celebrating the bicentennial. Dan worked at the grain elevator, back-breaking, filthy work, hauling around hundred-pound sacks of feed and generally keeping the local farmers in supplies and moving their product. It was a small elevator and never did much business (most farmers went to Despar), but at least there was one. In the seventies and early eighties, the train still ran to Ahnwee, but when that went out, it was the beginning of the end. The final nail in the coffin was when the freeway bypassed Ahnwee, making it almost impossible for truckers to service the elevator. Dan worked to the bitter end in 1993 when it shut down for good.

Now in his fifties, Dan lived off unemployment and looked for new work. At least he did at first. The unemployment ran out after the hope, and soon he sat for endless hours on the couch doing nothing but watching TV. Maggie, taking care of Dan's mother, was now taking care of Dan as well, who didn't seem interested in much anymore. Soon the house was in ill repair, the walk unshoveled, the lawn unmown. Maggie tried everything, but Dan wasn't budging from that couch. When Dan's mother went in the nursing home in 1998 Maggie's workload lessened. Or so she thought.

One day in 2003, after ten years of doing nothing, Dan was watching daytime TV as usual. He tended toward old sit-coms, always looking down on soaps as a waste of time. *The Brady Bunch* came on, with that insipid theme song. Dan started singing along. Soft at first, then at the top of his lungs. Screaming out all the stuff about hair color and curls. When the song was over, he kept on going, and going, and going. Maggie came into the room to see what the matter was during the third verse, took an aspirin at the fifth, called the doctor at the eighth, the ambulance at the fifteenth. Something was clearly wrong – Dan's eyes were glassed over, and he didn't even try to carry a tune. They took him to the hospital in Despar. It took sedation to shut him up. He spent a week there, undergoing every test anyone could think of. The diagnosis was a media-induced psychosis, complicated with the worst case of tinnitus anyone had ever seen or even heard of, plus a case of gout. In short, Dan had sore legs and his brain had turned to mush from sitcoms.

Maggie took care of him as best she could. She really gave it her all. He rarely went outside, instead sitting on the sagging couch watching TV all day and singing along to the theme songs at the top of his lungs. It was amazing Maggie didn't have a psychotic break herself. One morning she had enough and finally did one thing for herself: she died of a stroke right at the kitchen table. She might have sat there until she turned to dust, but a neighbor found Dan, naked, raiding the birdfeeder. Being Ahnwee, the neighbor obviously knew Dan, so instead of calling the cops, he walked Dan home, discovering the week-old corpse of Maggie in a housedress, a cold cup of weak coffee in front of her.

Sybil and her two brothers had a family meeting of sorts. No one mentioned institutionalization, but no one mentioned taking on being responsible for their father, either. Very quickly Sybil figured out that there was no question that she would be the person to care for him. Dan Junior and Ronny couldn't seem to get out of town fast enough after their mother's funeral.

Sybil moved back to Ahnwee.

That was two years ago. It was not that she didn't know what she was getting into – no, she knew well, being the youngest and getting a full dose of Dan's early years of craziness. On the other hand, Sybil's brothers had no idea, no idea at all what it was like for their mother to take care of Dan, nor did they know what Sybil was giving up. They knew even less about the current situation since neither had been home in over a year, when they appeared at their father's seventieth birthday, and Dan gave a good demonstration of his affliction, starting with sixteen choruses of the *Love Boat* theme song without a single change of tone. The brothers agreed that it was eccentric and entertaining, and they couldn't understand what Sybil was whining about. Sybil tried to explain that it may be eccentric and entertaining to watch your father smear marble cake all over his shirtless, concave chest once, but when stuff like that happens every day, the humor wears off.

She took a spatula and put the perfectly melted sandwich on a plate. "Come and get it, Dad!" she yelled into the living room. She put the plate on the table and laid a cloth napkin next to it. Dan came in, now wearing the throw from the back of the couch like a toga. Sybil was impressed how her father knew how to get it tucked just right to stay on.

"Sybil?" Dan said, looking up.

Sybil, who was wiping down the George Foreman grill with a wet paper towel, stopped. "Yes, Dad?"

"Sweetheart?"

"Yes, Dad?"

"Wouldn't you like to be a pepper, too?"

Sybil sighed. She resumed her work at the sink. "Yes, Dad. In fact, I would."

After he finished his sandwich and they sat in silence for too long at the table, Sybil put Dan in his chair and launched his TV Land sedative. She went back in kitchen for a strong cup of coffee and a little dose of reality via Zoom.

"Hey, babe!" Drew said, wearing a bathrobe, hair in a towel. Drew told her she was going to go to a new club with this basketball player she met at a party. "He's not NBA, but he's still hot," she said.

Sybil filled her New York friend in on the latest, and Drew was a good listener. "So, add in the wind turbine factory with the hog farm and casino, we have crumb-bums coming at us from all sides."

"'Crumb-bums'?"

Sybil could feel her face turning red.

"I miss you, Sybbie."

"I miss you, D."

They were quiet for a moment, then, "Tough love?" Drew hesitated. "Maybe it's meant to be. Maybe it's a sign that it's time to move back to the city."

"No matter what happens to Ahnwee, I have to take care of Dad." Lately Drew had become more insistent. It wasn't as if Sybil hadn't thought about it, and often. How could things get any worse? Sybil wondered. Really, how? Dad was deteriorating every day. She was not making money, or at least not enough. She had no friends. Now the town itself was in danger of dying.

"There are other ways. Maybe it's time, you know? What about your brothers? Can they take over with your dad?"

"They're no use. They don't even visit anymore."

"And what, 'cause you're a girl you have to be the care-giver? Seriously?"

Sybil shrugged.

"Just think about it, okay? Promise me?"

Sybil nodded. She admired Drew. How could she be so strong, and how could I get some of that mojo? Drew was from Nantucket, for Pete's sake; she grew up practically playing with Fabergé eggs. Sybil grew up where the weather was constantly trying to kill you. Yet she didn't feel strong at all; she felt more like she was dragging around a bag of rocks. People like Drew seemed to be born to polish rocks into diamonds, not drag them around.

After they ended their check-in, Sybil closed her laptop and leaned back. She wasn't sure if she felt better or worse for talking to Drew. Maybe Drew and Ruby were right. Maybe it WAS time to cut her losses, put her dad in the Good Shepherd nursing home in Despar, and go back to New York. She moved home to take care of her father, but maybe she was wrong to think she could take care of him in the first place. There are people who make caring for the mentally ill their profession. Sybil didn't repair her own car. She didn't pre-tend to be an architect or a bridge designer or rocket scientist. Maybe she shouldn't pretend she could take care of some-one with serious challenges. She decided she was in denial. She had to admit to herself how challenged Dad was. Not only that, she had to accept that he probably would never get better. Her mother and now Sybil always held out the hope that, just like how all of a sudden he fell into his mass-culture dementia, maybe he would fall out of it just as suddenly. She laughed. It had been years. He's not snapping out of it. She was fooling herself. She didn't like thinking like that, and she tried to move that thought out of her head, but she couldn't.

She went in the living room and sat on the edge of the coffee table, muting the Rifleman. "Dad, let me ask you something."

Dan continued to stare at the quiet TV.

"Are you happy, Dad?"

Dan didn't move or change his expression.

"Dad? Would you be happier where you could have more company, maybe people your own age, activities?"

Dan finally looked at her.

"I mean, am I really helping? Maybe it would be better to give you some professional help. I try, you know I do, but I don't know if it's enough, you know? And I don't know if I can keep doing this forever. What do you think, Dad?"

"What do I think?"

Sybil sat astounded by coherency of the question. "Yes, Dad?"

Dan looked right through Sybil, not saying a word.

CHAPTER 10: INTERESTING IS GOOD

After leaving Sig's, Ruby didn't go back to work, she just went home. She felt depressed. She wanted to be strong – she always wanted to be strong, stronger than her size and gender would automatically imply – but she wasn't feeling it. Alone time, that's what she wanted, and at Knotty Knits it wasn't guaranteed like it was at home.

She put on a pot of water and found a tea bag of Lipton, wrapping the string around the handle so it wouldn't fall in the water, and sat at her kitchen table, the same kitchen table she'd sat at for nearly a half-century. She had to admit that talking about Jerry for the first time in a long time brought back feelings, complex ones at that.

Ruby's clear stand on defending Ahnwee was built on one part a desire for justice for her and her neighbors, one part wanting to make sure Björn Björkman didn't win, and another part affection for the place she'd lived her whole life, short a spectacular four-year *rumspringa*.

Like everyone else, Ruby went to Despar High. Unlike everyone else of her gender, generation, and location, instead of getting married immediately after high school, she left Ahnwee. People were shocked. They shouldn't have been. It was the sixties, and times they were a-changin'. While people in Ahnwee didn't get to experience it firsthand, they got to see it on the television. Ruby saw The Beatles on Ed Sullivan as a little girl. She saw what was happening in San Francisco as a tween. She saw the roles for women as changing. She wanted some of that. Not a lot, mind you – she was still a young girl from the plains, but she knew she had to have a taste.

Her decision to leave Ahnwee was greatly facilitated by a story she saw in *Boy's Life* magazine about adventures in national parks. Rangers, guides, fire jumpers – all jobs the magazine talked about routinely. However, being a girl, her range of possibilities was greatly limited, so instead of a life of horseback and danger, she became a switchboard operator at the East Glacier Lodge at Glacier National Park. She had applied and gotten the job via mail. She had a going away party. Relatives came. Friends got drunk. Her parents cried. The next morning, her best friend, bleary-eyed and hungover, drove her to Fargo to catch the train that would drop her at her new life.

Her Glacier adventures were happy days for Ruby. Independence. Autonomy. Boys. Lou Reed. More boys. She was too responsible and sober by nature to have a summer of love thing in Montana, but she didn't think anything of going rafting on the south fork of the Flathead River with a group of like-minded peers of all genders, or going to a bar in Whitefish for a little dancing or riding around in muscle cars with muscly boys.

Her parents pleaded with her to return home to Ahnwee and get married like she was supposed to. She didn't. Not the first year, nor the second, nor the third. When her father had a heart attack, there was no saying no. He had worked in the bank as a vice president, which sounds more impressive than it was at that time, as he had to take over for tellers for their lunches and breaks and would mop the floor himself as needed. That was all fine, but the bank's president was a raging dry-drunk who made his life hell. Everyone said that's what brought on the heart attack, but Ruby thought it was the Pall Malls and his extra hundred pounds.

She returned to Ahnwee an interesting woman. Hers was a brand unknown to most Ahnweeians: adventure, cowboys, rafting. Yes, interesting. Most women in Ahnwee would never want to be described as "interesting," since it was usually a euphemism for "wanton." Ruby liked it.

Another person who liked it was Jerry Berlitz. Her future husband, eight years her senior, saw in Ruby the excitement he lacked in life. Ruby saw Jerry as her next chance to get out of the house, since helping her mother take care of her father was wearing thin. And she needed the money. No one would hire Ruby with the "wanton" thing metaphorically sewed to her shirt and with no jobs in the area anyway, and Jerry was a successful pharmacist, working for his father at Ahnwee's lone drugstore, Berlitz Drugs.

They married after a brief courtship, and he proceeded to suppress all the excitement out of her. Jerry liked the interesting part of Ruby, but that was in the past. Still, she learned to love him and their quiet life. Soon Jerry took over for his father when the elder Berlitz died in an unspeakable accident – still spoken about to this day – in his closet involving a tie and a chair and no pants. For the next four-plus decades, Ruby and Jerry ran the business together. Ruby spent those years at the register and taking care of most everything that didn't involve counting pills. They had three girls, all of whom left as soon as they turned eighteen, never to return but for brief visits. Life was the store and home. The one social outlet she had was a knitting circle, which seemed to involve as much wine as yarn.

Together Jerry and Ruby kept that pharmacy open believing he was offering a vital service to the community. When they finally closed, his last twenty customers transferred their prescription to Walmart in Despar. Then Jerry died. Well, not immediately, but in about six months. He had a massive heart attack – again, fatty food and no exercise equaled an extra hundred pounds – and died in Ruby's arms.

She was heartbroken. And, she had never felt so alone. She was a social person by nature, and after a lifetime of having that instinct hammered down, she didn't know how to restart her life.

The knitting group came to the rescue. In what remained of downtown Ahnwee, she owned a building, the old pharmacy, sitting empty with no hope of selling. "Why don't you open a yarn store?" one woman in the group said. "Or a wine store!" another added. She liked the idea, the knitting one. She had insurance and savings, and she could get it going, and all her knitting friends could come in and demand discounts. Knotty Knits was born. While it wasn't successful in a conventional sense, it gave Ruby a place to go and sometimes not feel so lonely.

She poured the water, swirling the bag around in the cup. She looked out the window at the bright day. She missed Jerry. Yes, meeting him had not resulted in the life she wanted, but he was a good man, a kind man, and good company. Now she was alone. She waited for her daughters to call weekly and visit once a year around the holidays, but that didn't make for a social life. Her now-once a week knitting circle at the store was all she had. She couldn't stand TV, never could. Now every evening she read and knit and listened to Velvet Underground records.

She missed Jerry. Boring or not, she missed the man, but even more, she simply missed the company.

CHAPTER 11: KICKING IT NEW GUINEA STYLE

After everyone left, Sig decided, like Ruby, not to go back to work. While he had meat to smoke, there was no hurry.

Sig hummed as he cleaned up. Entertaining at South Pacific Jerky wasn't typical for him; in fact, it had never happened before. Other than the five or six customers who stopped each day, and his wholesale customers who called in orders, Sig generally talked to no one, went nowhere, and never hosted a soul. Having people over made him feel at once happy for the social success and sad for exposing to him how alone he usually was. He had spent his entire life there, right there, smoking and selling and living in the double-wide, nothing ever changing except growing older and business slowly dropping off. He had often wondered if people saw him as some sort of freak, living alone behind the brightly colored, South Pacific-themed building. Like some sort of jerky troll. Not that anyone ever bothered him. In fact, there was no one *to* bothered him.

He plugged the pop machine, even though he had the key, got another Dad's Root Beer, and sat down behind the store in a lawn chair. He looked across at his house. His father had bought that house and had it delivered when Sig was a teen. It replaced an older, shabbier double-wide that leaned a bit to the south. This one had leaned to the west, but after his father passed, Sig had it leveled out.

South Pacific Jerky was originally Sig's father's business. He opened it after returning from World War II, having learned the art of beef jerky making in New Guinea. He was a friendly sort, and he soon connected with some of the Indigenous population over some primo illegal still-juice. These locals happed to have a thriving jerky business selling to the soldiers. They told him that jerky was an ancient native practice, but in fact the natives simply understood supply and demand, and the American soldiers demanded beef jerky. They took pride in their work and made top-notch jerky, and as the war was closing out, Sig's father paid one of the guys to teach him their method. It involved wood fire and special seasoning, but the native guy left out the true secret to his beef jerky: it wasn't beef. If Sig's father paid attention, he would have noticed a severe lack of cows in New Guinea, but a plentiful supply of deer, rat, tree kangaroos, dogs, and horses. The horses came with the Army, and for some reason they would often turn up missing. Still, while Sig's father didn't have keen powers of observation, it turned out he was a smart guy around a smoker, and he soon was making killer jerky.

Sig's father returned home to Granite Falls. At first, he continued to work the family chicken farm while he perfected his jerky on the side. His father thought he was wasting his time with his high-falutin' South Pacific ideas, when he should stay focused on the chickens. After about a year of working behind the chicken coop and getting some real traction wholesaling his jerky, Sig's father was soon making an okay living. He decided to strike out on his own. He found a great property on the main road between Ahnwee and Despar, guaranteed to deliver lots of tourist biz, and proceeded to build a cement block store and paint it with palm trees and, strangely, Miami

South Beach colors. He plopped a used trailer behind it for a house, and he was in business.

It worked. People liked his product, and the overhead was low. He met his future wife at a dance in Despar, and they successfully raised eight kids, all of normal height, except Sig. Eventually, the kids did what kids do: grew up and moved away. Except Sig.

Sig didn't meet a wife at a dance, or anywhere else. He had a hard time as a kid, being the only little person in school. How the other kids treated him didn't exactly warm him to his fellow man. He focused on the jerky and shied away from human contact. But that didn't work so well. He felt lonely. He saw other people having a life, and he wanted one too, but he had no idea how to do it and saw his situation as a little person as a major handicap. As a result, by forty, he was one-part loneliness and one-part anger, mostly at himself.

Then his dad died. His mother had passed many years before, succumbing to lung cancer, and eventually his father died of the same. Now he was on his own, both business-wise and life-wise. He took stock. He decided to embark on a campaign of self-improvement. For the anger, he decided to learn how to keep it together, to understand and practice the science of passive-aggression, but he seemed to go right to aggressive every time. He read a book – *Turn that Anger into Opportunity* – that recommended a Behaviorism technique of programming certain words as triggers for good behavior. The plan is to choose a word or words that work for you, and when you start to lose it, you take a breath and say your words. Sort of like counting. Sig was game for anything – especially since he was getting more and more attention from the sheriff – and he chose flowers since he loved gardening and thinking about them felt calming. Now, instead of yelling or punching, he would picture flowers and name the various varieties. Generally, he could get through tulips, daisies, marigolds, and pansies before blowing his top. He hoped to someday to make it to petunias.

Next, he decided to be around people more. If he wanted a social life, he knew it wasn't coming to South Pacific Jerky. He knew everyone in Ahnwee from high school and simply by being in the same place for a lifetime, so he decided he should start spending time there. That's why he was at Flump's Café that day Sybil and Ruby were talking about Björn Björkman's hog farm. He had previously decided, too, that he needed to say "yes" to doing more things, to take advantage of opportunities when they presented themselves. He got the idea from some blog he couldn't recall. That was why he volunteered to come with to visit Björn Björkman.

He felt proud of himself for following through, but he knew he had to do better with the anger piece. He didn't think that squirrel from Wind Energy Now he chased around was going to sue, but why put himself in that position?

He leaned back and stretched out, hands behind his head, looking skyward. He also felt proud that he was fighting for a good cause. As Sybil had pointed out, he didn't have a personal stake in it – his business and home weren't threatened – but it just wasn't right that those aliens at Wind Energy Now, that pus bag Björkman, and that self-righteous Malcolm Moose, wanted poor Ahnwee. Sig was just the guy to help with this fight; he had an enlarged sense of justice built from being a little person at Despar High. He knew what injustice looked like and it gave him the heightened sensitivity toward people being unfairly treated.

No, this was good, he thought. For him, anyway.

Chapter 12: What's Better Than Once? Twice.

Sybil parked her Prius alongside the old, boarded-up Independent Order of the Oddfellows Hall, the only parking spot she could find within a block or two of Main Street. She could hear music ahead and see the crowd of wholesome celebrants. She walked up the side street until the busted pavement turned into a newly paved sidewalk lined with young trees. A towheaded boy ran by, nearly pushing her out of the way.

At Main Street the parade paraded along. Sybil squeezed in at the curb. Maybe a couple hundred or so people lined the parade route for all of its five blocks. Old people sat in webbed lawn chairs while small children sat on the curb and teens stood back, looking uncomfortable in their own skin. American flags hung from light poles, and baskets of red, white, and blue petunias hung below. All in all, a Norman Rockwell Fourth of July.

Sybil tried to remember the last time she saw Ahnwee as busy as Despar was right then. She concluded it was never. She felt a little jealous, but not much. She went to school in Despar, went on dates to Despar, and generally regarded Despar as a second home, almost as an extension of Ahnwee. But she also knew that she was an exception. Among old-timers in Ahnwee, there was a great deal of animosity directed at their neighbor. It seemed to go well beyond the typical neighborly rivalries. She didn't know why that was, but she bet one piece was ethnicity: Ahnwee was German and Despar was Norwegian. She had heard the chatter growing up. Not that made sense to the modern thinking Sybil, but to old timers – well, there you go.

Sybil was correct on that assessment, but she didn't know the half of it. The bad blood between the towns went back to their founding, the Great War, and one ex-boxer by the name of Bruno Weyer.

To start at the beginning of Despar, after the Dakota land was stolen in 1862 and the land opened to easily sunburned settlers, one Anton Ásbjörn was one of the first settlers in the area with his wife and three sons. This was a good thirty-one years before Max Schroeder would come to start the chain of events that would be Ahnwee. Ásbjörn broke ground on his claim – about seven miles west of Max's future failure – built a first-class *hus*, and quickly became more successful than just about anyone in the area. Grain seemed the way to go, given the generally dryer climate of the area, and growing lots of it was easy. The hard part was moving it. There wasn't a train in the area yet, nor a grain elevator, nor much of anything else. The good news was that all the surrounding land quickly filled with Norwegian farmers, a group more willing than most to work together through the suffering. Norwegian immigrants to Minnesota loved suffering. They felt it was payback for their one big sin: that of sometimes enjoying things. A sunny day, a wildflower, the nape of a significant other's neck, all were enjoyments that needed to be answered for. Therefore, they got along wonderfully as a community, meaning Ásbjörn and all the other farmers soon banded together and brought their product to Willmar by wagon every fall.

Unfortunately, Anton Ásbjörn contracted chronic fatigue syndrome, and soon he could no longer farm. His eldest, Aksel, took over the farm, now over nine hundred acres, and worked it with his young wife, Anja, and his younger brothers, Alf and Arvid. Aksel was even more successful than his old man, who now merely spent his days sitting with a blanket across his lap on the porch, being waited on by his wife and daughters-in-law, and writing poetry about his condition. He suffered and thus was happy, and therefore deserving of more suffering.

Eventually Aksel and Anja had children, whose names are of no consequence other than to mention that to no one's surprise they started with A. Soon, and as prescribed by long farming tradition, it was time for Aksel's younger brothers to move off the farm and make something of themselves on their own. In 1890, Alf and Arvid moved just a mile-and-a-half away to a nice little spot on the Minnesota River, where they purchased a quarter section from Lazy Emil, a rare lazy Norwegian. Actually, that was unfair – he was simply out of his skill set. In the old world, Emil was a fisherman, and, after following the rest of a boatload of new immigrants to this land of milk and honey, he expected to pursue his vocation. However, the river didn't have anywhere near enough cod to make a living – in fact, it didn't have any cod at all since it was a river and not an ocean – so he resigned himself to trying his hand at farming. In this, he had no skill. After thirty years he had barely cleared enough prairie to grow food for himself, much less to sell. His property looked terrible, brush and garbage surrounding his hovel, his horses gaunt and boat left to rot. Soon his wife left him and moved to Minneapolis, and Emil decided he had enough of this sod-busting game.

Alf and Arvid went to work. Arvid saw a need to move grain and, lo and behold, there was a river adjacent to their new property. They built the grain elevator and a barge to move the product downriver to Granite Falls. On the trip back, they brought goods to sell from the elevator, such as fabric, pianos, fireworks, salt, poetry books, and other necessities of life. Soon a town grew up around their elevator, and they were fabulously wealthy. His success was sealed when the Great Northern Railroad finally came to town. It put their barge out of business, but that was a minor concern compared to all the grain they were now able to move east and all the new consumer goods they could now sell.

In fact, the town got its name from the railroad. Before that, it was just a cluster of houses around a grain elevator. When the Great Northern laid a spur to the town from nearby Montevideo, one of the railroad workers said to another railroad worker as they started down the new track, "Wheres we-a-go-in?" The other guy replied, "Down this spar." But the first guy couldn't hear, given how much noise your average steam engine of the time made, and yelled, "Where?" To which the other guy yelled back, "Down this spar. THIS SPAR!" Later, when yet another guy asked the first guy the same question, he answered "Some-a place named Despar." Soon there was a railroad sign at the station saying, "Despar," and the deal was done.

The grain empire was mostly Arvid. His brother Aksel... no, wait, Anton...or whatever, wasn't napping, either. Alf − that's it − like his brother Arvid, saw a need and filled it, in his case opening a brothel behind the elevator. Alf reasoned that bachelor Norwegian farmers don't live for hard work alone; they need distractions and reasons to feel guilty. And he was right. Like his brother, Alf became fabulously wealthy.

The town grew quickly. In Norway the economy was in the toilet, and farmable land scarce. Young men by the thousands left for the new world, and when they found places with other Norwegians, they settled it. By 1901 when Ahnwee was founded, Despar numbered an impressive nine hundred and fifty-six souls. By 1910, it was up to over fifteen hundred, a considerable town for the time. Grain filled train cars and ladies of the evening plied their trade.

Life was good for this town of Norwegians.

Unfortunately, good-for-nothing, untrustworthy immigrants were moving in too close for their tastes, bringing down property values and stinking up the neighborhood with strange cooking smells. Never mind that the Norwegians of Despar were all immigrants themselves; these Huns were different. They watched warily as a German town grew up to the east. Right away, the first few interactions didn't go well, starting in 1901 when Max Schroeder stiffed Arvid for the wood for the Ahnwee lodge, and Alf for a two-night binge at his house of ill repute. More importantly, few in either town spoke English, preferring to stick to their mother tongues. Thus, they couldn't communicate, leading to deep suspicion that whenever they interacted, the other was talking smack about them.

Right out of the gate, the towns were very competitive. Not a good move for Ahnwee, given that there were so many more Norwegians in the area than Germans. This tension came to a head with the incident of 1917. The Great War was three years old, but just now getting underway for the United States. This caused a great deal of tension directed at the German population of Ahnwee. Sure, Norway was neutral, but by this time many of the young men in Despar and the surrounding area were born in the U.S. and were now far more American than Norwegian. Given this climate, the more conspiracy-minded believed that Ahnwee was a hotbed of spies. Clearly, all those Kaiser-lovers were plotting something. Where better to begin the takeover of America than in the hinterlands of Minnesota? When Harve Johnson's horse died for no good reason one day, the young men were sure it was the Germans. When Torgle Turnblad's hen house burned to the ground one August evening, the only conclusion they could draw was it was the Germans. The young men had to do something. Being not only Norwegians but also Minnesotans, they decided to have a meeting.

A resident of Ahnwee, German immigrant Bruno Weyer, a red-faced, bulb-nosed, bowlegged former boxer living above the new mercantile, was indeed plotting something. Hard to say what exactly, since being drunk pretty much twenty-four-seven meant he rarely made sense, but he thought it his duty to fight for the Fatherland. No, he didn't poison a horse or burn down a chicken coop, but he did talk a lot of smack. The rest of the town tried to talk him down, telling him to "Relax, we're in America now." But that didn't deter Bruno from making plans, and the drunker he got, the bigger the talk. And drunker he did get, and often. To say Bruno liked the bottle is like saying the *Titanic* had a little mishap.

After downing a bottle of rotgut he bought from one of John Big Moose's grandsons, Bruno decided one clear, unusually warm October, to act. He didn't know how, what, or why, but he did know where: Despar. After dark, he rode his old u-backed nag the seven miles to Despar, just in time to discover the meeting going on at the IOOF hall. He knew something big was going on; the meeting was quite loud. He looked in the window as thirty or so blond men in their twenties debated. There were no streetlights and no moon, so they couldn't see him just a few feet from the open window looking in. Bruno watched and listened. Then he knew what to do: he gathered straw and sticks and laid them around the foundation and under the low wood porch and stairs. Then he took another bottle of rotgut and poured it around, lit a match, threw it in the hay, and yelled, "Long live the Kaiser!" and ran away. The straw and sticks and cheap booze caught fire immediately, but the people inside heard Bruno yell. They ran outside, saw the fire, and tried their best to put it out. They had no fire department to call, no ready source of water to tap, not even a shovel at hand. They tried to kick the flaming straw and branches away from the wood building, but it was no use: soon fire engulfed the IOOF. No one died, but the hall was a total loss.

Tired, dirty, and angry, the young Norwegian-Americans had had enough. This was proof positive that the war was coming to western Minnesota. Rumors spread like wildfire. The fire was set by a team of well-organized terrorists. The fire was set by spies as the first salvo of taking over Despar. The fire was set by company of German regulars, spiked helmets and all. There was only one thing to do: twenty-five of the young blond men got their guns, their hunting dogs, and their horses and set off for Ahnwee.

They arrived in town not five minutes after Bruno, whose old horse didn't move very fast. It was now four in the morning, the town dark, and no one was around except Bruno, who now sat in front of the Mercantile, passed out. They approached him, and the point men noticed immediately that the dude smelled of cheap booze, just like the booze they smelled in the fire. Actually, he always smelled like that, but indeed, they did have the right man.

The next morning, when the town's citizens arose, they found Bruno's body in the middle of Broadway, face stuffed with lutefisk, having died of either choking or the taste.

The lutefisk calling card was unmistakable. This was a Norwegian act of terror. They feared it was merely the first salvo of an ethnic cleansing of Germans from western Minnesota. Many of the younger, more hotheaded Ahnweeians wanted to seek vengeance. However, cooler heads quickly prevailed in the persona of Pastor Schultz, an elderly, nearly deaf Lutheran minister from Baden-Baden in the northern foothills of the Black Forest. The minister from Third Lutheran rode into Despar and made such an imposing figure in his vestments that he was not molested by the still-angry residents. He met with his counterpart and, to make a long story short, both agreed the towns should bury the hatchet.

Which, eventually they did. The sheriff investigated the fire and the murder and called it even. Despar rebuilt the IOOF hall, now out of brick, and the people of Ahnwee decided they were better off without that good-for-nothing Bruno anyway. The war ended a year later, removing the cause of a good deal of the tension between the towns.

Still, the competitiveness remained. Add their checkered histories and the German/Norwegian thing to the normal competitiveness nearby towns are bound to have, and snarky things were bound to be said. Every year, students from Despar High climbed the Ahnwee water tower to paint "Despar High," painting over the previous year's contribution. Ahnwee boys would go to Despar every Halloween and set bags of dog shit on fire on doorsteps, toilet paper Despar High, and generally make pains of themselves. The Despar Phone Company wired all of its town and westward, but for years wouldn't run wire to Ahnwee. Meanwhile, Ahnwee put up a public beach and boat launch on the north side of Lake Ahnwee, just west of town, and made it free to Ahnweeians, but if anyone else, namely Desparians, wanted to use it, they would have to buy a yearly pass for ten dollars.

Even in recent years, when cell phone towers went up, Despar businesses along the highway and Big Moose Casino were all were taken care of by the major carriers. Ahnwee was forgotten, and everyone felt sure it was because of Despar. Three-G coverage? They had no Gs at all. To get bars, the people of Ahnwee had to drive to Despar.

So it went, a campaign of vandalism on the part of the towns' teens and a passive-aggressive war on the part of the town's elders. Despar always had the advantage. It had the high school that even kids from Ahnwee had to attend. It had the population advantage. It had the allegiance of all the Norwegians in the surrounding area. For an example of how the latter worked, the Norwegian farmers would go out of their way to bring their crops to the elevator in Despar, riding right by Ahnwee, so that even in the best of times the grain elevator in Ahnwee languished, only the few Germans and outlier nationalities of the area using it.

With this nearly century-old competition, Ahnwee was losing, and now, with the likelihood of Ahnwee getting torn down, Despar would finally get their vengeance for the IOOF fire.

Sybil watched the marching band as they played their way down the street. What is that song? Sybil wondered; it sounded familiar but not as a Sousaphone-style march. No, some young band teacher got creative. Which was fine with Sybil, if only she could place the song. After the marching band, a seventy-five white Cadillac Fleetwood convertible slowly rolled by, a large magnetic sign for "Ben's Body Shop" on the passenger door, with Miss Ahnwee – a pretty blonde high school kid – sitting in the back, butt on the top of the back of the seat, waving a well-coached wave of royalty. She wore a tiara and a strapless sequined evening gown that reminded Sybil of Ginger in *Gilligan's Island.*

Sybil suddenly realized what song the band was playing: Lady Gaga's "Bad Romance."

Following Miss Despar was another white vintage Cadillac convertible containing Commissioner Harry Balzac. He looked right at home, waving and pointing, smiling and sweating.

Target acquired. Sybil didn't come to the Fourth of July parade for the high school band and the cultural anthropology, she came to plead Ahnwee's case to the one man who could do something about it: the sweaty commissioner.

Sybil had first met Commissioner Harry Balzac four years before at the ribbon cutting for the wind turbine, when Sybil happened to be visiting from New York. He spoke for a good twenty minutes, taking credit for something he had nothing to do with, until, after he cut the ribbon with cartoonish giant scissors, the blade came swooping down for the first time, taking out the commissioner's H2 Humvee. He swore loudly – unfortunately, right into the microphone, to the disapproval of the many voters gathered – as his prized vehicle flew across the county road and landed upside down in a drainage ditch. She hoped he didn't bear a grudge about that. The turbine was no worse for the wear, other than developing a squeak each time the offending blade passes the exact spot. The next time Sybil met the commissioner was after she was elected mayor. The good commissioner paid a call at New York 'Tique in that first month, telling Sybil about the importance of unfettered capitalism and gun ownership. Sybil, having run as an independent, listened respectfully, until it was time for him to go. He went in for the hug – something not unusual in New York but unheard of in the plains of Norwegian and German farmers – which Sybil returned, going with the turn sideways technique. He pulled her tight, grabbing her ass to boot.

In some ways, County Commissioner Harry Balzac was a typical politician. Not the ass-grabber piece – okay, sometimes that too – but in his assent to power. A local boy, he was a high school hockey star who went on to play for the University of Minnesota, Duluth, where he was considered a pro prospect until he blew out his coccyx on a power play, an injury that left him five percent permanently disabled. After dropping out of college, he parlayed his two drops of local fame to become a sports guy for a ten o'clock news show in Duluth. After being fired (TV is so fickle), he returned to Despar and made some money as an auctioneer during the farm crisis of the early eighties. After the farm economy improved (much to his chagrin), and after a few other careers in collections, asbestos sales, and cable TV customer service, he started his career as a seed inspector for Monsanto, where he tested crops to see if farmers were using proprietary GMO seeds without a license. About that: for thirty thousand years farmers have been holding back enough seed to plant the next year, but in the modern world of genetically modified crops that's against the law; farmers had to buy new seed from Monsanto every year. Therefore, the giant multinationals needed someone to inspect fields for scofflaws who thought they could plant their own seeds. Balzac was just the man for the job. This continued to be his day job, the role of county commissioner being part time.

Balzac had been a county commissioner for twenty years. He first got into politics when, after finding God at a right-wing fundraiser, he ran and won on a platform of Jesus and mutual backscratching. He took to politics like a bird takes to pooping on a bald man's head.

Now it was time to put that cunning and clout into play for Ahnwee.

But it wasn't going to be easy. The day after Sybil, Ruby, and Sig decided to talk to Commissioner Balzac, Sybil called his office in Despar. No one answered and she had to leave a message. Sybil tried again on Friday. On Monday when she called, she actually talked to a real person, and she told the receptionist that the three of them wanted to see the commissioner. She was told he didn't have an appointment available until after Labor Day. Sybil identified herself as the Mayor of Ahnwee. The receptionist put Sybil on hold, and when the receptionist returned, she said the commissioner wouldn't be available until after Thanksgiving. She insisted on seeing him, and the receptionist hung up.

Sybil, Ruby, and Sig decided that ambushing Balzac was their only chance. Sig knew he usually worked out of his car driving from farm to farm, so staking out his office would be a waste of time. The one place they knew for sure where he'd be was at the Despar Fourth of July parade.

Sybil suggested she go alone. Maybe they had made a mistake with calling his office; three likely-to-be-angry citizens wanting an appointment may have intimidated the commissioner. Maybe she'd have better luck by herself. Not via an ambush, but politics – one elected official to another. Besides, Sybil thought, the last meeting, and how it ended, was still fresh, and she didn't want a repeat. She had considered bringing Ruby, whose idea it was in the first place to approach Commissioner Balzac. She admired her skill. In fact, Sybil thought Ruby was abler than she was, since, when the pressure was on, Sybil got nervous and didn't know what to say. She knew that. Ruby, on the other hand, when the pressure was on, she just knitted a fraction faster. Sybil admired that. Problem was,

Sybil didn't know how to suggest that only Ruby should come along without hurting Sig's feelings. Sybil decided it was high time she man-up and did her job, to be strong like Ruby.

That was the plan. The plan only extended as far as Sybil crashing Despar's big Fourth of July celebration. After that, she would have to improvise.

Sybil watched Balzac's convertible move on down the street. Next came yet another white Cadillac convertible, this one with Jon Fjord riding and waving, wearing tight jeans and a plaid shirt. Got to hand it to him, she thought: he knew how to look the part of a man of the people. Behind him was a fire truck with town volunteer firefighters riding on top. Next came last year's homecoming float from Despar High, with the theme of "The Warriors will scalp the New Prague Trojans," featuring a large two-by-four framed papier-mâché tomahawk moving slowly up and down, chopping a papier-mâché Trojan soldier (who, technically, looked more Greek) in the face (it probably was meant to be going for the scalp, but it landed right between the eyes). After the float, an antique wood Chris-Craft boat rolled slowly by pulled by a Ram truck, and on the side of the boat was the sign, "Sven Svenson's Realty, Serving Greater Despar Since 1998." Next, a Model T with a magnet sign of Lar's Lawn Care. The Oscar Mayer Weiner Mobile. Some seemingly drunk guys on their riding lawn mowers, trying to do some sort of formation, but instead having several near-misses before resorting to swearing at each other, much to the horror of many Lutheran mothers of young children.

And so it went. After the last parade contingent – the living members of VFW post 805 – walked and wheeled by, no one in the crowd left. A few people took the opportunity to cross the street, but otherwise the old people stayed in their lawn chairs and children still sat on the curb and the teenagers were still uncomfortable. Sybil had been to this parade several times before – in happier days with her father, and a year ago when Drew came to town – so she knew what to expect: given the brevity of the parade and the shortness of Main Street Despar, it was a tradition that the Fourth of July parade would go around the block at the end and come back down Main Street for a second pass. Some years they were good for a fourth pass or, so Sybil has been told, one time even a sixth (always even numbers, of course, since their cars would be back at the beginning). Sure enough, five minutes later, the marching band came marching back, and this time Sybil recognized the song right away: "Smells Like Teen Spirit." Miss Despar again followed the band, the beauty queen still sitting in her vintage limo waving. As Miss Despar rolled by, Sybil took note of the magnetic sign on the car door: "Norm's Hardware." She could have sworn it had said something else before. Again, Commissioner Balzac followed, still waving but now showing serious pits in his beige suit jacket. After the fire truck and the homecoming float came the antique wood boat. Its sign said, "China Grand Dragon Buffet." The Model T rolled by, saying "Thad Thorgaard, Pain-free dentistry." Could the signs be different on each side of the vehicles? A block away, the band stopped playing and began to scatter toward waiting relatives; there would be no third and fourth pass this year. Sybil, along with many from the crowd, walked down Main Street following the last of the parade. Ahead, Commissioner Balzac's white Cadillac was diagonally parked by the Gifts and More shop. On the way, Sybil ran across the street and checked out the sign on the last vehicles. Yes! They are different on each side! A detail that was either new or at least she never noticed before. It seemed bizarre, but she wasn't sure why.

The end of the route was quickly mobbed with the drunk

guys on mowers and their wives, high schoolers in marching band outfits, and elderly men wearing medals, and all their relatives. In the center of it all was Commissioner Balzac, holding court with his hand around Miss Ahnwee's waist. Since she was a foot shorter even in her heels and thirty-plus years younger, it made for a creepy, child molester moment. To her credit, Miss Ahnwee didn't look to be enjoying it at all, and she peeled Balzac's hand slowly off her as she squirmed right, escaping his grasp. He didn't seem to notice, focusing instead on pontificating for a number of men with their arms crossed about how farm support reform was just one example of how America has become the Soviet Union.

"…You see, it's like this then," Balzac said as Sybil approached. "We need to continue to subsidize the big farmer; God rewards those who are most successful. If a man has managed to amass, say, two thousand acres, well then, he shouldn't get punished. If a man is making, say, a million dollars a year, we should reward that. That's what Jesus would want. We need him to grow corn and keep us all fed. He earns that subsidy." The men, most dressed in well-worn Walmart clothing, nodded.

Sybil hovered. How to do this? She tried waiting Balzac out. He kept talking, and people kept listening. Soon it became apparent waiting was hopeless; Balzac didn't seem to be winding up anytime soon.

"Well, what a surprise! Always nice to see our good neighbor to the east come to our humble Fourth of July celebration," said Jon Fjord from behind.

Sybil jumped like someone grabbing an electric fence.

"Whoa, there, Cindy. Decaf. Consider decaf."

Sybil composed herself. "It's Sybil."

"It's not Cindy?"

"Nope. Sybil."

"Old Harry said it was Cindy."

"Yet another thing he's wrong about."

Jon Fjord laughed.

Sybil wondered if he could turn on the twinkle in his eyes at will. "Nice parade, Fjord. Great touch having businesses sponsor only one side of the floats so they could be sold twice."

"Thanks. That was my idea. Why not?" He said, clearly rhetorically. He followed Sybil's eyes. "Are you waiting to see the commissioner?"

Sybil nodded.

"Trying to save your town?"

Sybil nodded again.

"Good luck with that. I heard about Wind Energy Now. That on top of Big Moose Casino, on top of Björn Björkman's shit pond."

"You know about all that?"

He waved and nodded at someone behind her, before focusing again. "That's tough. Really, good luck, okay? Seriously. If I can help, just say the word."

Sybil wasn't sure how sincere he was, if at all. She settled on not at all.

Meanwhile, there seemed no end to Commissioner Balzac's conversation with an old woman talking about the need to outlaw sports bras. Sybil didn't like interrupting people, but she took a breath, clenched her jaw, and waded in. "Commissioner Balzac? Commissioner Balzac?"

Sybil was in luck – the commissioner jumped at an exit strategy from the crazy conversation. "Yes? Cindy! Mayor, so great to see you. How can I be of service?" he said, turning away from the complainer and putting his hand on Sybil's shoulder so as to block any attempt the old woman could make to cut back in. Jon Fjord stood near, enjoyment crossing his face for the scene in front of him.

That was easy, but I wish Balzac would take his hands off me, Sybil thought. "Commissioner, my town has a problem. We have the government trying to take our homes." She came up with the strategy right on the spot, and felt proud of that, as well as nervous.

"Now, Cindy, that's just not right! Eminent domain?" he said in a too loud voice so that all could hear.

"I guess so."

"Ya, this is just what I'm talking about," he nearly yelled, looking around at the people nearby. "What right does the government have to come in a take people's homes? It's just not Christian."

Jon Fjord looked around and laughed, shaking his head in disbelief.

Balzac smiled for everyone. "Walk with me, my dear," he said, leading Sybil away from the crowd, now using his inside voice outside. Jon Fjord trailed. "I was saddened to hear that Ahnwee may go away. Growing up in Despar, I have many fond memories of Ahnwee, especially in high school and your water tower." The commissioner moved as if uncomfortable, perhaps from the coccyx, or possibly hemorrhoids. When out of earshot of the crowd, he said, "See, I understand the thinking was that with Björn Björkman filing lawsuits, something had to be done. The county can cut him off at the pass if they condemn the land and let the courts later decide who gets compensated; the main thing is that old sack of farts shouldn't get that land."

"I imagine you do feel that way, Commissioner," Fjord said, "I recall Björn Björkman has run against you in every election since the mid-nineties."

The commissioner gave Mayor Fjord the skunk eye. "Björn Björkman is a godless atheist."

Sybil ignored the redundancy. She knew the story: Every

117

four years Björkman would file as an independent or as a representative of some fringe or made-up party and make Balzac's life hell. One year Björkman ran on the "Balzac is a Crook" ticket. Björkman on a couple occasions actually got invited to a debate, where he would read off a litany of crimes and misdemeanors – most of which weren't true – that Balzac supposedly did. Sybil scratched her chin. "So that's why the condemnation. But what about Wind Energy Now?"

"Wind Energy Now employs a lot of people around here, and pays lots of taxes."

"What about Big Moose Casino?" Sybil asked.

"What about it? Like we're going to start giving land back that we took fair and square? Can we get a refund on the beads for Manhattan? Look my dear," he said, sliding his hand down her back, making her shiver. "Even if Malcolm Moose pulls it off with his treaties and lawyers, Björn Björkman doesn't get it, so we win either way."

Sybil was confused, so she went back to her ask. "I – I mean we, the people of Ahnwee, would like you to help us save our town, regardless of who wants to take it. We don't want to leave; Ahnwee is our home."

Balzac grinned. "Sweetheart, that just may not be possible. I believe the hearing already happened, and all that remains are some formalities."

"We don't care, commissioner. We're not leaving." Sybil was having an out-of-body experience, as if someone else was being this putting-her-foot-down, we're-not-leaving gal. She liked it.

Balzac looked at Fjord, who stood a few feet away, arms crossed. Balzac shrugged. "Well, then, Mayor, how can I help?"

"Can you put a stop to the 'formalities'?"

"Maybe. I'll have to make a few calls. Pull a few strings."

He put his hand around her waist.

Sybil noticed for the first time that Balzac was wearing makeup, some sort of foundation. His sweat made the makeup start to run. "You'll do that for us?"

"Certainly, my dear. For the God-fearing constituents of Ahnwee? Certainly."

He reached down to squeeze her left butt cheek.

Sybil, with Ninja-like skill, grabbed his hand before it could find its target, twisted, and turned the physical encounter into a handshake. "Thank, you, Commissioner."

He smiled, gave a huffing laugh, and moved onto the next constituent.

"Yeah, that can't fail," Mayor Jon Fjord said.

"So Balzac promised to pull a few strings, to put a stop to the blighted thing. I think we might be okay," Sybil told Augie and Sig back at Flump's Café.

"Wow, that was easy," Sig said. "Way to go."

"Yeah, nice work," Augie added.

Sybil felt proud. She had finally done something right as mayor.

"Ahnwee isn't going to be torn down?" Pastor Farber said.

Sybil hadn't noticed the good pastor at the end of the counter, as always reading a small paperback. Pastor Farber didn't look happy at all. Sybil wondered if she should ask him if he was okay, but Sig solved her dilemma.

"Pastor, you don't look too happy," Sig said.

"Oh, I am, I am. I'm just not feeling well."

Sybil looked at him, and then at Augie and Sig, who both shrugged.

CHAPTER 13: A LITTLE DRAMA WOULD BE NICE

Pastor Fabian Farber spent the rest of the day at the church, moping. At about 10:00 p.m., when he would normally have been in bed reading some depressing dead French author, he instead put on his best cassock, shaved his stubble, and poured a chalice of sacramental wine. Then another. And a third, what the hell. Cheap nasty stuff, but he was starting to feel it.

When Sybil had told him it looked like the town was saved, he felt truly happy for Sybil and all his neighbors and parishioners. On the other hand, he was miserable. He wanted the town torn down. Or at least the church. Whatever got the job done.

Fabian Farber didn't grow up in Ahnwee; he hailed from Kansas City, middle of five very devout Lutheran children. He was a normal child, if a little desperate to be noticed by his parents – being the middle child and all – but nothing out of the ordinary. His parents finally noticed him and were very proud when he enrolled in the seminary. His calling was driven less by the love of Jesus and more by his love for Charlton Heston in *The Ten Commandments*, a movie he must had seen over a dozen times. In seminary he did very well – he combined a natural inquisitiveness with an eagerness to follow – and so he graduated on time and worked in various congregations until being ordained. Finally, he got his first, and to date only, parish assignment: Third Lutheran in Ahnwee. He arrived at a church on the decline, the average age of parishioners growing one year older every year, until fewer and fewer old Germans occupied the deteriorating pews. The elderly minister who had been there twenty-plus years took Farber under his frail wing. In exchange for the senior minister's mentorship and long-winded stories, Farber helped his elder in every way, from the pulpit to the bathroom, until the old minister passed and the historic church was all his.

He was happy. Sure, it was quiet in Ahnwee and in his church doubly so, but Farber was something of a loner anyway, and he liked the quiet. Plus, he was a voracious reader, and for that quiet is helpful. Nearly every day the Despar library was open one could find Pastor Farber at a table, head down in some book, leaving at closing with stacks of the same. Then, after Ahnwee got its broadband, Amazon boxes started appearing on the parsonage doorstep.

He was open-minded in his habits, reading everything from Dietrich Bonhoeffer to Sylvia Plath. But maybe he read too much. When ordering *How to Know God* by Deepak Chopra, *Being and Nothingness* by Jean-Paul Sartre appeared under "Customers Who Bought This Item Also Bought." He hadn't heard of it – Sartre not being the stuff of seminary classes – but it sounded interesting. And it was. That would be the first of many books he would read on existential philosophy. It would change his life. He concluded that Sartre, Kierkegaard, and Camus were right: not only is there no God, but that none of it matters, anyway.

Not good. Being in your mid-thirties and a pastor of a congregation is not a great time to have an existential crisis. He considered quitting, getting on the next Greyhound for wherever, but that wasn't really an option for Fabian Farber.

While it was a free county, it wasn't for the good pastor with his outsized sense of responsibility and an undersized reserve of personal go-get-it-ness, not to mention the lethargy that often came from what was probably clinical depression. So, he kept on going as best he could, increasingly phoning it in to the ever-shrinking congregation, keeping his atheism to himself. In his spare time, he kept on reading, often sitting at the end of the counter at Flump's Café with a book and a cup of weak coffee, and when he wasn't there, he was back in the church contemplating various methods of suicide.

No one knew any of this of course. All the people of Ahnwee knew about the meek, quiet pastor was that he seemed increasingly ill-suited to the job. Lucky for him, no one cared.

While he had little interest in life and no longer feared the consequences of ending it, one thing kept him going: saving the church building itself. A wonderful example of Christopher Wren meets gothic (he liked architecture and had read many books on it), it was in bad shape with a leaky roof and a crumbling foundation, among lesser problems such as wiring and heat. That was why he had gathered the last of his interest in life and energy for the church and tried to raise money with the bake sale at Ahnwee Days. That was why, when it went bust, it was the last straw, and his head went in the oven.

After he heard that the town would likely be torn down, he was happy. Forget about the architecture, the rotten old church. It gave him hope, hope that the bulldozers would deliver to him a new life, any life, anywhere else.

It was a short holiday for Reverend Farber. Less than two weeks later, when Sybil told him and everyone at Flump's Café that the town was saved, his hope was smashed once again. He went into his pity mode. He prayed (for old times' sake) that the church would get sucked up into a tornado, himself included.

And thus, Pastor Farber was wearing his best cassock and drinking sacramental wine; he wanted to go out in style.

He considered his options. Option one: he could hang himself from the rafters. That had a lot going for it: very tidy, fast, and memorable. But maybe too memorable – some poor person would discover him swinging sooner or later, and probably be traumatized, and if that happened, the Pastor couldn't live with himself, no matter how dead he was. Plus, he didn't have a rope. Option two: a bullet. Also fast, but messy, and he didn't own a gun. Option three: sleeping pills. Not fast, no poetry, but clean, painless, and a good corpse. Yes, he thought: three.

He got out a bottle of sleeping pills he had been prescribed a few years back, as if a pill would fix his nihilism. He didn't like taking medications, so after he had tried one to be compliant, forty-seven little tablets remained in a plastic bottle with a childproof cap in the medicine cabinet.

Next question: where to do it? He decided a little drama would be nice – maybe it was the wine talking – and he took the candleholder off the altar and hopped up. This was a new experience in itself; he liked sitting on the altar. It felt bad, as in good, bad. He lay down, stretched out flat, looking at the ceiling, one hand holding the chalice. It was a nice ceiling. Dark wood, big old-growth timbers. Good luck to the next guy getting it fixed up, he thought – if there is a next guy. He leaned up and emptied the pill bottle in his mouth. He drank the last of the wine in the chalice and laid down to what he hoped would be a permanent sleep.

Chapter 14: Optimism Is Overrated

The next morning Sybil rose feeling optimistic. County Commissioner Balzac practically promised to put an end to this "blighted area" stuff, and if anyone could, it was Balzac. For all of his obvious faults, he did believe in property rights, and he did have a great deal of seniority. Maybe the town would be okay, she thought. More: maybe *I* saved the town. Maybe I'm a good mayor after all.

Even though it was Monday – she usually took Sunday and Monday off – Sybil went into the shop at ten on the button, ready to do business. She'd neglected things that last couple of weeks, missing some days, not getting her work done; the weight of Ahnwee holding her down. Now, Monday or no, she had some eBay orders to ship and needed desperately to update her website. Still, when Ruby stopped in on her way to her own shop at eleven, she took a break and told her the news. Ruby was happy, to be sure, but maybe not as happy as Sybil was. She didn't know what to make of that, so she decided to make nothing of it. When Ruby had to leave to open up her shop for the day, Sybil invited her over for dinner. Perhaps Ruby would buy into Sybil's upbeat attitude over food. Plus, Sybil's father seemed to respond well when Ruby came over, seeming more coherent and tracking better than usual. Maybe having someone else around helped. Maybe their long history made his father remember something of the person he used to be.

At five thirty sharp, Ruby appeared at the back door carrying a casserole dish. "I hope I'm not late."

"Not at all. Come in." Sybil thought about how before all this insanity they were passing acquaintances, now Sybil wanted to consider Ruby a friend, something she had sorely been missing. One thing Sybil liked about Ruby was her rep: many of the older folks in town saw her as something of a radical. She did, after all, move away from Ahnwee when everyone else got married to local boys and had babies by eighteen. Not only moved away, but moved west. Granted, Glacier National Park wasn't exactly San Francisco, but it was west. She did move back, and she did marry a local boy in Jerry, and they did have two children (both of whom moved away at eighteen also, only they never moved back), but none of that changed the fundamental fact that Ruby must be some sort of flower child. Proof? She ate at the late hour of five thirty, when most civilized Ahnweeians were already done with the dishes. All qualities Sybil admired about Ruby, or anyone from that generation.

Sybil took the casserole and put it on a trivet. She lifted the lid to find a hotdish of cream of mushroom soup, green beans, canned chicken, and crumbled-up Triscuits.

"Ruby!" Dan yelled at the top of his lungs. He stood in the doorway wearing an old suit, double-breasted, navy-blue pinstriped, and way too big for his emaciated frame.

Ruby gave him a big once-over. "Well, Dan, don't you

clean up well. Expecting company?"

He looked befuddled, looking down at his clothes, to his right, to his left, straight up in the air, and then at Ruby again. "Will you marry me, Ruby?"

"No, Dan. But I did bring Triscuit hotdish."

"Yahtzee!"

The suit was indeed Dan's idea. Sybil had no idea why, but no harm in his wearing a suit if he wanted to. And now she knew why, and it made Sybil happy, because it actually made sense. Her dad did do better with Ruby around!

They ate in the dining room, first time it had been used for its intended purpose in a long time. Dan usually ate in front of the TV on a folding TV tray. Sybil served a salad of kale and arugula with Craisins. Ruby's hotdish sat in the middle of the table, serving spoon keeping the lid from closing completely. For dessert, they had coffee and peanut butter bars. Dan didn't say anything more, eating quietly as if he were the only person in the room. Sybil knew better, though. If her father was alone, more likely he would have eaten the hotdish with his hands, or possibly dumped it on his head or generally thrown it around the room. No, this was the best behavior she'd seen in quite a while.

All three sat at the rustic oak dining room table, with Dan slowly nibbling at a second peanut butter bar. Sybil and Ruby talked about the Wind Energy Now, Big Moose Casino, Björn Björkman, and Commissioner Balzac. "What do you think, Ruby? Balzac can do it, can't he?"

Ruby poured water in her coffee. "I would imagine so, Sybil. If he wants to."

"Wants to?"

She took a sip of coffee, put it down, and poured more water from her glass into the mug. "Honestly, I don't trust that fart bag any farther than I can throw him."

"He said he'd make a few calls." Sybil desperately wanted to hold onto her optimism.

"Let's hope for the best." Ruby took a bite of peanut butter bar. "How are you holding up, Sybil? Seems like you've taken on a lot with this."

"Well, I guess I have to, being the mayor and all."

"Trust me, Sybil, there are a lot of people in this town who've taken their turn as mayor, but not many would actually have lifted a finger."

Sybil never thought of it as "taking a turn." She did run unopposed, and that always seemed a bit off to her, as if the first person to volunteer got the job.

"You should be proud of yourself for all the work you've done for Ahnwee. We're all proud of you."

"Proud? Loud? Shroud? Browed?" Dan said staring straight forward.

The music stopped, and Sybil got up and walked over to the old RCA console under the window. "Requests?"

Ruby had none, so Sybil squatted in front of the cabinet, flipping briefly though the records before pulling one out.

"Sybil?"

She lifted the tone arm and set it down. "Yeah, Ruby?" Django Reinhardt began playing guitar.

"You didn't answer my question."

"What question?"

"How are you doing?"

She walked back and sat back down at the long side of the table, exactly where she would have sat as a child. She took a drink of coffee, gathering her thoughts. "I guess okay. Funny. If you told me five years ago that Ahnwee was going to be torn down, I probably wouldn't have cared one bit. Oh, don't get me wrong – I only wished the town well, but I thought I was done with this place, and I thought the town was just plain done with its boarded-up storefronts and vacant houses, glow-in-the-dark lake and miniature golf wind turbine. Yet here I am."

"Here you are."

She realized how that sounded. "Sorry, Ruby. I don't mean to say I don't really care. I do. A lot. Look at the town. Augie, Pastor Farber, yourself: why should you have to take that? It's not right. This is your home."

"But it's not yours, is it?"

Sybil paused. No. Certainly not, but she didn't want to say that. She loved the people, she did, the old people she'd known all her life, all her neighbors, Ruby and Sig and Pastor Farber and Augie. Good people all. Rural people are not like New York people. You don't see them once in passing on a corner or in a café and never again. No: you know these people over the long haul. They come with the place, and you have to take it as it is, since they are yours. Yes, small town life can be wonderful, she thought, but not for me.

"How's it going with you, Dan?" Ruby asked, before taking a sip of coffee.

Dan said nothing, nibbling ever so slightly on the last corner of his bar.

"Good peanut butter bar?" Ruby asked.

Sybil's father stared unblinkingly at the center of the table.

"What day of the week is it, Dan?" She asked.

He got up slowly, carefully, stiffly, and walked out of the room. "Your chocolate is in my peanut butter."

Ruby and Sybil watched, both taking a drink of coffee.

"Well," Sybil said, "he was eating a peanut butter bar, so it wasn't a complete non sequitur."

"I'm sorry, Sybil."

"I remember my mom taking care of him and wondering how she could do it. I guess she couldn't."

"Sybil, you can't let it kill you." She politely left out *like it killed your mother.* "Has he been to the doctor lately?"

"I took him in April." Sybil had a sip of coffee, looking at the living room doorway after her father.

"He looks thin. Thinner than usual." They sat quietly. Then, "Have you considered that nursing home we talked about?"

Someone banged on the back door. Sybil all but leapt to her feet to answer it.

Sybil looked out the window first – an old habit from New York where no one would just open the door without checking if the person on the other side had an ax – but didn't see anyone. At first, she thought kids, but before she walked away, someone knocked again. Then she knew, and she felt ashamed. She opened the door, and on the bottom step was Sig.

He sat at the kitchen table as Ruby carried dishes to the sink. His eyes set on the plate in the middle of the counter. "Those are some fine-looking bars."

"Help yourself," Sybil said, pouring more coffee from the Bonavita carafe and passing the mug to him. Sybil never made bars the entire time she was in New York. Not once. In Ahnwee, bars were like crème brûlée. Sybil had her mother's recipes, all kept neatly in a plastic box, and now she made bars regularly, with the thought that every little bit helps when trying to fit in.

"I've got some news." Sig carefully picked out a large bar with his fingers, bit in, chewed, and said, "Yum, that's different. Is this how you make bars in New York?"

She started to say what do you mean by that, but Ruby jumped in first.

"So, what's the news?"

"I did some checking. A crazy thing called the internet. I know who's been pushing the 'blighted area' thing."

"Who?" Ruby said.

"Balzac."

"What?" Sybil nearly yelled.

"Seems he's been working on the county board for a couple months to make that move. It's right there in the minutes. Then in May, he apparently packed the room."

"Balzac is behind all this?" Sybil said. "This is all that big…" she searched for a biting insult but couldn't come up with one "…meanie's doing?" She didn't know if she wanted to cry or scream or both.

"That complete asshole?" Sig said. "Yeah, he's the one."

"That old windbag wouldn't bother with this if there wasn't something in it for him," Ruby said. "No doubt someone's pulling his strings."

"And I think I know who," Sig said, Taking another bar from the plate. "Wind Energy Now funded his PAC to the tune of three hundred thousand dollars, just last year. It's all public record."

"Moving on up!" Dan yelled from the living room.

All the newfound hope Sybil had from talking to Commissioner Balzac was gone. Ruby called Balzac a toad and Sig called him a shit heel. They promised to reconvene at Flump's Café and talk it through with Augie and Pastor Farber and whomever else, but the hopelessness of the situation was painted on their faces. Sig gave Ruby a ride home, but not before he took a third bar for the road, guessing correctly that the secret New York ingredient was a pinch of cayenne.

Sybil started the dishes. She could hear her father in the living room watching *The Jeffersons*. She did a couple plates before stopping, wiping her hands on the dishrag, leaving the rest for later.

She joined Dan in the living room. Mr. Jefferson was yelling about something, but she didn't know what, only that an audience found it hilarious. How can this be? How can that man be so dishonest? All she wants to do is save her town, but everywhere she turned, it got worse, worse, worse.

She tried to zone out, to forget about it over *Chico and the Man* followed by *Petticoat Junction*. No luck. It was getting dark. "I'm going to go get some air, Dad," she said to no response. She had to get out of the house, maybe have a cry.

She liked walking after dark. There was something she didn't do so much of in New York, at least not in her neighborhood. In Ahnwee, she usually walked to Broadway, seeking the reassurance of the few streetlights in town, but this night she decided to try another direction, walking west. Here, there were no streetlights to help her, but the yard lights on garages, above doors, and on the occasional pole in the front yard were enough. The streets were empty of people, but not only that, empty of cars, both of the moving and parked variety. Houses that were inhabited had their vehicles in or in front of their garages. She could hear the familiar and pleasing night music of frogs and crickets, plus the muffled sounds of televisions behind walls. At a corner house she heard an argument going on and then saw it in action through the kitchen window as she passed. The woman yelled and pointed at her husband, and he slapped the sides of his head. That would be the Schwartz's. On the next block, she saw a sight that was abnormal for its normalcy: a man stoking a bonfire in his yard while his wife and two adult sons watched. That would be the Benz's. She went to school with one of his sons, Jan, at the time a lean young blond Aryan, now an oversized bald man. "Hi, Mayor!" he yelled. She waved back. That act made her at once happy and sad – happy to be acknowledged with some degree of affection, sad that she will be the one on watch when they come and take his parents' house.

The street sloped gently downward. It was new moon dark, and she tried to be careful where she stepped for fear of twisting her ankle in a pothole or something. A dog barked. As she passed a house with its lights on, she could see a woman in a window, Sybil guessed doing the dishes. It was too dark for her to see Sybil, but Sybil knew her as the mother of a high school pal, now long gone on to a more successful zip code. What was her name? That's right: Mrs. Weyer. She wondered how many years she had lived in that house. It was small, but it was hers.

Sybil kept walking, houses thinning out at what would be the equivalent of three blocks from Broadway. The street ended at a field. Across the field was an eerie green light. She started across the field. She dodged an engine block in the weeds and then a roll of barbed wire. It was treacherous walking in her Danskos, and she moved slowly, carefully, judging every step.

She arrived at a familiar spot on the shore of Lake Ahnwee. When she was a kid, this was where she and her friends would go swimming, an informal beach – no sand, but a big oak tree with a rope swing daring kids would use to jump in the water. The tree was still there. Dead, but there. At the water's edge, she sat down on a hot water heater lying on its side. She thought the color of the glow was like nothing else, except maybe Green Lantern. It didn't smell, and, happily, the hog farm was down-wind at the moment. No birds, or bugs, or anything else living, except Sybil, animated by the post-apocalyptic scene. Across the lake were the white lights of Wind Energy Now; they lit their property to day-like brightness, and maybe a bit more.

A dragonfly did a loop-de-loop, surprising her. It hovered

in place as only a dragonfly can do, right in front of Sybil. She smiled. The dragonfly flew out over the shore, and, once over water, turned upside down and dropped as if it were hit with Yard Guard.

Yeah, right, she thought. Maybe taking bulldozers to Ahnwee would be a blessing.

She started walking back home, but decided to take another street back for variety, one bringing her back downtown. On Broadway, all was quiet on a Monday night at ten, as it was on any night at ten. The one exception was Dirty Girls, a block away. She walked toward it. No real reason why. No one was about, even though there were several pickups in the lot. She started to walk by, but instead turned and walked in.

She had never been in Dirty Girls. She had never been in a strip bar of any stripe. Her first impression was how boring it looked. She had thought such a place would be a party. When she'd been to a couple bachelorette parties, back in the day when her friends did such things, the gals whooped it up with the male dancers, hooting and hollering, dancing along. She expected it'd be like that. Instead, a bored-looking young woman she'd never seen in town before was buck naked doing some acrobatics on a brass pole. Loud Credence Clearwater Revival played. A handful of men slouched at small tables around the room, all of them sitting alone, all of them look-ing miserable. It was quite the opposite of a party.

"Mayor!" Jackson said, holding his arms up as if to hug, but thankfully dropping them before trying. "What brings you in?"

She said she was just passing by.

"You never passed by before."

"Yeah, well…"

"Let me get you a Red Bull."

She said no thanks, a Diet Sprite would do. He led her to the "bar," where she sat, and he went behind and poured her a Diet Sprite in a tall, frosted glass with a tiny straw. She watched the redheaded woman leave the stage and walk to the men at the tables. She was a trim, attractive girl with too much makeup, a pierced bellybutton, and a tattoo of a unicorn on her left butt cheek. The naked young woman smiled at each man in turn, saying something to each up close, each either ignoring her or shaking their heads no, until finally a man laid money – Sybil couldn't see how much – on the little table and the thin young lady proceeded to straddle him, rocking back and forth, as if having intercourse.

"Are you kidding me?" she said out loud.

"What, you've never heard of a lap dance before?" Jackson said.

All this was stranger than a glowing lake. Stranger than a wind turbine obstacle course. Stranger than strange. The club was considered by most if not all in town to be a black mark against Ahnwee. No one ever spoke about it. Or to Jackson. If Jackson ever noticed he was getting snubbed, he didn't let on; he in fact seemed to be living the good life. Jackson looked young to Sybil, college age. Somewhat chunky with a poor growth of beard, he wore a Calvin Klein jacket over a black Metallica t-shirt and jeans, flip-flops and a Twins cap with sunglasses on top. Bottom line, he was a garden-variety nerd, but he came off like he believed he was super suave.

"How did you get in this business, Jackson?"

"Kind of a long story," which he proceeded to tell from start to finish. A graduate of Despar High, he was voted most likely to be arrested in a derivatives scandal. He had a house he inherited from his mother; God rest her soul. He couldn't find a job that paid him what he thought he was worth, and he had a lot of house equity to work with. He decided he was born to be an entrepreneur. He considered fast food franchises, but, after getting *The Sopranos* box set for

Christmas and watching every episode in some lonely, crazed, body-odor-inducing marathon, he decided to go into the strip club business. His theory was that there was nothing to do in this godforsaken part of the country, both for men of all ages and for young women who needed work.

The first problem was that a liquor license was out of the question, not just because of his age, but because in Minnesota full nudity isn't allowed in establishments serving booze. Instead, he set it up as a "juice bar," serving mostly Red Bull. He bought the old Legion Club, long out of business after the last World War II veteran moved away to live his last years with his daughter in New Jersey, and he reopened it as Dirty Girls. He had no experience in such matters, so he modeled it on Bada Bing, the strip club in *The Sopranos*. Who knows what the future holds, he said, but so far his theory of young women in the area needing work had proved true, and that young men, mostly from the turbine factory, needed diversions was also spot-on.

Sybil couldn't deny it: he probably – no, certainly, by a mile – had the only successful business in Ahnwee.

All the time he was talking, Sybil was observing like Diane Fossey in the bush: pure anthropology. It occurred to Sybil what was going on at Dirty Girls: it had nothing to do with sex. No, it was power: these lame, ugly, powerless men get to have beautiful young woman approach *them*. If it weren't for the money, the beautiful redhead wouldn't even look at those losers, and they knew it.

"Enough about me. Have you saved my town yet, Mayor?"

"What?" Sybil was startled, not realizing how mesmerized she had become with this strange scene.

"How's the 'Save Ahnwee' campaign going?"

She hadn't heard it called that, and she wondered if Jackson just thought of it or if other people had been saying that.

"Terrible," she said. She told Jackson about all that had been going on. "In short, we are in deep doo-doo."

"Deep shit, indeed." He scratched his head. "What are you going to do?"

"I don't know. I was thinking of moving to Minneapolis this time."

"No, I mean the town. Don't tell me you're going to give up." He seemed genuinely concerned.

She shrugged. "I don't know what else to do."

"Look, Mayor, we're all counting on you."

She both liked to hear that and didn't like it, all at the same time. "Seems like everything is stacked against us."

The music started – "Achy Breaky Heart" – and a new woman came out. This one taller, with jet-black hair and per-fectly defined abs. She was dressed like a cowboy. Sybil's inter-est became less anthropological and more lustful. Not the first time a woman turned her head, and, considering there didn't seem to be a decent available man her age in the county, maybe it was time to change teams. She shook her head and smiled at herself.

Jackson didn't seem to notice Sybil's distraction. "Well, sure. But there are things we can do."

She noted the "we" part.

"You know what happened when I wanted to open Dirty Girls? Augie Flump, who was mayor at the time, called a town meeting. Everyone came. Really worked me over. Maybe you should try that."

She thought it interesting that Jackson would suggest a strategy used against him, with no apparent hard feelings. Sybil wanted to dismiss the idea in favor of continuing her pity party, but she had to admit it was a good one. But "wait, it didn't work."

"What do you mean, Mayor?"

"You opened. Dirty Girls is here; the town didn't stop you."

"Yeah, well, nothing works a hundred percent of the time."

The next morning Sybil rolled out of bed late. She had had trouble sleeping, finally dropping off at about two, but when she slept, she slept hard.

Walking barefoot into the kitchen in her PJs, her father greeted her, "Good morning, sunshine! Look who's the sleepy head!" He said.

She scratched her noggin, scrunched her eyes closed, opened them, and he was still there.

"I have waffles. Want a waffle? And lox. Cream cheese. Bagel. You name it." He put a cup of coffee on the table in front of her.

"Dad?"

She started up in bed. The drapes were closed, and she couldn't see if it was day or still night. She picked up her clock, red numbers saying it was nine-fifteen. Dang, just a dream.

She walked in the kitchen in her PJs to find her father eating dry cereal. "Let me get you some milk, Dad." She went to the fridge, got milk, and poured some in his bowl. "Say when." He didn't say when, and she stopped where she usually stopped. As she put the milk back, Dan yelled, "It's GEER-REAT!" making Sybil jump, look back, and then start laughing, before starting to cry.

Instead of going to the store, Sybil decided to go to Flump's Café. All this craziness had not been good for business, but she needed something money can't buy: people who can talk and listen. She half-ran from her car through a steady rain to the café. Inside, she sat at the counter and Augie came over, commenting on the weather. She ordered a sticky roll. At least a few of the extra pounds she'd put on over the past two years could be credited to sticky rolls. Augie brought her the gooey pastry and a coffee. She never liked his coffee, finding it to be more like tea, but she didn't care at the moment.

The place was empty, so she filled Augie in on the latest news.

"I don't get it, Sybil. If he's behind everything, why would Balzac tell you about Björn Björkman at Ahnwee Days?"

"He's not behind all of it, just Wind Energy Now. The way I figure it, he was hoping we could stop Björkman for him."

"So Wind Energy Now wouldn't have his lawsuit to contend with." He laughed a short belching laugh. "Balzac belongs in Louisiana. He's just a damned county commissioner, not the boss of the county."

As Sybil made short work of her roll, she looked at Augie. Jackson was right. Fighting for the town wasn't about her. Heck, it might be doing her a favor if it meant she could move back to New York without guilt. But, what about people like Augie? For her, Flump's Café has always been there, a constant. When she was a little girl, her father would take her there for a hot fudge sundae, and she would sit at the counter, maybe at that very stool, her feet not touching the floor. Has Augie aged? He must have, but he didn't seem to. Maybe a bit bigger, a bit balder, but still the same Augie.

It was easy for her to forget, but Sybil loved Ahnwee. Not logical, she could never explain it to anyone, but she did. It was a community. It was their community. Their shared history, shared success and failures. In the edge of town was a cemetery. The markers reveal all the people who made a home in the area, all the people who roughed it to make it what it would become, and could be again, all the men who came home in a box from whatever war. Ahnwee was on the ropes, but it was a great place, if you could see it through the right lens, if you could spend time with its inhabitants, all good people who would help a neighbor. People like Augie. Like Ruby. Sig. Even G, the shaky dude in the grain elevator. And heck, maybe even Jackson, she conceded.

Augie came over, took the empty plate, and put it somewhere beneath the counter. "Looks like you enjoyed that sticky roll, Mayor."

"Augie, have you lived here your whole life?"

"Ya, you bet."

"In the same house?"

"Ya. My great-grandfather built it when he moved here."

"And it didn't burn down?"

"No. Why would it burn down?"

Sybil decided to change the subject. "Augie, I was at Dirty Girls last night…"

"Is that so."

"Not for the girls, to talk to Jackson."

"I understand. I'm a modern man."

Sybil thought, no you're not, but plowed ahead. "Jackson told me that when you were mayor you had a town meeting to try to stop him from opening."

"Fat lot of good it did."

"Should we try it now? We have to tell the town what's going on, that Ahnwee may be torn down."

He shrugged. "Might as well. What do we have to lose?"

Chapter 15: Always Dispose of Unused Prescriptions

Pastor Fabian Farber awoke to water dripping on his face. He thought those stupid existentialists were wrong: there is an afterlife. Maybe not heaven, since it was the same leaky ceiling, but an afterlife, nonetheless. He realized he was still on the altar at Third Lutheran. It must be like the movie *Ghost*, and he was invisible. Where's Whoopie? He sat up and looked around. He hopped down, thinking everything seemed normal. He walked outside into daytime. It was raining, and he could feel the chill and wet. Strange, he thought, I would have guessed a ghost would get a pass on temporal concerns like those. Finally, it occurred to him maybe he was alive.

He had to know.

He walked to Flump's Café through the rain, drenched from head to toe. Augie stood behind the counter and the mayor sat at the end. He sat down at the other end. He didn't say anything. He looked rough, hair a mess, his cassock weighing down like a towel. He was a ghost. He was sure of it. He looked around for a light he could walk to.

Sybil looked down the counter and wondered when the good pastor came in, and how she could have not noticed. He looked terrible, both in his wet dress and his long face.

"Pastor, how are you today?" Sybil said, genuinely concerned for the wet, rumpled man.

He slowly looked at her. "You can see me?"

She chose not to answer the question and pressed on. "I got bad news on the town. It's not saved yet after all." She went on to give him all the details.

"The town may be torn down after all?" He looked like he won twenty on a scratch-off.

"You almost look happy about that, Pastor," Augie said.

"No, no, not at all. It's so disappointing!" he seemed positively giddy.

"Can we use the church for a town meeting?" Sybil said. "We're not letting them take Ahnwee without a fight." Augie and Sybil looked at him. "Pastor?"

"Sure, yeah."

"Seriously, you okay, Pastor?" Augie asked.

He nodded. They both looked at him for a moment, before getting to work on planning the meeting.

Later, when he went online to find out what went wrong with his suicide, he discovered that old pills lose their effectiveness, and his prescription sleeping pills were outdated by years.

Chapter 16: Ace in the Hole

The church filled up, much to Sybil's joy. No one could predict what would happen when she decided to call a town meeting, least of all her. Sure, she, Ruby, and Sig, as well as Pastor Farber, Jackson, and Augie were excited about saving Ahnwee, but beyond that group, sometimes it seemed like no one else cared. More than that, Sybil wondered if there weren't those who would just as soon have the town put out of its misery.

Sybil and the crew had hung flyers all over Ahnwee, and in the two weeks leading up to the meeting they – Sybil and Ruby especially – knocked on every door in town. Sybil thought how she'd known all these townspeople all her life, and they all knew her as well, so she thought it would be easy. It wasn't. Few answered their doors. The ones who did mostly gave uncommitted answers, "Oh, on a Saturday? At noon?" "I need to mow, but I guess I could." "Isn't there a sale on at Walmart?" "My son the doctor may call, and I should stay by the phone." "Hum, maybe, but that's usually when I play backgammon online." Those were the best answers. One man greeted Sybil at the door with a shotgun, saying, "I don't have to listen to your government," and one woman yelled through the screen door that she has told her and told her, she will not be needing any more Amway, and that she was going to sue because the laundry soap gave her boils.

Still, thought Sybil, they would not go down without a fight. Once people see that they can win this, maybe they'll join in. Maybe if they think about how important Ahnwee is, they'll fight to save the town. Maybe.

Now that the church was packed Sybil felt vindicated. She stood in the front with Ruby while Pastor Farber stood behind the altar. Sybil was dressed in her best black silk pants and black blouse, Ruby in her muumuu and Birkenstocks and the pastor in fashionable black, sporting a white collar.

"Okay, everyone, settle down and we'll get started," Pastor Farber yelled in his high, falsetto voice. When Sybil asked if they could use the church for the town meeting, he looked less than enthusiastic, not to mention very wet. She figured he was depressed about the situation with Ahnwee. Now, to Sybil, he looked happy. He had probably never seen this many people in his church since… well, ever.

Sig sat in the front row, and he gave Sybil a thumbs-up. Three big red-meat-loving guys sat behind him with seed caps laughing about something. Gilbert, or "G," came in, looking all around, paranoid as all get-out, before standing in the back in the shadows in the corner. Bud, the old yellow lab, wandered in behind G before the door closed, slowly sauntering up the aisle, tail in a slow, sweeping wag. Now maybe the dog's owner would be revealed, Sybil thought. But no, the old pooch flopped his hindquarters down in the aisle, not paying attention to anyone in particular.

Jackson came in with the redhead and the raven-haired women Sybil had seen dancing in his club, plus a new one, who was way too thin to be healthy. All three were wearing mini skirts, midriffs, and high heels and carrying rolled-up cardboard. Heads turned as they sashayed down the aisle like a Robert Palmer video. The girls settled in the front pew next to Sig, who seemed to be happy about that, ahead of the three big homies, who were extremely enthusiastic about the women's choice of clothes and seats. One of them said something to the redhead – Sybil couldn't hear what – and the redhead turned and smiled, obviously well acquainted with him.

Jackson walked up to Sybil, leaned over and said, "My ace in the hole."

"Ace in the hole?" Sybil repeated.

Jackson winked and rejoined his girls.

Ruby leaned over to Sybil, "Who are these people?"

"Jackson's 'ace in the hole.'"

"No, not his dancers, all these people. I see some townies, but who are all these other people? I don't recognize ninety percent of them."

Sybil, like Ruby, knew everyone in town. Looking around, she spotted a couple neighbors and elderly parents of former classmates, but Ruby was right: who were these people? But she didn't have long to consider it.

"Let us pray," Pastor Farber said. People bowed their heads, including all the atheists in the crowd, including Sybil, just to get along. The pastor proceeded to say a prayer for the success of their mission to save Ahnwee, for the people attending and all the people who ever attended and all the people who should attend. He continued to pray for the health and happiness of all relatives living around the country, for the leaders in St. Paul and Washington to have wisdom, and all the little babies in Africa. He kept praying, and one by one people had to straighten up due to developing kinks in their necks and generally being tired of it all. Ruby and Sybil's eyes met, and Ruby rolled hers. Conversations started in the nave. Finally, apparently realizing that he had completely lost the congregation – er, meeting attendees – Pastor Farber said a quick "Amen."

Sybil stepped up to the lectern on the altar. "Ahnwee is under attack." She had practiced that line in a Stickley mirror at New York 'Tique for hours. "Good people," she thought that would sound mayorly, "we are under attack from three sides." She went on to brief everyone about the Big Moose Casino, Björn Björkman's hog farm, and Wind Energy Now. She explained how Commissioner Balzac was behind it all. She explained that if they wanted to save Ahnwee, save their homes, the time was now. She wrapped her speech up, the speech of her life, with the big ending she also rehearsed in the two hundred dollar mirror she has never been able to sell. "Most of you have lived here all your lives," as she said this she thought about how, like Ruby, she didn't recognize a vast majority of the people there, but plowed ahead, anyway. "And you know what a great town Ahnwee was and can be again. Sure, we've fallen on hard times, sure, nearly all our businesses are gone, our young people move away as soon as they are emancipated, sometimes sooner, our lake glows in the dark, and the wind turbine takes some getting used to. But we can come back. We can make Ahnwee a place to be proud of again. But first, we need to keep it from being torn down. We can do this! We have the power! Nothing can stop us!" Sybil yelled, fist in the air.

Feet shuffled.

"Who's with us!" Sybil yelled, trying again.

Someone coughed.

Sig jumping up on the pew, making him almost as tall as the scantily-clad redheaded stripper sitting next to him. "Yeah!" he yelled, power to the people fist in the air.

Someone cleared his or her throat.

Ruby said to Sybil, but loud enough for everyone to hear, "Well, that's not good."

"Socialist!" someone yelled from the pews.

Sybil was flabbergasted. The non sequitur-ness of the comment set her speechless, or nearly so. "Wha…"

A man in the back, fat, suspenders, baby bird hair, lumbered to his feet and pointed at Sybil. "You're the problem. You're a socialist!"

Sybil looked at Ruby, who shrugged.

The man pulled out a red MAGA hat and put it on – or tried, since it was too small, so it more perched on his big melon.

"Yeah, definitely not good," said Ruby.

"Listen, everyone," the man continued, "the mayor here would have you believe that the government will solve all your problems. This so-called 'mayor' wants to stop a good, decent citizen and honest businessman from using his property the way God intended, as the biggest hog farm he can possibly build. Once again, Big Brother wants to tell you what you can do with your property."

What was there to say? Not much apparently, because Sybil, Ruby, and Sig were slack-jawed. The audience murmured, talking amongst themselves, except for three fat townies in overalls who laughed.

Finally, Sybil said, "But that makes no sense. We are trying to get the government to NOT take our land…"

"Liar! Look at this would-be mayor – dressed in black like some E-You-Row-Pee-An. People, you can't trust a socialist! Björn Björkman is a God-fearing Free Man. As such, he has the right to do whatever he wants with his property, and any property he legally claims as his own. I and many people here are Free Men and stand with Mr. Björkman to defend his right to not pay taxes, to feed his family fatty foods, park in handicap spots, and do whatever he wants on his land."

"But we're talking about *our* land…" Sybil said.

"Björkman doesn't have a family…" Ruby said.

"What's fatty food have to do with this?" Sig said, pleading more than asking.

"Socialist liars! People," the fat man in the back said, now turning to the audience, "we've already shown that these people are socialists, and the mayor thinks that government belongs in your kitchen…"

"You're the liar!" yelled a man from across the room, jumping to his feet and pointing at the guy.

Sybil finally exhaled, happy that someone was going to come to her defense and talk sense. She was sorely disappointed.

"People, that man and all these Free Man characters are racists, dedicated to wiping out the Red Man," said the pointing guy. He had long black hair and was wearing a Pendleton shirt even though it was ninety-plus outside. "This town is on our land, Dakota land, owned by the Dakota people, more specifically the Big Moose family. Now, we would appreciate it if you all packed up and moved. Today. We'll be in touch about any back rent. Don't you worry about that."

The group of big guys sitting around the Free Man guy, now with their own MAGA hats, jumped to their feet and started yelling across the room. A group of native men sitting around the Pendleton-wearing guy leaped to their feet and yelled back.

Pastor Farber retook the altar and pleaded for restraint, charity, peace. "This isn't helping anything," the minister yelled, his voice hitting a Minnie Riperton octave, not making a dent in the cacophony.

A woman wearing a hemp shirt ran forward and threw an ice cream bucket of some thick red liquid on the altar, splashing it all over the hapless pastor. The church instantly fell silent. The woman turned to the gathered so-called townspeople. "This red paint symbolizes the death of our environment due to nuclear power and fossil fuels! Protect the environment! Wind power!" A group of mostly middle-aged women in tie-dye t-shirts jumped to their feet and unfurled a banner that said Our Planet Is Dying" and began to chant, "Wind power! Wind power!"

The Free Men guys yelled at the wind power people, "Socialists! Socialists!"

The native guys yelled at the Free Men, "Racists! Racists!"

Sybil and Ruby, side-by-side, motionless as a stunned hamster in a cup, breathed through their mouths unblinking at the show. Pastor Farber, a short distance away, looked down at his ruined clothes and the likely ruined altar.

Just when it couldn't have gotten more confusing, the three dancers from Jackson's Dirty Girls got involved. They leapt to their feet, held up white signs saying, "Save our town," "We're excited about Ahnwee," and "Ahnwee girls do it better" and started whooping and cheering and generally bouncing up and down. The crowd stopped everything, as the men took in the three bouncing, braless someone's-daughters. One of the old fat townies behind them yelled, "Now that's a position I can get behind!" sending his two friends into hysterics. The chaos resumed with the dancers dancing and cheering, and the Free Men, wind power, and Native rights people all yelling at each other. And the cherry on top was the dog, who got in the spirit by barking like crazy at the crowd.

"Well, that went rather well, didn't it?" Ruby said to nasty looks. Sybil, Ruby, and Sig settled around a table at Flump's Café, breathing hard from panic and from running away from the crowd to the café. They had escaped the church through a door behind the altar, a feature the builders had included just in case of such uprisings.

Out the window of the café, they could see people getting in cars up and down the street and driving off. Sybil observed that while the wind power people seemed to prefer bicycles and Priuses like hers (Prii? Priora?), it was interesting that the American Indian activists and the Free Man people both seemed to prefer the same vehicles, namely big diesel Ram king-cab trucks. Curious, given they had so little else in common.

Augie brought them all coffee. "I could hear the racket all the way down here."

Pastor Farber walked in, jacket and pants now hard with dried red paint.

"Oh, I'm so sorry," Sybil said. "Are you okay?"

"My church…"

"Sit down, Pastor, sit down," Sig said.

"…They wrecked it. The pews, broken, red paint…" He lowered his head, shuffling over to the table. Augie reflexively laid a cup of coffee in front of him.

"Well, it could be worse," Ruby said, "It could have been real blood."

G came in. "Whoa, dudes, that was nuts." He said, pulling a chair over and joining them. G looked pretty bad, skinny as a telephone pole, a deathly pallor, and rotting teeth. Sybil thought how you really know things have gone to heck when the town meth addict thinks the situation was nuts.

Jackson and the three dancers from Dirty Girls came in, heels clicking on the terrazzo floor. Jackson waved at the group, and they sat at the neighboring table.

"'Ace in the Hole'?" Ruby said.

"Well, I thought we might need more turn out, so I got my

girls here to come. Plus, it worked when Augie had his town meeting against Dirty Girls. How was I to know…"

"Let me get this straight," Ruby said, "You thought bringing some of your floozies to the CHURCH to argue for saving a town was a good idea?"

"Well, yeah, I…"

"Who are you calling a floozie?" the black-haired raven said.

"Yeah, you little Weeble!" said the redhead.

"Since when do you care about this town, Jackson?" Ruby said, bitchier than Sybil had ever heard her.

"I have twenty employees working for me, from wait staff to cleaners to dancers," Jackson said.

"I grew up five miles from here," the too-thin one said. "Where do you expect me to work? Walmart? I make more in a day dancing than I would in a week at Walmart. More on a Saturday."

Ruby was taken aback. For Sybil, that was a first. Sybil decided to try to calm things down. "Listen, fighting among ourselves isn't going to help us. The question is, what are we going to do now?"

"Give up?" Pastor Farber said.

"But this is my home," Ruby said. "My husband and I raised our kids here."

"They're not taking my home and business without a fight," Jackson said.

"Here's my question," Sig said, "who invited the Big Moose people, Björn Björkman, and Wind Energy Now?"

"It was open to the public," Ruby said.

"Yeah, but how did they hear about it?" replied Sig.

Sybil debated to herself whether to come clean and decided yes. "Well, I guess I invited them," Sybil said.

"What?" "What were you thinking?" "Genius move" and

other similar comments erupted from around the tables.

"Well, I thought it only fair that they have their say, too. I didn't know…"

"You know now. This is war," Jackson said.

"Yeah, war," G said.

"Now they made me mad," Ruby said, knitting away.

"Yeah, mad," G added.

"Whatever it takes," Sig said.

"Whatever," G opined.

"How can we fight this?" Sybil said, more complaining than asking. "Darn it, they've all got the money, the lawyers, and are obviously able to marshal a constituency and pack meetings. What do we have?"

"We have Jesus on our side," Pastor Farber said, obviously out of habit, not sincerity.

"Oh, pa-lease," Ruby replied.

"I think we should do a brainstorm," Sybil said.

Everyone groaned.

"What?"

"Mayor," Augie said, "does anything good ever come from a brainstorming exercise?"

Sybil was flummoxed, but G came to the rescue with an actual brainstorm suggestion.

"I know! I read this book once, called the *Monkey Wrench Gang*."

"Edward Abbey," Ruby said.

"They were a band of radical environmentalists led by this guy Hayduke, and they set out to blow up the Glen Canyon Dam."

Jackson looked puzzled. "And?"

"Well," G continued, "we could blow up the hog manure pond."

"The hog manure pond?" Jackson said.

"Do you know the hog manure pond is uphill?"

"Sure, G. But why? Do you know what that would do?" Sybil asked.

"That would show him. Teach him a lesson."

"You'd flood the town with pig shit," Ruby added.

"I have the chemicals," G said, undaunted. "I bet I could make a fertilizer bomb from the stuff at the grain elevator."

Sybil wondered why G would have such chemicals.

"Does anyone have a useful suggestion?" Ruby said.

"What we need is attention. What we need is for people to come here and see what's going on, bring popular opinion on our side." Jackson said.

They sat silently, drinking their coffee.

"Bam!" G said. "Up goes the shit pond!"

"Shut up," Augie said.

Chapter 17: The Fourth Estate Strikes Again

Sybil took a drink of coffee and opened the laptop. Her dad was in the living room, occupied for at least the next hour with back-to-back episodes of *Green Acres*.

"Hi, Sweetie!" Drew said.

Sybil smiled.

"How'd the meeting go?"

"Not so well." Sybil gave her the news, and Drew looked as if she were going to laugh but kept it together.

"Oh, I have to write this all down. What a story! You can't make this stuff up." Drew adjusted the webcam, centering herself up better. "What are you going to do now?"

Sybil said she didn't know.

"Didn't you say that County Commissioner – what was his name?"

"Balzac."

"Yeah, Commissioner Balzac – didn't you say he was taking bribes?"

"Not bribes. He has a political action committee and Wind Energy Now is a big supporter. That's why he wants to condemn the land."

"Yeah, that. You know what I'd do? I'd call the press." Before Drew was a personal trainer and yoga instructor, she was a publicist for a PR firm that crashed when their best customer died of autoerotic affixation.

"The press. Yeah." Sybil was upset with herself for not having thought of it herself.

"Or you could move home."

"Drew…"

"I'm just sayin'."

"Green Acres is the place to be!" Dan yelled from the living room.

Sybil looked at her friend, and, as she did more and more, longed for New York.

Sybil gave Ruby and Sig coffee, and they sat at the fifties table at New York 'Tique.

"A press conference, eh?" Sig said, taking apart a Russian nesting doll with great interest.

"Great idea," Ruby added, taking a sip of coffee. She made a face as if she were sucking a lemon.

"We can call the Twin Cities media – TV and print – as well as town papers in the area. We could even try the national media. Maybe they'll find it to be a great story from the heartland."

"We could call *The Daily Show*!" Sig said, the seven round female figures now lined up in descending size. "So, what are these for?"

"Focus, please," Ruby said. "You ever throw a press conference?"

"No. but it doesn't seem like it should be that hard."

"I bet the hard part will be getting anyone to care," Ruby said.

They decided Sybil would write up a media release for Friday. Ruby would talk to Pastor Farber about using the front of the church for the event, since it was the most photogenic place in town and used a building as a backdrop some people may agree was worth saving. Sybil thought she'd once again recruit poor sickly-looking G to hang a banner, which reminded her of a question that had been bugging her.

"Why would G have chemicals in the grain elevator he could use to blow up the hog manure pond dike?" Sybil asked.

No one said anything.

"What?" Sybil said.

"Well, his lab," Ruby said.

"Lab? What lab?"

"He has a meth lab," Sig said. "Everyone knows that."

"I didn't."

Ruby and Sig couldn't seem to make eye contact.

"Really? A meth lab? Like *Breaking Bad*?"

"Sort of," Sig replied.

"And everyone but me knows about this?"

Still no eye contact.

"I feel like an idiot."

Ruby, knitting what appeared to be a one-armed sweater, said, "Don't feel bad, Sybil. It's what everyone likes about you. You see the best in everyone."

That made her feel better, a bit. "Should we call someone?"

"Who?" Ruby replied.

"The authorities?"

"As in the cops?" Sig sad, smelling but not tasting the coffee. "On G? I don't know."

"Yeah, I guess," Sybil said, wanting to take it back.

Sybil didn't know what to think, so she decided not to think about it at all. Instead, she considered if her self-image of a confident Hilary Clinton type was inaccurate. Maybe she should settle for being an Unbreakable Kimmy Schmidt type instead. Maybe the whole Save Ahnwee thing was an exercise in fooling herself. No, she thought, it's not that. She wasn't fooling herself; she knew didn't have a chance. Still, she had to try. Maybe she could think of all this as an exercise in hopelessness, like a suicide mission, or being a Republican in Minneapolis. "Ruby, if we don't win, what will you do?"

"I don't know. I'm old enough to retire. Jerry's 401k leaves me in reasonable shape. I really don't know what I'd do."

"Would you move to Glacier?" Sybil asked.

"Back to Glacier? No, certainly not. Well, maybe a vacation, but not to live. I'm not a kid any longer looking for adventure. I'm looking for…well, basically this."

"A world of trouble? Your home threatened?" Sig said, putting the Russian dolls back together.

"Of course not. But until all this started, it wasn't so bad."

"We could use a few customers," Sybil said.

"Well, yeah, sure. But I like it here. No, I love it. I love Ahnwee. I've known everyone in this town my entire life. Except for people younger than me, those I've known for their entire life. You know what I mean. Take you, Sybil. I remember when your mom brought you in the drugstore for the first time. She was so happy to have a girl. I think your brothers were driving her nuts running around the store, being high-spirited toddlers. She looked so proud of you. Dan, too. He would show me pictures every time he was in. Now multiply that by a couple hundred, and you have a real community. There isn't anyone in this town I wouldn't trust my house keys to. If I need help, I have two hundred people I could call. No, you can't find a place like Ahnwee. Ahnwee is my home, and I don't want to be anywhere else."

Sybil had never heard that story about her folks, and it

made her choke up. And it made her think, too. Not the story about her parents, but what Ruby said about Ahnwee. All along Sybil was hoping for an exit strategy from their hometown, while Ruby wanted nothing more than to stay.

"But, I don't mind telling you," Ruby continued, "that it's been pretty lonely since Jerry died. Counting on my neighbors in a pinch is one thing, but company is another. My house is so empty."

They looked into their coffees as if expecting to see something.

Sig looked up. "Yeah, but this is nice right now. This minute."

"It is, Sig. It certainly is."

Sybil rubbed Ruby's shoulder as if to say, "Me too."

"There's only one thing," Ruby added, "That would make this perfect."

"That is?" Sig asked.

"If Sybil would learn how to make a decent cup of coffee."

Sybil looked in the mirror. Urgh. Her clothes didn't fit so great anymore. Maybe she needed a new look. She could see that her signature black, common as pigeons in New York, made her an oddball on the prairie. If being an oddball was extra credit in New York, it was radioactive in Ahnwee. So instead, she opted for a red power suit she hadn't worn in ages. She hoped it made her look powerful, like Gloria Steinem, but it bulged in all the wrong places and her pantyhose were cutting off her circulation. She remembered wearing that outfit for the first time. It was for a date. This guy, this broker guy, asked her out on Tinder, and she decided she should dress right for someone of his class. Turned out he wasn't a very good broker, so she looked a bit overdressed for a Roy Rogers, even for the one in Times Square. She went out with him a couple more times, going to a Rangers game once, which she hated, but she also gave him credit for trying hard to court a Minnesota girl. She slept with him that night. It was awkward and short, but it was also better than most of her relationships, which were awkward and short from the get-go. She wondered how their relationship would have turned out if he hadn't turned state's evidence on his Ponzi-scheme of a firm and went into a witness protection.

She tugged on her silk blouse. In the mirror, the buttons strained a bit too much, but that blouse was her best option.

She went in the living room. "Dad? Are you going to be okay by yourself?"

Dan didn't say anything, intense gaze fixed at the TV as Eddie Albert and Eva Gabor fought about something.

"You're going to stay here and watch TV, right? I'll be back in probably a half hour, an hour at the most."

Dan said nothing.

Sybil let the screen door slam as she walked down the front steps. It was a strange sight; Sybil dressed in a suit walking on the edge of the sidewalk-less streets of the dusty little town. She wished she hadn't worn heels, but she couldn't take them off because her hose would run for sure. Why didn't I drive? She wondered. On the corner she waved at a man on his knees weeding a gold tractor-tire planter. He had one arm – when did he lose his arm? Had she simply not noticed since she returned to Ahnwee, or was she not as wired into the town gossip as she thought she was? Aha! The sweater Ruby was knitting. He whistled. She smiled, not in the least offended by the old man joking around. It occurred to her that a one-armed old man was as close to an offer as she'd gotten since she came back.

Yup: slim pickings in Ahnwee. That Malcolm Moose guy was attractive; but while he didn't wear a ring, he still seemed unobtainable, considering the circumstances. Sig? For some reason, being the queen of Beef Jerky wasn't very appealing. Plus, while she now thought he was a great friend, he was also a hothead. Sybil dated hotheads before – especially in New York – and never wanted to again. In the big city she didn't meet a lot of native New Yorkers, although she understood there were plenty in the boroughs. All she met were these guys who moved to town to become rich in the stock market or advertising or publishing – like that broker guy – and they all seemed angry or self-absorbed or both. She'd had a few relationships with women over time, during and after college. Her most serious was a friend of Drew's – actually, Drew's yoga instructor – and that was nice. It was New York so it was no big deal to anybody, maybe not even to Sybil. They drifted apart when the limber waif moved to Brooklyn – Flatbush being the new SoHo or something. Sybil could see swinging that way again. Still, no help there: even if she cast a wide gender net, the dating pool was a shallow one around Ahnwee.

Ten minutes later, she was in front of the church, where they were ready for her. The wind was light and from the south, so things were looking good on the stink issue. She looked over the setup. "It looks great, Pastor."

Pastor Farber had set up a podium on the landing in front of the church, run an extension cord, and connected a mic and speaker. He smiled. He was happier than he had been in a long time. Having something to do can be a great antidepressant – besides getting ready for the big press conference, he worked all week hammering and gluing and nailing the pews back into some shape after the misbegotten town meeting.

A brand new banner hung across the church entrance. Sybil had sent a rush order to Let's Go Crazy Printz in Despar (the money coming out of Sybil's pocket), and G had once again done the honors of hanging it up. Sybil looked at him all askance, knowing what she now knew about him.

"We just need the press to come," Pastor Farber said.

Sybil had written a release and sent it around. The press conference was to begin at one, and at twelve-thirty Sybil could see Ruby a block away lock up her store and slowly walk to the church.

"Sybil," Ruby said.

"Ruby."

"Pastor."

"Ruby."

"Sybil, what didn't you do this time?" Ruby said.

"I didn't call Malcolm Moose, Björkman, or Ms. Hoffman."

"Good."

Sybil became aware of feeling moist under her arms and feared that she had already sweated through her suit. She lifted one arm and then the next to check, and sure enough, her red suit now sported enormous wet patches. Dang, she thought, I knew I should have worn a black suit, summer or no.

"Suggestion, Sybil," Ruby said. "Don't lift your arms like that at the press conference."

G came up, pointing. "Do you like the sign?"

"Yes, I do, G; you did a good job hanging it." Sybil said. "G, we don't talk often enough."

"We don't?"

"No. How are you?"

"A bit nervous at the moment." Which was how he indeed looked.

"Well, if you ever want to talk."

"About what?"

"About how you are doing." Sybil began to regret starting this.

G looked at Ruby, and at Pastor Farber, and said, "Okay."

"Say, Sybil, did you use Let's Go Crazy Printz in Despar again?" Ruby asked.

"Yeah."

"That explains it."

At first, Sybil didn't understand. Then she looked at the banner, really looked at it, and noticed for the first time that it said "Shave Ahnwee."

"Dang it!" she yelled. She looked at the good pastor. "Sorry."

He shrugged. "'Dang'? No problem. No problem at all."

"'Dang,'" G said with a smile, not about the banner, but about Sybil's best effort at expressing frustration.

Sig pulled up across the street in his 1975 Cadillac Fleetwood. "Well, hot mama," he said, walking up the steps looking at Sybil. He looked up at the sign and recoiled. "Really? Oh, come on. You have to be kidding me!"

A car drove confidently through the wind turbine on the other end of Broadway and continued down into town. Sybil watched the car roll toward them, and she finally recognized it.

The 1956 Chevy convertible parked across the street next to Sig's Cadillac, having some sort of vintage car show of their own. Mayor Jon Fjord got out and yelled across the street. "I heard about your press conference, and I thought I could lend some support." Bud wandered up to Fjord, who reached down and scratched his ear.

"Support?" Sybil whispered to Sig. "With support like his, we don't have a prayer." A woman Sybil didn't know got out of the passenger side of Mayor Fjord's Chevy, banging her door into Sig's Cadillac.

"Hey, watch the paint!" Sig yelled. She was a young woman, skinny, a face like a Pekingese and carrying a notebook and sporting a camera around her neck.

Mayor Jon Fjord said, "This bright young lady is an intern at the *Despar Tattler*."

The Pekingese waved awkwardly, self-consciously.

Dang, Sybil thought. Is this child going to be the only press? Surely someone else will come, won't they?

Pastor Farber went into the church and returned with a cooler filled with bottles of water for everyone. It was already probably close to ninety degrees. Other than the handful of people already there, no movement could be seen anywhere in town, including Bud, who was sleeping in his customary spot in middle of the street. Mayor Jon Fjord and the Pekingese chatted off to the side. G was on the ladder, putting some white paper tape over the letter H. Pastor Farber took the opportunity to pull weeds around the church sign on the lawn. Sybil sweated, standing next to Ruby.

One o'clock came. Nothing. Ten past one came. The dog rolled over.

At one fifteen Sybil decided to get started. She had written the speech, the mic was set up, she might as well read it. Ruby called everyone to come around and pay attention. G got off the ladder, job half done. The Pekingese snapped pictures before picking up her notebook and clicked her pen. The wind shifted and the familiar aroma of the shit pond wafted in like a brown tsunami. Sybil got behind the podium and began.

"Members of the press, fellow Ahnweeians, and guests. We stand here today in a town threatened with extinction. This proud town was founded over a hundred years ago by pioneering and farsighted immigrants who believed in the American dream, a dream that says all men are created equal. While the obvious misogyny of that statement is unquestioned, the sentiment still holds true: we all deserve a place to live, to be treated fairly, to be rewarded for hard work, and to trust that the deeds to our houses are in order."

Even before seeing it, everyone could hear an engine approaching from the west. All eyes went to the red and white truck as it approached the wind turbine, almost not seeing the problem before squealing its breaks, then taking a left, the usual route for the uninitiated. Sure enough, a few moments later the truck came onto Broadway from a side street, took a right, and stopped right in the middle of the street, chasing Bud to the curb. The truck was more like a van or one of those boxy ambulances, with a folded down satellite-type dish on the top and a big, logo-y "seven" painted on the side and the words, "Eyeful News."

The doors opened, and the driver got out, stretching his back. From the passenger side swearing could be heard. "Jerry, what the fuck? This can't be it. Nobody wants to save this shithole." A woman, forty pushing thirty, tight lime-green business suit, orange complexion, multi-colored hair with a bump-up, walked around the front of the van, stumbling in stiletto heels. "What is that smell? I mean, seriously, is that you, Jerry? You have to eat healthier. No more gas station hot dogs," she yelled, loud enough to be heard for blocks around. "Hey, you! Behind the podium! Do you know where Unweed is? We're looking for a town called Unweed."

"Ahnwee," Sybil said.

"Yeah, whatever. Jerry here is stoned and now we're lost."

Jerry was already unloading the van in the street: tripod, battery pack, black boxes that looked like they've been thrown around quite a bit.

"This is Ahnwee. You found it."

"I told you so," Jerry said, not slowing down.

"Don't get smart with me, camera monkey." The woman walked up to the church and Sybil. "Cara Carrington, Channel Seven news. Don't mind him. He's union so he thinks he is allowed to talk to the talent." She held her hand out. "You must be Mayor Voss."

Sybil shook her hand, the reporter sporting a mean business animal grip. "We're just getting started," Sybil said.

"What's the deal with the big fan? This town is like a miniature golf course, and I was the ball." She didn't seem to want an answer, but instead said that it would be a few minutes while they get set up. "Sorry we're late. We had no idea how far it was. I mean, I don't think I've ever been this far west of the cities. I don't think I've been past Minnetonka, to be honest. I think my producer is punishing me. That's what it is. He's mad because I won't sleep with him anymore. What is it with people? Shouldn't he be happy I slept with him at all? But no. In fact, to see this guy, he should be happy anyone ever slept with him, not just because of his gut, but because he's got a disability."

"Disability?"

"Yeah. He suffered from a micro penis. Have you heard of it? To tell the truth, I never minded, but he had such a complex about it, it was all he could talk about in bed. You ever sleep with a man with a micro penis?"

"Ah…"

"It's not the meat, it's the motion, as they say. But it is a funny little thing, and it got lost in his fat folds. That wasn't so attractive. But a girl's gotta do what a girl's gotta do. Am I right?"

"Um…"

"Now, I used to date a baseball player. For the Twins. Now

that slugger had a bat…"

Sybil tried to follow along, nodding and smiling, as Cara Carrington talked at lightening speed. Eventually she realized it didn't matter what she did, so her mind wandered.

"Who's that hunk-a-hunk?" Cara Carrington said. "I know he doesn't have a micro penis."

Sybil followed Cara Carrington's eyes to Jon Fjord, and Cara Carrington was gone, standing next to Fjord in a flash. He looked at Sybil and smiled.

Everyone stood around as Cara Carrington flirted and Jerry the camera monkey dragged cables around.

"Ready to go, Ms. Carrington," Jerry the camera monkey yelled from behind all his junk.

"About time." Cara Carrington returned to the front of the church and went over the plan with everyone. Sybil would read her statement and they would film it, and after that, Sybil would take questions.

Sybil started her speech over again. She laid out the issue of Big Moose Casino, Björn Björkman, and Wind Energy Now. She told them about County Commissioner Balzac and how Wind Energy Now is giving him massive campaign contributions. She framed it around how the little guy is getting pushed around by powerful interests, and all they want to do is save their homes. She finished with, "Ahnwee isn't Minneapolis or even St. Paul. We are simple people, small town people, and we want to stay that way. It's not just Ahnwee; small town life is endangered from all sides, from big box retailers siphoning off main streets to struggling farmers not being able to support their communities; from a lack of investment in infrastructure like schools and roads and freeway exits, to depopulation due to a lack of opportunity for young people. We are not going to solve that today; all we are asking is to be allowed to have our town."

"And maybe a few customers once in a while," Sig called out.

"And a proper-sized mast for the wind turbine," Ruby said.

Right then, as if on cue, Jackson and three dancers, the redhead, too-thin girl, and raven-hair, each wearing their usual little miniskirts, midriffs, and high heels and carrying the same cardboard signs from the failed community meeting, crossed the street. They ran yelling and cheering behind Sybil, waving their signs in the air, "Save our town," "We're excited about Ahnwee," and "Ahnwee girls do it better," and generally bouncing up and down. Sybil could read Cara Carrington's lips as she said to Jerry the camera monkey, "Are you getting this?" Fjord laughed and the intern scribbled furiously in her notebook.

Sybil tried to quiet them down, and eventually they did, since they received little encouragement from the few attendees.

"Mayor, question?" Cara Carrington said into a microphone with the cord snaking its way back to Jerry the camera monkey. "What does this all have to do with 'slave'? Are you saying this is some kind of sex thing? BDSM?"

"What?" Sybil said, feedback from her microphone almost knocking her over. She followed the reporter's eyes up to the banner, where G had taped over only part of the "H," so that it now said "Slave Ahnwee."

Sybil talked fast, explaining about the rush job and Let's Go Crazy Printz and G and the banner coming out of her own money.

"Mayor," Cara Carrington said into the microphone, "some say that Ahnwee is blighted, that it smells like a giant sick pig flew over and laid a big dump, and that if you're not careful that squeaky wind turbine will four-iron your Escalade into that glow stick of a lake. And, worst of all, no one is making money. How do you respond?"

"Sure, Ahnwee is just an antique shop, yarn store, diner, strip joint, and meth lab, but it's OUR antique shop, yarn store, diner, strip joint, and meth lab."

As the last words left Sybil's mouth, she noticed her father walking down the street. She shuddered but was consoled that he was wearing pants and looking fairly normal, if distant. He came up to the van in the middle of Broadway, unzipped pants, pulled his bat out, and peed on the black boxes stacked on the ground.

"Hey!" Jerry the camera monkey said.

"Okay, let's review," Ruby said, knitting something long. "Where did we go wrong? Anybody?"

After the press conference, after Ruby escorted Dan home, after Jerry the camera monkey quit swearing, and after Cara Carrington was done with Sybil, the gang had rendezvoused at Flump's Café.

Sybil, Ruby, Sig, and Pastor Farber sat at a table, with no one else in the place but the dog and Augie cleaning something. Sig had his head in his hands. "All I can say is, Déjà-fucking-vu."

"Déjà-fucking-vu indeed," Pastor Farber said.

"Pastor!" Ruby said in mock surprise.

"Perhaps we should have made clear to Jackson that kind of help isn't helpful," Pastor Farber said.

"Perhaps," Ruby said. "What else?"

Augie walked over to their table from behind the counter, wiping his hands on his apron. "How'd it go?"

"Shut up, Augie," Sig said. "Hey, where were you?"

"Somebody in this town has to work." Augie left and returned with coffee cups and a carafe, pouring everyone a cup. The crew stared at the table.

"What else?" Ruby said.

"Well, the good mayor could stop going to those donut-heads at Let's Go Crazy Printz in Despar," Sig said.

Ruby nodded. "Good. Good. Sybil?"

"Yeah?"

"Thoughts?"

"I can't leave my dad at home alone anymore. That's for sure." They stared at the table some more. "You know, it's not all bad," Sybil said. "Channel Seven did come out, and they're going to do a story. That's good news."

They all nodded.

"And Sybil did cut a fine figure in her red outfit," Sig said, "At least when she kept her arms down."

Cara Carrington did an interview with Sybil after the so-called press conference, asking her all about the town, the businesses, the lake, and the stupid wind turbine. She talked more about Björn Björkman's hog farm, Big Moose Casino, and Wind Energy Now. Jerry the camera monkey filmed Sybil walking down the street in her red suit looking purpose-ful, and then again making believe she was doing something useful at New York 'Tique. "B roll" he called it.

"Well," Ruby said, "You're right. Let's hope for the best. Tomorrow night?"

"That's what she said. At five and ten."

Just before five p.m. the next day, Sybil, Ruby, and Sig all gathered in front of the television in Sybil's living room.

Dan watched *Petticoat Junction* on an old, portable TV in the kitchen. Sybil wished he would stay in the living room with her and everyone — especially Ruby — but he seemed pretty determined to follow his usual routine. Ruby made it more okay by suggesting, "Don't worry about it."

Sybil was worried, but hopeful, that Cara Carrington would do a good job, especially after spending a good deal of time with her explaining the situation carefully and thoroughly. "What do you all think?" Sybil asked.

"About what?" Sig said.

"About the report. I think it'll be good."

"I hope you are right, Sybil," Ruby said, knitting as usual. "I don't have any experience with the media, but from what I've been told, they are usually looking for a story."

"That's okay, right?"

"Yeah, as long as it's the story you want them to tell."

Sybil didn't know what to think. She wanted to be optimistic; she needed to be optimistic.

"It's on!" Sig said, turning up the volume with the remote.

"A small town in western Minnesota may go the way of the dodo bird, raising issues about what happens when outsiders take on local interests. Cara Carrington has the story," said a man with Ken-doll hair and a perfectly knotted tie.

"That's a good start," Ruby said.

Open to a shot of a map, with an arrow shooting across to Ahnwee. "Here in the prairie, far, far from the Twin Cities..."

"Well, it's not *that* far," Sig said.

"...outside interests are threatening the fabric of a community, their very way of life." Björn Björkman's face appears on the screen. He appears to have a tear rolling down between the boils on his cheek. "I don't know what I'm going to do. My family has farmed this land for generations, and now we will have to go out of business if we can't solve this."

Sig leaned forward. "What the f…"

"What is threatening this man of the earth, this modern-day American Gothic?" A shot of Björn Björkman standing next to his wife, looking off, concerned. "The neighboring town of Unweed has been hijacked by interests from the East." Now the B roll of Sybil walking down the street in her smart red power suit. "Sybil Voss moved to Unweed two years ago, some say in order to take over the town and fashion it into New York of the Prairie." The TV showed a close up of the New York 'Tique sign.

Sybil perched on the edge of the couch, watching herself on TV say, "I lived in New York for eight years."

"'Before moving home!' That what I said, 'I'm from Ahnwee, I lived in New York for eight years before moving home!'"

A shot of Cara Carrington holding a microphone. She's someplace, not Ahnwee, that looks familiar to Sybil. "And now, Mayor, some would say you fashioned this poor little town into a new New York, a den of drugs and sex."

"We have a lot to offer here," TV Sybil said, before switching to a shot of the four strippers bouncing about below the banner saying "Slave Ahnwee."

"That's completely out of context!" flesh and blood Sybil said.

"Drugs and sex? You can't even swear," Sig said.

"And indeed, they do," Cara Carrington's voice said, over a shot of the outside of Dirty Girls.

Back to a shot of Björn Björkman, who is petting a pig, with voice over by Cara Carrington. "What does this have to do with this paragon of American virtue, the small farmer? The New York interests have taken it upon themselves to fight Mr. Björkman with all their wealth and influence…."

"'Wealth and influence'?"

"…threatening to scuttle his plans for improving the environment through proper handling of waste from his family farm."

Ruby dropped her needles next to her chair and leaned forward. "That old pussbag son of a…"

"I used to go there all the time, but now I feel shunned," Björn Björkman said.

"According to anecdotal evidence from people unwilling to go on record, this is a scenario playing out in rural areas across the country, with strange people coming in and taking over," Cara Carrington said over a shot of Sig walking down the street.

Sig leapt to his feet. "'Strange people'? Did she just call me 'strange people'?"

They go back to a shot of Sybil standing in front of the church, dancers bouncing around behind her. "What makes this different is its brazenness."

TV Sybil seems to proudly proclaim, "…Ahnwee is just an antique shop, yarn store, diner, strip joint, and meth lab…"

"And there you have it. Not the small-town life we remember and idealize."

Missus Björn Björkman is on camera, holding onto her husband's arm. Both of them are crying rivers. "I don't know what we are going to do. I just don't know what we are going to do."

And back to the Ken-doll-hair anchorman. "Thank you, Cara. Cara Carrington, from somewhere far, far west of the cities."

Sybil turned it off with the remote. Sybil, Ruby, and Sig sat, silent, looking like stunned sparrows in a towel.

"Forget about your cares. It is time to relax. At the junction. Petticoat Junction!" Dan yells from the kitchen.

Chapter 18: Always Know When You Are Licked

On the corner of Second Street North as she walked home from New York 'Tique, Sybil saw Mrs. Schmidt, as she saw her most days, working in the garden. Sybil smiled and waved. The old woman stood up, wiped her hands on her apron, and flipped Sybil the bird, yelling, "I knew you were trouble when I caught you steaming up the windows in that boy's car!"

Sybil quit waving. Well, Sybil thought, there's at least one citizen who saw the news report.

Sybil had gone into work bright and early in an attempt to remember what a normal day might look like. It didn't work. Her walk to the store was surreal at best, with the two people she encountered crossing the street to get away from her, followed by people driving by, pointing. The end came when a man called New York 'Tique asking how he could get in on the drugs, sex, and slavery thing.

Time to call it a day. At eleven o'clock, she locked up and set off for home.

Walking past the oh-so-familiar little homes, when she wasn't getting flipped off, she had time to think. Yup, she decided, the wheels were completely off the wagon. Not only was just about every power broker in the area out to get Ahnwee, now the media was on Ahnwee's back as well, and specifically on Sybil's. "Den of drugs, sex, and slavery?" Sybil thought. With me in charge? When a little old lady in a Minnesota prairie town gives you the middle finger, the wheels are definitely off.

How did this all happen? she wondered. In the span of five weeks, Sybil's life had gone from boring and depressing but normal, to disaster area. She knew she was different. New York had changed her, at least outwardly. She liked dressing in black. She liked strong coffee. She missed subways. But she was sure she was the same girl who decorated the gym for prom at Despar High, the same girl who didn't have a date to the prom. She had been a girl scout, for Pete's sake. She probably sold cookies Mrs. Schmidt those long years ago.

"I give up," Sybil said aloud as she walked to her house. Good to know when you are licked, and Sybil knew she was and then some. Time to move. Time to move away, far, far away, where no one had heard of Ahnwee, the Big Moose Casino, Wind Energy Now, or certainly Björkman, not to mention sex, drugs, and slavery. So, Minneapolis was out. Time to go back to New York. Drew would let her use the couch until she could find some ridiculously overpriced walkup in Brooklyn. No more Manhattan. Seinfeld was fiction. No, all she needed was a place with a cute wine bar and coffee shop within walking distance. Maybe she could open a new store. That would be problematic, since her customers from Midtown wouldn't dream of going to a borough, but there are always new customers. Nothing wrong with ironic pink flamingos for Flatbush nouveau riche hipsters or even non-ironic card playing dogs for visitors from Queens. Twelve million people, she could get lost and forget about all this craziness. Meet a man or woman of her dreams, settle down, get a trendy dog, go to a show once or twice a year. New York wasn't all that the first time around, but maybe she just needed to try again. Lower her expectations.

And what about fair Ahnwee? Ruby and Sig and the rest might be relieved, she considered. Her father, well, it's probably for the best to put him in a home. Probably long past due on that one. Walking up the walk to the back door, she decided she would call the nursing home in Despar right away to start the ball rolling. She would tell everyone else as well; there was no reason to wait.

She went in the kitchen. "Dad! I'm home!"

He said nothing, but she could hear *Sanford and Son* on the tube. She looked in. Sure enough, Dan was in his usual chair. Yes. It's for the best. "Dad? I want to talk to you. It's important."

She heard the mail slot by the unused front door bang. It startled her. One in the afternoon was not a typical time for Sybil to be home. Plus, they got very little mail, since Sybil paid all their bills online, and, well, who mails stuff anymore? To Sybil's surprise, Dan got up from his chair and walked over to the front door, opened the mailbox next to it, and took the mail out. Wow! She thought. I suppose he'd been doing that his whole life, and somehow his muscles remember. It looked like two letters. He carried the mail back toward his chair, but before getting there, he pulled open the drawer in the end table and tossed the mail in. He sat down.

"Dad…" Sybil started to say but stopped. She never looked in that drawer. She never used it, why would she look in it? She walked over, standing next to an oblivious father, and opened the drawer. It was full of mail.

Ruby added water to her coffee and tasted it. She added more. She sat down at the table. "So, you saw the *Despar Tat-*

tler story?"

Sybil sat across from her. "No, I didn't. But get this…"

"It wasn't bad. No mention of 'slave' anything. 'Ahnwee Fighting for its Life.' A certain amount of gloating about how successful Despar is, and a certain amount of painting Ahnwee as a small-town Gary, Indiana, but still, not bad."

"Ruby, let me tell you…"

"You came off pretty well. Even the picture…"

"There was a picture of me?"

Ruby took a sip of coffee. "You bet. Above the fold."

"Above the fold!" Sybil flung her arms in the air.

"On page seven. Let's keep some perspective."

"Still, it's something." Sybil had her picture in the paper!

"Anyway, what did you want to tell me?" Ruby asked.

"Huh?"

"You called, invited me over for 'coffee,'" Ruby made air quotes, "and said you had news. I assumed it was the *Tattler.*"

"The news! Yes." Sybil went on to explain about Dan had been throwing the mail in a drawer. She laid the pile in the middle of the table.

"Sybil, let me get this right: Dan has been hiding the mail."

Sybil nodded. "That's why we never heard about the hearings." She pulled out the top letter, already open. "Here's the notice about the lawsuit from Björkman." She pulled out another, "Here's the hearing at the County Board about condemnation." And another, "Here's the eviction notice from the Big Moose Casino. It's all right here."

Ruby looked at them, each in turn. Then yelled toward the living room, "Way to go, Dan!"

"Three-hour cruise!" Dan yelled back.

"Well," Ruby said, "There's not much to do about it now, is there."

"Maybe there is. Look at this one." Sybil pulled out one

more, handling it almost gingerly. "It's the notice about the County Board's final action regarding the condemnation. The meeting hasn't happened yet. It's next Wednesday."

One minute Sybil was ready to quit and move on, but now that there was hope, quitting was the furthest thing from her mind.

Ruby took another sip of coffee, inspecting the letter carefully. "Wednesday – so we have a time to maybe stop this craziness."

"Yup. We have a chance."

CHAPTER 19: DEPENDS HOW YOU DEFINE "BLIGHTED"

Sybil put on her red power suit once again. She had asked a neighbor, a mother of a high school friend who somehow must not have heard about her supposed ambitions for Ahnwee, to watch over Dan. With the discovery of the letter, Sybil back-burnered the call to the nursing home, but it was clear that the days of leaving Dan unattended were over. Sybil told herself she would deal with it soon enough, but for the time being she would bring him along with her to the store, where there is so little walk-in business it didn't much matter what Dan did.

Sig volunteered to drive to Willmar, the county seat, saying that Sybil's Prius was too cramped for the journey. Sybil couldn't argue with that. Sybil, with Ruby shotgun, drove to South Pacific Jerky, where they got in Sig's 1975 Cadillac Fleetwood, Ruby in back, knitting up a storm. The car was immaculate and smelled of Armor All and beef jerky. The driver's side seat was more than all the way forward and up, and Sybil wondered if it was in the range of normal for the car seat, or if there was a special kit or something to make it possible for Sig to drive. She had no intention of asking.

"Hey, nice picture, Sybil," Sig said.

This was the first time Sybil had a chance to see Sig since

the *Despar Tattler* story came out. Sybil just happened to have a copy. She thought she looked statesperson-like at the podium, if a bit puffy. She read it aloud as they drove through Despar onto the freeway.

"'Ahnwee Fighting for its Life,'" Sybil began. "'We all know Ahnwee as the little ghost town to our east whose water tower annually sports Despar High's best artwork. Now the town is fighting demolition in the face of progress.'"

"Progress?" Sig said.

"'The town of two hundred is trying to hold off development from all sides. "We like it here," Mayor Sybil Voss said at a press conference.'" It went on to explain the issue, before getting interviews from Ms. Abbie Hoffman, who was quoted as saying, "We need to stick together in the face of oppressors!" Malcolm Moose, who was quoted as saying, "What part of get off my land don't you understand?" and Björn Björkman, who was quoted as saying, "No one reads your crummy paper but parakeets. Go away."

Sybil folded it up so as to look at her photo one more time. "Not bad. A number of misspellings, but not bad."

They drove through Despar, onto the freeway, past the big boxes into the flat, treeless expanse of Great Plains farms. They made small talk driving past fields of corn – not the eating variety, the fuel and fake sugar variety, yellow gold – as far as the eye can see. They had gotten a late start, but they were making it up in a hurry. Sig liked to open up the big engine of the Cadillac to "blow the carbon off," whatever that meant. Sybil was terrified and was happy beyond reason when they arrived in one piece, making the forty-mile drive in just over thirty minutes.

At five minutes to one, Alfonse Schreiber waited for them by the steps to the high-style modernist county courthouse. Ruby wore a red and yellow muumuu, while Sig had on a sports jacket and tie. Schreiber, unbelievably, wore flip-flops and cargo shorts, but still the Abboud suit jacket.

"What is wrong with you?" Ruby said.

"What?"

Sybil wondered if her father and Schreiber might not be sharing a room in the puzzle house in a month or so.

"Okay, here's the situation," he said, standing on the steps above them. "In May, the county board declared Ahnwee a blighted area after Wind Energy Now testified that the lake was toxic and unfit for people to live in the vicinity, and the town is closed and in ruins and a hazard to anyone who comes near. Now they are meeting to finalize condemnation and pay for having the land cleared, and then to sell it to Wind Energy Now for one dollar."

"What about Björkman?" Sig said.

"And the Big Moose Casino?" Ruby said.

"Those issues are destined for court. These County Board people probably don't know anything about it, that is, they didn't until that Channel Seven report." He looked right at Sybil. "Speaking of: really, Mayor? You brought strippers to a press conference? I mean, Brenda and Tiffani are hot, but how could that help you?"

"Schreiber, how is it you know their names?" Ruby said, shading her eyes from the sun.

"What do we need to do?" Sybil said.

"Well," Schreiber continued, ignoring Ruby's question in favor of Sybil's, "it doesn't matter if they declared the town a blighted area if they don't condemn your houses and clear the land, and then approve selling it all for a dollar. That's what matters. What we have to do is convince them to not approve either motion."

As they entered the courthouse, the transition from the clear midday sun to the relative darkness of the building blinded Sybil.

"Cindy! Pleasure to see you again," came Commissioner Balzac's voice out of the shadows. Sybil closed her eyes tightly and opened them, eyes slow to adjust, the shape of what appeared to be a Macy's parade float coming into view. The commissioner held his hand out for a shake.

Sybil, flanked by Sig and Ruby, stood with hands on hips. "Commissioner, the last time I saw you, you promised me you would make a few calls, and let me know what you found out."

Balzac pulled his hand back. "I did my dear, I did. I found out Wind Energy Now is an important part of our community, and they need to expand so we can have more jobs."

"And more campaign contributions for you," Sig said, pointing.

Sybil hadn't noticed Ms. Hoffman from Wind Energy Now standing by the hearing room door. "I just want to say," Ms. Hoffman, jumped in, "how sad I am that beautiful Ahnwee is soon to be no more. It's just not right. Small towns are under attack from all sides by special interests. Not to mention the complete lack of environmental justice in this country, what with the hazardous lake and Björkman wanting to build a hog manure pool. Darned shame."

The Ahnweeians stared at her, mouths agape. Finally, "But it's you who polluted the lake!" Ruby said.

"And it's you who wants to take away the town!" Sig said.

Ms. Hoffman, wearing an all-hemp power suit, looked aghast. "No, certainly not! We are on your side. If they level your town and burn the soil, we're going to do everything in our power to make sure it doesn't fall into the hands of that devotee of animal cruelty, Björkman."

"But we don't want our town leveled," Sybil said.

"And, we don't want our soil burned," Ruby said.

"Fight the power!" Ms. Hoffman said.

Commissioner Balzac laughed. "Young lady," he said to Ms. Hoffman, even though she wasn't young, "someday, you're going to be president."

Our heroes made their way into the hearing room, which was undergoing some sort of remodeling with paint-less, taped, and spackled drywall walls, plywood floors, and very temporary-looking yellow shop lights hanging from the metal framework of what was destined to be a drop ceiling. Sybil, Ruby, and Sig sat in the front on rental folding chairs and Ms. Hoffman more in the middle of the room. The only other person there was a big body builder in a tank top toward the back.

Fifteen minutes late, five hefty white men – all with grey hair save one, Commissioner Balzac, whose hair was suspiciously dark black – filtered in, laughing and wiping their mouths with napkins. The beefy men in jeans and sweatshirts – except Balzac who wore a too-tight three-piece blue pin-striped suit – took their place in high-backed faux-leather chairs behind folding tables in front, ignoring everyone in attendance. The future angioplasty customers talked amongst themselves, one with his head down looking at an iPhone, about the going away party they just had for one of their support staff: pizza and silly gifts for the young lady who was off to get married to her soldier boyfriend in the fall. Sybil wondered if drinks weren't part of the celebration, considering the way they were acting.

Just as the biggest county commissioner in the middle was about to gavel the board into action, the door behind them opened and in came Mr. and Mrs. Björkman, arm in arm. Björn sported a MAGA hat but otherwise looked like he just got out of the barn, and smelled it, too. Mrs. Björn, no MAGA hat, wore stretch pants plus a baggie blouse pulled tight in all the wrong places. She smiled a stoned-looking smile and waved to the body builder guy who didn't wave back.

The commissioners watched them walk down the aisle, the commissioner in the middle with the gavel hovering in mid-air. "What do you want, Björkman? Just so you know, I'm armed."

"Don't worry, Chas, this is business." He motioned as if hammering a nail. "Don't you think you should get to it?"

The man in the middle paused for a moment, shrugged and said, "Well, the sooner we start, the sooner we end." before banging the gavel three times.

The door opened again, and in came Malcolm Moose and ten men with long black hair all wearing t-shirts saying, "LOOSE SLOTS!"

"Well, look who's here," Björn Björkman said. "Long Dong, are you still on the war path?"

"Shut your blowjob hole, shit farmer. We are here to get back what's ours."

"Wait – that's right: you're not 'Big Moose' like your great-granddad, just 'Moose.' Maybe more like 'Tiny Moose' then?"

The commissioner in the middle banged the gavel. "Now, gentlemen, let's be civilized."

Malcolm Moose and the rather fit and handsome young men sat down, looking about uneasily.

The gavel-wielder got right to it. "Well, I think I know why you all are here. Well, maybe not the beefcake in the back, but the rest of you." He turned to Balzac. "This condemnation thing is yours, isn't it Harry?"

"Indeed," County Commissioner Balzac stood up. "I think it's pretty clear what needs to happen. We need the town of Ahnwee condemned; that's why we are here today. That much we agree on, am I right?"

Björkman stood up. "I don't care about that. You can't give away my land to that earth mother and her communist wind turbine factory because it's my land."

Malcolm Moose leapt to his feet. "Your land, you say, shit pool boy? That is our land. We have title, legal and binding, even for you colonizers."

Björkman pointed. "Don't act all wounded. We kicked your ass in 1862 fair and square."

One young man yelled, "'Fair and square'? How are smallpox blankets 'fair and square'?"

"You just wish you thought of it first!"

"Well," the young man said, "considering everything, yes I do!"

"What do you guys want, anyway? The liquor store's on the next block."

One young man started to get to his feet, but Malcolm Moose put a hand on his shoulder, and he reluctantly sat back down. "Björkman, I got to ask," Malcolm Moose said. "Seriously, be honest: did you go swimming this morning in your big brown swimming pool? I never understood how white people can put up with smelling so bad, but you! You are a whole 'nother species."

Balzac, still standing, held his hands out, looking the embodiment of reason. "Gentlemen. We can settle this. All we need is to get the land condemned and then Wind Energy Now here can work it out with each of you, depending on how accurate your alleged paperwork is."

Schreiber jumped to his feet. "I object, your honor!"

The commissioner in the middle said, "'Object'? What are you, stupid, Schreiber? This isn't a court of law. There's no objecting."

"Your honor, the good people of Ahnwee have a right to…"

"Seriously, Schreiber?" said the guy in the middle. "You're

wearing cargo shorts? Don't you know how out of style those things are?"

"Yeah, but they have a lot of pockets," Schreiber whined.

Balzac sat down, eyes rolling. The gavel-wielder looked uncomfortable, and the remaining three seated commissioners looked miserable, not looking at anyone, with the one still working his iPhone.

Sybil was lost, but Ruby had game. "Commissioners, you have to hear us out," Ruby said. "We live there. Those are our homes. I ran a business on Broadway with my late husband since the Vietnam War. I'm living in a house that was my husband's father's, and his father's before him. No one can tell me that's not ours."

"Right on, sister!" yelled Ms. Hoffman, fist in the air. "Make sure you get compensated for the condemned land. Don't let these men push you around," she said with no small amount of derision with the word, "men."

"Oh, Christ on a bike," said the commissioner in the middle. Here we were having a fun little party, and now this."

"Anyone have any Pepto Bismol?" said the commission to his left.

He looked to his right and left. "Do you gentleman need this?"

They all grumbled at once, iPhone guy yet to look up.

"I didn't think so. I think we should table this to a later date."

"Why?" Commissioner Balzac asked.

"To study it. Right, guys?"

Again, they all grumbled at once.

"Let's put it on the agenda for…I don't know…October?"

The commissioner on his left whispered in his ear.

"Let's say mid-November, AFTER the election." He banged his gavel. He called the next piece of business, the proposal to install a chin-up bar in the county park in Despar.

The body builder stood up to make his case as everyone else filed out.

"Schreiber, you are as useless as tits on a bull," Sig said, shaking his head.

Schreiber stood, gesturing with both hands. "Hey, success, right?"

"Was it?" Sybil said. She worried she sounded sarcastic when she was quite sincere. In fact, she felt lost, as if she had fallen in a well, so deep down that all she heard was echoes.

After the gang left the hearing, they reconvened at Flump's Café just in time for lunch. When they arrived, Augie was working on his laptop at the counter while Pastor Farber read *Being and Nothingness* to his left. Meanwhile, G washed the windows with a floor mop, and Jackson read a magazine in the window.

Sybil, Ruby, and Sig — benefiting from Sig's blowing the carbon off — all had their coffee and soup du jour in front of them before Schreiber even arrived. "Sig," Schreiber said, "when you finally get arrested for your driving, be sure to give me a call, okay?"

Sig gave him the one-fingered salute.

They told Augie and Pastor Farber all about the hearing, and Augie said he knew, since he'd been following the tweets of one of the commissioners. "Did you know the park in Despar is getting a chin-up bar?" Augie said.

"Look, this is pretty good," Schreiber said. "You have a reprieve of over four months to get organized."

"Get what organized?" Ruby said.

"You know, organized," Schreiber replied.

"Tulips," Sig said.

"Schreiber is right," Sybil said, not wanting Sig to get to daisies. "This is good, right? Now we can come up with a plan. Let's brainstorm."

Everyone groaned.

"What?"

"Not that again," Sig said with a companion eyeroll.

"Mayor, I'm not getting out the whiteboard," Augie said.

Jackson laid his magazine, *Strip Club News*, on the table. Sybil thought how magazines have taken specialization too far. He stood up. "I know some people," he said.

"'Some people'?" Sybil said.

"Yeah, you know. Some people."

Ruby turned. "'You know some people'? Have you been watching *The Sopranos* again?"

"I don't think knee-capping everybody will help," Sig said. "As personally satisfying as that would be."

G leaned on the mop handle. "The offer still stands for bombing the manure field."

"See?" Augie said. "This is why no one likes a brainstorming exercise."

"BAM!" G threw the mop handle on the floor, making everyone jump. "Up goes the dike!"

"Shut up," Augie said.

Schreiber snapped his fingers in a clichéd "I've got an idea" way. "The election is between now and the hearing, that's why they postponed it. They will be too busy to meet, plus, they can get the campaign contributions and put them to use before pissing anyone off by taking what may be a controversial vote."

"Maybe that news piece did us a favor after all," Ruby said.

Schreiber smirked. "Well, I'd say the glass is one-tenth full on that one, but for sure, it also gives us a chance to unseat one of them."

Ruby looked at Schreiber like he was nuts.

"Hey, maybe Balzac will lose the election," Pastor Farber said, finishing his brainstorm with a sip of coffee.

"Who's running against him?" Sybil asked. She never followed county elections before. Who does? She heard said once that county commissioners are the most powerful people no one ever heard of.

"No one, I think," Schreiber said.

"What difference would one seat make? Wouldn't we need to replace three of the five?" Sybil said.

"Well," Augie said, looking at his laptop, "not really. The guy who was tweeting said the last thing he was going to do was hand over the land to 'that lesbian.'"

"Ms. Hoffman?" Sybil asked, after at first thinking the tweet was referring to her.

"Of course," Ruby said.

"So we have one, if for completely the wrong reason. But we'd still need one more."

"I know for a fact that the chair hates Wind Energy Now," Schreiber said. "He is a pipefitter for a regular job – not little plumbing pipes, but big oil pipeline pipes. He is personally invested in making sure 'green' anything doesn't succeed."

"One would do it, then," Pastor Farber said. "We just need to defeat Balzac."

"Easy to say; hard to do, don't you think?" Ruby said.

They sat. Sybil and Sig looked down at their soups. Pastor Farber rustled a packet of crackers. Ruby took out her knitting. Jackson read the back cover of his magazine. Augie checked his Facebook.

"I know just the person," Schreiber said.

"For what?" Ruby replied.

"To run against Balzac."

"Who?" Sig said.

"Mayor Sybil Voss."

Sybil appeared more surprised than anyone by hearing her name, and they all looked pretty surprised.

"What are you smoking, Schreiber?" Augie said.

"What are the chances of that succeeding? Hasn't Sybil's name been dragged through the mud lately?" Sig said. "No offense, Sybil, but after the 'New York of the Prairie' story, you rank lower around here than a dog pile on a sidewalk."

"Lower than heel crud," Augie said.

"Lower than tobacco juice in a gutter," G said.

"Give her a break, boys," Pastor Farber said. "Wait! I have one: lower than a bugger on a park bench."

"Wouldn't tobacco juice in a gutter be lower?" G said.

Alfonse Schreiber said, "Have you ever heard 'there is no such thing as bad publicity'?"

Everyone nodded.

"Well, it's not true. But the fact is, Sybil is already an elected official, and the 'New York, a den of drugs and sex' thing is already old and forgotten, in favor of whoever is on *The Voice* tonight. It's an off-year election, so no one will be showing up to the polls, anyway."

"Yeah," Sig added, obviously enthused by the idea, "We just have to get more to the polls than Balzac."

Sybil really, really liked the idea, but didn't want to show too much interest, out of Minnesota modesty.

"Is this going to work?" Augie said.

"Does anyone have any better ideas?" Ruby replied.

No one said anything. Sig ate a cracker. Farber fidgeted. Jackson opened his magazine to the ads in back. G developed a tremor. Augie looked on eBay.

Sybil stood up, proud. "I'll do it!"

CHAPTER 20: CHILIDOGS

"Are you crazy?"

Sybil knew Drew wouldn't approve, but she still recoiled from her reaction.

"Don't they all think you are some sort of East Coast pervert?"

Sybil wanted to defend her decision to virtual Drew, but she didn't know how. It really didn't make sense, even to her. Just when her stock couldn't sink lower – as the gang seemed all too happy to elaborate on that – she decides on participating in the darkest, meanest, most deceptive, manipulative, back-biting, masochistic popularity contest (next to Miss America) ever invented by mankind: An American general election.

"It's hard to explain…" And it was, other than to say it was not without precedent for Sybil. In fact, it should have been expected. For example, when Sybil was a girl, she tried out for hockey. That she didn't know how to skate didn't hold her back. She tried. And she failed. Did she give up? No way. She strapped on those skates and learned. She learned how to skate backwards; she learned how to handle a stick; she learned the rules. Did she eventually make the team? Well, no. Not even close. But the point is, the more she failed, the harder she tried.

"Sybil, there aren't enough Upper-Westside therapists to set you right."

Not only did her running against County Commissioner Balzac reveal a deep character flaw of stick-to-it-ness in Sybil, it was personal. She hated that man. She had never hated anyone before. Hate is so firm, so final. She took pride in seeing other people's points of view, often to her detriment. Hate? It must all be a misunderstanding. But Balzac — well, that old pseudo-Christian windbag, he lied to her right to her face. Not only that, he seemed to take joy in it. Sybil thought he was one smug so-and-so who needed to get a lesson in humility, and she wanted nothing more than to be the deliverer of said humiliation.

"I can do this, Drew," she said, leaning on her elbows, coffee mug on the kitchen counter next to her. "I know I can. We have a plan."

"A plan? Even General Custer had a plan."

"It's a good plan," Sybil said, not having any idea what this plan might be.

After they finished their chat, Sybil prepared dinner for her and her father. She placed a plate of two hot dogs buried in canned chili — another of her father's favorites — in front of him. Sybil went with a bag of salad from Walmart and some grape tomatoes, plus a bit too much Italian dressing. "Dad, guess what." She didn't really expect a response. "I'm running for county board."

Dan used his fork to cut up the hot dogs into bits.

She ate a forkful of salad. "What do you think?"

He looked up, blue eyes dull. "Three hour."

Sybil looked at him, long and hard. "Yes, Dad. Three-hour tour. But what I want to tell you is that I'm running for county board, and I'm going to be very busy for a while."

"The ship's aground."

"Yes, it sure is. But Dad, I think it's time we found you professional help."

"Uncharted desert isle."

"I can't do it any longer. I want to, darn it, but I can't. I have to take care of myself, and I have to see to it that you are taken care of. I'm doing a crummy job of both right now." She choked up and tried mightily to keep it together. "Maybe there's help for you. Maybe there's some sort of programming that can make some kind of difference. Just because your doctor gave up doesn't mean there isn't something that can be done now. Maybe that quack you've been going to forever needs to be fired. Maybe I haven't been helping you at all by keeping you home and parked in front of the TV. Maybe I'd given up when I should have gotten excited, taken action, driven you to the Mayo Clinic or something. I don't know, Dad. I just don't know. But this isn't working, is it? You can't sit in front of the TV until you die. And I can't sit next to you until I'm good as dead. I think you need to live in a place that can take care of you properly. I can't do it. I just can't." By the end of her rambling speech, she was a puddle.

Dan kept his stoic glare forward. "Farm living is the life for me."

Sybil looked at him, considering if that was an actual response to what she was saying. Dan picked up a piece of hotdog, barely visible from the chili, and flung it at Sybil, hitting her on the forehead. Sybil didn't move. Dan licked his fingers and returned to eating. Chili dripped down between her eyes and hung off the tip of her nose.

I deserved that, she thought.

CHAPTER 21: FICKLE FASHION

The first thing Sybil, Ruby, and Sig did was set up a campaign headquarters. They had their pick of Broadway Street buildings, and they didn't so much rent one as commandeer one, pulling the boards down off the windows and getting a locksmith out. With a couple dozen empty storefronts to choose from, they chose one next door to Ruby's former pharmacy now yarn store so they could run some orange extension cords over for juice (why involve the electric company?). It had been a TV repair store back in the day, but the shell-shocked Korean War vet who ran it had a bit of an alcohol use issue and, even when sober, didn't really know how to repair TVs. When big boxes in Despar started selling TVs for a couple hundred bucks, and since he charged a hundred an hour with little hope he would succeed, it was time for him to retire and move to Arizona. He abandoned an inventory of dusty little boxes filled with every tube ever used in the twentieth century, all useless now.

They cleaned the place up, tossing the little boxes in a big box in the back of the store, since it was illegal to throw the tubes in the trash given their use of a bouquet of heavy metals. They gave the store a good sweeping and scrubbing; G washed the windows and helped Sybil carry over a couple desks from New York 'Tique. Voilà! Campaign headquarters.

Almost. They needed a sign. Back to Let's Go Crazy Printz! Why in the world go back to Let's Go Crazy Printz? Ruby and Sig asked Sybil on separate occasions. Store credit, she replied. They owed her from their past blunders. This time they came through: "Dump Balzac!" spelled success-fully on the twelve-foot canvas. Given the New York thing, the brain trust decided their best bet was to campaign *against* Balzac, rather than *for* Sybil Voss. Thus "Dump Balzac." Sybil didn't like it, but she kept it to herself. That part of her where her pride didn't live knew they were right. "Go negative and stay negative," Sig said. Pastor Farber even agreed. So came the banner, and about ten thousand flyers, laying out Sybil's argument:

Dump Harry Balzac!
Since when did the county board become
a lifetime appointment?
Time for new blood!
Harry Balzac has been county commissioner for over twenty
years. What has he done?
Take money from polluters? March in parades? Pinch butts?
Throw him out! Vote Voss, Tuesday, November 9.

They looked good, Sybil thought, in trendy orange and Twentieth Century MT font and a black-and-white picture of Balzac with a red circle and slash over his face.

Next step was an image change.

"I don't want an image change," Sybil said, as they drank coffee at the new campaign headquarters.

"Trust me, Sybil. Blending in is your best bet," Ruby said.

"It's not that you don't look good in black," Sig said. "Think of it as branding. Do you think Paul Ryan wants to lift weights all day? Tucker Carlson wants to wear a silly bowtie? Donald Trump wants to have a bird's nest on top of his head? It's their brand."

"Can't my brand be black?"

"Not if you want to win," Ruby said.

Into Despar they went, Sig driving at warp speed. Through the wind turbine, north of the lake, and out on the highway, where a world of merchandise awaited. Ruby and Sig didn't talk about what they had in mind for Sybil, and she wondered if they had a plan or if they were winging it. They drove past Super Target and Walmart, and even Dollar General, before pulling into Fleet Farm. They must have a plan, she thought.

Fleet Farm was a regional big box with farmers as a target audience, focusing more on hunting gear and tools than clothes. Sybil had never been to a Fleet Farm; it seemed like no place she'd be interested in. It seemed as if there would be as many women in Fleet Farm as there would be men in a Pink store. Need a bed liner for your Ford F-150? Cement blocks for a retaining wall? Large caliber ammunition? Fleet Farm is the place. A new wardrobe; sorry, "brand"? Not hardly.

The lot was half-empty, and Sig parked far from the door.

"Can you find a spot further out?" Ruby said in sarcasm.

"Good to get exercise," Sig replied.

As they approached, the double doors swung open automatically, as if snapping to attention. The three walked in almost shoulder to shoulder, and the huge store opened up before them. Sybil felt dizzy. The place was an aircraft hangar. Highly-polished cement floors, stadium lights hanging from the ceiling casting an otherworldly yellow light, merchandise on scaffolding-like metal shelving reaching a good two stories high. Sybil thought that the entirety of Broadway would fit in the building, length, width, and height. A hot dog stand sold one-dollar red hots, condiments across from the counter, a line of plump people snaking toward the ice-fishing department. It struck Sybil that it was three in the afternoon and thus nowhere near lunch or dinner, yet there were more people in line than Augie will serve at his café all day. Heck, all that week.

"This way," Ruby said, walking on with Sig at her side.

Sybil realized she was frozen in place like a doe in a poacher's sight. She ran to catch up like a child to her parents, even though she was a good head taller than Ruby, who was a good head taller than Sig. She noted that the chunky people in line were all staring at them.

They wove their way along, through pet, electrical, camping gear, supplies, tombstones, artificial limbs, and garden gnomes. Sybil wondering all the way where they were going. Ruby and Sig said nothing, reinforcing for Sybil the thought that they had a plan long worked out. They walked past the fishing gear and then guns and rows of ammo, which freaked Sybil out. Sybil looked up at a tree stand. It never occurred to her that hunters bought tree stands. Sure they did – why not? Why trust your life to some flimsy thing built out of scrap wood by a drunk hunter, when you could sit in a Deer Master 3000, with a built-in cup holder and Wi-Fi?

Ruby and Sig stopped. Sybil, still looking up at the tree stands, almost walked into them. She looked around wondering why they stopped, but then she realized why. "Oh, heck no."

Ruby touched her arm. "Sybil…"

"Nope, no way."

Right then, out of nowhere, "Sybil! What brings you to fair Despar?"

She didn't turn, hypnotized by the display in front of her, but she knew the voice. "Hi, Fjord."

"We're doing a little shopping," Ruby said.

"What's it to you?" Sig said.

Jon Fjord ignored Sig and continued. "Shopping? I have to say, none of you look like the hunting type." He picked up a pair of camo pants, folded neatly in a bin.

"We're full of surprises," Ruby said.

He snapped them unfolded, and held the pants up to Sig. They were as tall as him. Sig snatched them away, threw them on the floor, and said, "Tulips."

"Those are in the front of the store." Jon Fjord turned back to Sybil. "Speaking of surprises, I hear you're running for County Board."

Sybil was amazed. They hadn't announced it to anyone; how did he know? "Yup, Fjord. I am. And I'm going to win."

"Okay, Sybil. I hope you know what you are in for, but either way, I wish you luck."

Sybil leaned back, arms crossed. "Really? You wish me luck?"

"You bet. I'm on your side." He picked up another pair of camo pants and held them up to Sybil this time. "So what's up with the camo?"

Sybil was too stuck on Fjord saying he was on her side and almost seeming to mean it, to answer his question, even if she had the answer.

"Oh, I get it. You're pandering. Not bad, but it's a bit far. If you were a man, sure, people would buy it. But I would suggest sticking with your red suit, knee-length skirt. Hilary Clinton, right?"

Ruby looked up at him. "Fjord, now you give fashion advice?"

"No, I give political advice. Plus, you look good in that suit," he said, not taking his eyes off Sybil. He tossed her the pants. "But hey, desperate times demand desperate actions. I get it."

"Hey, Fjord, the boner pills are over by the pharmacy. Why don't you go get some?" Sig said.

Fjord laughed a brief, snorting laugh. "Seriously, good luck, Mayor. I hope you kick his ass." He walked off, not in the direction of the pharmacy.

They stood silent, each trying to get their heads back on task.

Jon Fjord liked how I looked in my red suit? Sybil thought. Then Sybil looked at the display of camo wear, shirts, coats, hats, socks, shoes, backpacks, briefcases, computer bags, computers, flashlights, canteens, and more and more and more, and said once again, "Oh heck no."

Sybil, dressed head to toe in camouflage – Desert Storm variety – stood next to Ruby and Sig on the stoop of the old one-and-a-half story sort of bungalow. To Sybil, the peeling paint was incongruous with the carefully arranged planters full of petunias under the windows on the right and left. She stared forward at the closed door, doing nothing. Sig reached around her and knocked loudly. The door opened, and the smell of a litterbox attacked her nose. An old lady in a beyond-stretched-out t-shirt and underwear said from behind the screen door, "Can I help you?"

Sybil steeled herself, stood up straight, and said, "Good morning. My name is Sybil Voss, and…"

"I don't know a Sybil Voss. You must have the wrong house."

"No, no…I'm Sybil Voss, and I'm…"

"Barney!" the woman yelled, not turning her head, almost

knocking Sybil off the stoop with her onion breath.

"No, I'm…"

"Barney! Do you know a Sybil Voss?!"

From somewhere behind the woman, a man's voice yelled, "No! Sounds German!"

The woman in her huge panties behind the screen said, "Is she German?"

Sybil started to say what difference does it make and what does that have to do with anything before deciding instead to go with "Yes," since she was, after all, of German descent.

"We don't know any Germans." She looked past Sybil. "Is that a midget?"

Sybil started to say what difference does it make and what does it have to do with anything before deciding instead to say nothing.

"Lady," Sig said, "Those are really beautiful tulips."

"Those are petunias," the lady of the house said.

Ruby nodded to Sig, and whispered loud enough for Sybil to hear, "Well played."

Sybil bucked up. "Ma'am, I'm running for County Board, and I'm here to ask for your vote."

The big woman behind the screen door looked her up and down. "Okay."

Sybil looked at her, unsure what to do next, expecting any answer but that.

The woman continued, "Time women ran the place. Those big meat-eating moochers need their comeuppance."

Sybil said thanks, and that she agreed, and that she would leave some literature for her to look at being only September, knowing that the woman would need some sort of reminder when November came.

"Right on, sister. Stick it to the man. Take Barney, my husband. He thinks he's in charge. The old booger isn't even in charge of his own hygiene."

Sybil couldn't think of one thing to say or do.

"Sisters are doing it for themselves, right? Am I right?"

Sybil nodded.

The pants-less woman looked Sybil up and down. "By the way, are you going hunting?"

Sybil said thanks for her support and to have a nice day. Sybil, Sig, and Ruby walked back down the semblance of a sidewalk to the street, not wanting to cut across the lawn to the next house.

"Well, that went well," Ruby said.

"I feel ridiculous," Sybil said, referring to her new fresh out of the duck blind look.

"You heard Fjord," Sig said, "Pandering is a good thing. You just wait. She wasn't the target audience."

When Sybil ran for mayor, there was no real running. Ruby asked her, she paid the ten-dollar fee, made a flyer, "Sybil Voss for Major," got them printed and then reprinted correctly, didn't do anything to distribute them, and was elected in a landslide. She was the only candidate on the ballot. Now she had to actually campaign. No one outside of Ahnwee knew who she was, and those in Ahnwee weren't necessarily on her side, so she started with Despar, the only other town in the county board district. Door to door. Pressing the flesh. Pounding the pavement. Retail politics. High touch. All that.

At the next house, a gold-painted tractor tire planter sat where a sidewalk should have gone. In the center was a lawn butt. Sybil wondered if they bought it from the couple who sold lawn butts at Ahnwee Days. They walked up to the door, and this time Sybil knocked.

"Yes?" the man said. He had on a t-shirt and boxers. Sybil wondered what it was about this block that people not only sit around in their underwear on a Saturday afternoon but answer the door in them as well.

She did her spiel.

"So, you want to be a county commissioner, do you?" the man said. "What is your experience?"

Sybil thought that a refreshingly sane question. She told him she was the Mayor of Ahnwee.

The man looked her up and down. "Well, good work. I'm glad you got that crazy New York stripper mayor out of there. My god, she was an embarrassment to the entire state. Now you, you look like someone I can trust."

Sybil started to say how unfair that was and that she wasn't an embarrassment to the state and that she was trying as hard and she could and she won in a landslide last year before she settling on "Thanks."

She left a flyer, and as they walked back to the street Sig said, "That's what the clothes are for."

"I'm incognito, right?" Sybil said, looking down at her crisp new togs.

"No dear," Ruby replied, "just well-marketed."

At the next house, a grey-haired man in pants but no shirt (Sybil thought this a victory) greeted her at the door. Sybil gave her sentence, and he said, looking her over, "Nice to see a solid local girl running for office. Who is the county commissioner now?"

She told him.

"That toad is our county commissioner? Seriously? I went to school with him. I gave him a swirly once after math. Hell yeah, I'll vote for you." He took a flyer from her. "And if you want, I'll give him another swirly, for old time's sake."

She said she'd keep it in mind.

Back out in the street, Sig said, "See? See?"

Sybil had to admit, at least to herself, it was going better than expected. Three houses, three people committing to voting for her. No matter how it got done, the main thing was that it got done.

They kept walking, banging on doors, walking across lawns, occasionally getting chased by dogs. Most people didn't answer, even though Sybil could hear TVs on behind closed curtains. Sybil understood; she didn't like answering the door to solicitors, either.

Only a week into pounding on doors, and Sybil was already getting sick of it. There was a lot of repeating yourself. There was a lot of walking. There were a lot of doors slammed and dogs barking. But, true to her nature, no way was she quitting.

The sun cast long shadows as they left the last house for the day.

"I had no idea campaigning would be this tiring," Ruby said.

"We're just getting started," Sig replied.

They walked to Sig's car and in no time flat, they were driving back south and east, past South Pacific Jerky, around the lake, into the pig shit zone, through the giant putt-putt windmill, and to Sybil's house. She waved bye and went in the house to her next set of problems.

"How was he?" Sybil asked the long-haired high school senior she hired off Craig's List. The girl reminded Sybil of herself when she was that age.

"Good. He just watched TV, as usual."

Sybil apologized for it being so boring, and the girl said it was fine, since she could get her summer reading done. Sybil asked what she was reading.

"*Mrs. Dalloway*. You ever read it?"

Sybil said no.

"It's old. It's all about a couple characters, mainly a woman who is throwing a party. She seems to be full of regrets. That's what I think, anyway." She said Sybil should read it and handed her the book, saying she was finished, and no hurry getting it back, that she'd rather read Dan Brown.

Sybil took it and thanked her, fanning through it. She thought about how long it had been since she read a book, and thought yes, she would read it. It might be good to take her mind off…well, everything.

The girl left, and Sybil went in the living room and kissed her dad on the cheek. He didn't react. Two stacks of three boxes sat along the wall. A lifetime of buying stuff, Sybil thought; all the proud possessions, great buys, and good memories reduced to a handful of boxes.

"Dad? You're going to like it there. Remember visiting Grandma? I do. It's a nice place. They recently remodeled. They have poker night."

She had her hand on his shoulder. He didn't react; he might as well have been made of wax. Since she told him about his going into a nursing home, he hadn't said a word. No anger. No sadness. Nothing. She wished he would sing a sitcom theme, or even a commercial jingle, something. Was he resigned to his move? Was it good-ol' Minnesota passive aggression? Or was he simply oblivious to what was going on? Sybil thought she'd need a Ouija board to find the answer.

She knew it was the right decision, but it didn't make it one bit easier.

Chapter 22: We Are Going to Like It Here!

Dan didn't say anything and cooperated completely. The nurses and support staff at Good Shepherd were extremely nice and said "we" when they meant "you" or "he." "We're going to have fun, Dan!" one blonde girl with a tattoo of a dragonfly behind her ear said. Dan said nothing. "Here's our room, Dan. We have our own TV!" said a short quintessentially Irish-looking girl. Dan said nothing. Sybil whispered to Dan, "Say the word, and I'll kill them both for you." Dan said nothing.

Sybil hauled in the boxes and set up her father's remaining possessions in as pleasing a way as possible on shelves, the windowsill, on the dresser. A few books he will never read again. Odd memorabilia – a baseball signed by Rod Carew, a glass paperweight Sybil gave him for his birthday when she was in high school, a fake bowling trophy with the little gold man rolling the ball from between his legs. Frames. His photo in his Army uniform. Pictures of his sons and their families, the very same sons who were too busy to help move him into what was sure to be his last home. Next to his bed she set up a photo of him with Sybil's mother. She looked at it. She thought how with everything going on and all that had gone on – especially with Dad – it was as if she hadn't given herself permission to miss her own mother. Sybil felt like she lost a chunk of herself – not a limb, more like a major organ.

"Dad? Do you miss Mom?"

Dan sat in a vinyl chair in the window, sun crossing his face, his eyes looking forward. Still not a word since Sybil told him about his new home.

"Are you going to be okay here?" Sybil looked around. There was nothing more to do. Yes, there was: she turned on the TV, switched it to *Good Times*. Dan looked up at the set mounted in the corner.

Sybil kissed him on the top of his head and left.

Going home to an empty house was strange. No TV blaring. No veneer of tension from not knowing what could happen next. No one to wait on. Ruby had offered to come by, but Sybil said there was no need. Ruby called, and insisted on coming over, but Sybil said she wanted to be alone. She had gotten some Kemps vanilla ice cream from the Stop and Pop, and sat by herself in the kitchen. She finished the whole quart as she had a good cry.

Time passed.

Sybil tried to read *Mrs. Dalloway*, but she couldn't figure out what the hell was going on. I mean, stick to one POV! She put it aside in favor of a Judy Blume book.

Sybil poured herself into the campaign. She found it an effective analgesic, deadening the pain of her father going to the nursing home, the pain of having to admit she couldn't save him. As long as she kept running around from campaign stop to campaign stop, as long as she made herself bone tired so when her head hit the pillow she was out for the night, as long as she had other people around keeping her distracted, she felt strong, even excited.

But when she was alone, she was in her own personal pity-pit.

Ruby and Sig were great, serving as her co-campaign managers and keeping her reasonably sane through the process. But she also knew her task was huge, stressful, and unlikely to succeed. Was her running against that entrenched sack of meat Balzac really the best plan they had? Even if she won, that would only fix the condemnation problem and keep Wind Energy Now away. They still had Björkman and Malcolm Moose to deal with. Sig said, "First things first," and she knew that he was right. And she also knew she didn't have a better plan, so there it was.

When she wasn't campaigning, she was visiting her dad at Good Shepherd, or, on increasingly rare occasions, she could be found at her store, or simply at home. Being home was strange. The abject quietude of her father's – now, by default, her – house was unnerving and unprecedented. Around her were the ghosts of her childhood, her missing brothers, her mother, and Dan. Christmases past, birthdays, graduations: yes, but more, the little moments: the Christmas tree that her oldest brother knocked over, watching *Taxi* as a family, making ice cream with an ice cream ball or at least trying (it came out as more like cream soup). Never had the house been that quiet.

She was, for the first time in her life, completely on her own.

She thought about her brothers. She asked them to visit Dan, and they both said they would. They didn't. Why did she expect anything from them? They didn't help out when Dan was still in his home, so why would they step up now? Still, disappointing. Sybil understood – boy did she ever –

211

how hard it was to watch one's father deteriorate, but that doesn't mean you get to run away and make believe nothing is wrong. It took days before they visited Dan, coming as a pair, and, even then, they were out of there like a rocket after maybe half an hour.

Not that Sybil could honestly say that her father cared. He no longer sang commercial jingles or even sitcom theme songs; he just sat there in a big faux-Naugahyde recliner locked to not recline (insurance issues, a helpful first-person-plural nurse told her) watching whatever was on TV in the common area. She wished he would wander pantsless out in the yard, pee on a flagpole, dance the tango in the dining room, anything, something, other than just staring ahead. She would read to him, she would ask him about the past, and she would talk trash about the nurses, but he still stared ahead.

Chapter 23: A Glimmer of Hope

Being a small election, there were no polls, so it was impossible to know how Sybil was doing. After slogging through September, knocking on every door in the county, it was hard to tell if she was making headway. For sure, people were talking. "Oh, you're that vet who is running against that old box of boogers!" "You're that girl who is opposing that fat fossil!" "You're that girl from *Duck Dynasty* who is running against that constipated old seal!" were but a few of the comments she heard at doorsteps. Never mind the complete inaccuracy; they at least got her opponent right.

Finally, October brought a glimmer of hope. The campaign had a breakthrough when Balzac finally referred to her at a campaign stop in front of a reporter for the *Despar Tattler*. Quote: "My opponent? All I can say is, it makes me happy – no, proud – to live in a country where an atheist New York lesbian dominatrix can run for any office she so whims."

At the campaign headquarters after a lunch of Flump Burgers they met to figure out what to do next. Most of Sybil's brain trust was there – Ruby, Augie and Pastor Farber, G and Jackson. Sig was a conspicuous no-show. The dog was lying by the door. How did he get in here? Sybil wondered. One of these guys must be his owner, and maybe now she'd find out who.

They sat on folding chairs around the door on sawhorses they were using for a desk, drinking coffee. Sybil wanted to make it, but Ruby insisted, and now Sybil suffered through what she considered to be dirty water. Sybil wore her now signature camo pants and shirt and, considering the season, a light camo jacket. Jackson brought his girls: raven-haired, and too-thin, barely dressed in halters and yoga pants, regardless of the season. Sybil wondered two things: Does Jackson ever go anywhere without arm candy? And aren't they cold with their flat, beautifully marbled stomachs out in the fall breeze? She couldn't take her eyes off them.

"He's scared," Jackson said.

"Definitely scared," Augie said.

"An 'atheist New York lesbian?' Is that even good English?" Ruby said.

"Is it 'lesbian atheist,' or 'atheist lesbian'?" Jackson asked.

Sybil felt a chill run down her spine. How did he know she had dated women in New York? And, what's supposed to be bad about being an "atheist New York lesbian" if she was one or not? Well, maybe he was close, a bisexual and humanist, but the point is...her head swirling, she wasn't sure of the point, but seriously, how could he know she had dated women in New York? But, of course, she thought, he didn't know, he made it up hoping it would be damaging.

"Earth to Sybil!" Ruby said.

She snapped back from staring at the raven-haired girl's abs. "Sorry. What was the question?"

"What to do now." Jackson smirked at Sybil.

"Keep at it, I suppose," Pastor Farber said, with no smirk at all.

"The camo worked," Ruby said. "People don't know who she is."

They decided Pastor Farber was right: keep going with what was working. So, on the to-do list went even more door knocking and "Dump Balzac" flyers. Augie suggested they needed more attention than that, and they debated how to get free media in the absence of being able to pay for paid media. Fine, but how could she get the attention of the press?

"I could do like we talked about before and blow that shit dike," G said.

They all looked at him.

"Well, that would generate attention, wouldn't it?" Ruby said as she knitted what looked like a couch throw cover.

"I think it's time my girls got out there and helped knock on doors," Jackson said.

To Sybil's surprise, the idea of door-to-door strippers gained traction in the room. Men, Sybil thought. "I don't like it," she said. "I want to run a campaign of ideas."

They all stared at her in silence, before bursting into laughter. Even Ruby. Sybil laughed too, as if she meant it as a joke.

"I think we should revisit the shit dike," Augie said to more hilarity.

"Seriously, we'd help door knock," the tall raven-haired beauty said. "Right?" she said to her counterpart sitting next to her.

"Ya, sure, you bet," the slightly-too-thin girl said in a perfect Minnesota accent.

"Sweetie, thanks but no thanks," Ruby said.

"Well, 'Sweetie,' I think this campaign needs all the help it can get," the too-thin one said.

"It's true, Ruby," Jackson said. "We expect Balzac to get most of the men's votes, but maybe we can chip away at that a bit."

They all looked at Sybil for guidance, which at once frightened her and made her feel powerful. "You know where we can really use your help?" she said to the women. "Getting businesses to post the Dump Balzac posters." Most of the businesses in the area – well, all areas anywhere – were run by men, and seemed to be firmly in Balzac's camp. The girls might have persuasive powers with that audience. Sybil was proud of her strategic thinking, hoping to both win the strippers' support and avoid having them door knock in midriffs. She felt like King Solomon for strippers. It was a short-lived pride.

"I'm not sure you guys are taking us seriously," the raven-haired unnamed girl said. "I've been to college; I can help with this."

"Listen, toots," Ruby said in an even harsher tone than her usual truth-telling, "If you want to be taken seriously, put on some clothes."

"What – a muumuu?" Raven said.

"What – a wool sweater?" The skinny one said, high-fiving Raven.

"Ladies," Jackson said. Then turning back to the rest, "Seriously, we need to take advantage of this tiny sliver of momentum."

And then, as if through some sort of divine intervention, an actual oh-so-rare potentially good break for Sybil and the good people of Ahnwee presented itself. Sig burst in the campaign headquarters causing the door to bang against the wall, adding emphasis to the "burst" piece. The dog jumped, but not quite to standing.

"Guess what?" Sig said, panting, as if he had just done Zumba.

"You're late," Ruby said.

"I'm late because I got a call right as I was leaving. It was Balzac's campaign manager – they agreed to a debate!"

Early on, when the campaign started, Sybil called Balzac's

campaign to challenge him to a debate. No one answered, and she left a message. She followed up two more times, with the same result, and tossed in an email for good measure. Nothing. Now…

"A debate!" Sybil said. Mixed feelings once again, as she knew this was an opportunity for people to hear about her and to make serious traction. Plus, it meant she was being taken seriously. On the other hand, she had never been in a debate, not even in high school. It came up once, in middle school civics, but she faked being sick that day rather than do her part arguing for "the Second Amendment is the most important right in America." Actually, faked would be incorrect, as she was sick, throwing up all night thinking about the next day.

Team Ahnwee got to work. There was a lot to plan. What the process would be to choose a venue. How to prep Sybil. What needs to happen to not screw this up. And after they were too tired to continue, and it was time for dinner anyway, and after everyone filtered out, Sybil sat there by herself. She had a feeling that she hadn't felt in a long time: hope. Plus, a bit of disappointment, because she hadn't noticed who the dog had left with. But mostly hope.

"Cool – an actual debate?" Drew said on Sybil's laptop screen. "I would be scared to pieces."

That evening, after the meeting, Sybil wanted to talk to Drew, bad, since she was indeed scared to pieces. She waited until morning. It was early, and Sybil could see Drew was still in her bathrobe. She apparently didn't take her makeup off the previous night, and she looked like she used to look after a hard Saturday night back in the day.

Drew asked for the details, as to when and where, but the only detail Sybil had was the date: October 13, only a week away.

"Are you ready?"

"No, I'm certainly not." Sybil put on a confident face for her campaign team, but she knew no one bought it, least of all herself. "But we are going to rehearse. I'll be okay."

"More than okay: you're going to kill him."

That made Sybil smile. That was why she Zoomed Drew first thing.

"How's your father?"

Sybil told Drew about visiting him at least every other day, and how he was not his usual disruptive self; he seemed to be shut down, sitting there saying – or singing – nothing. She didn't tell Drew that she was worried, and wondered if she made a mistake putting him at Good Shepherd. But what else could she do, she told herself, but logic and reality didn't stop her guilt from stacking up. Instead of telling Drew all that, Sybil changed the subject, asking her about her goings on. Sybil got the distraction she was looking for with stories of late-night parties and star sightings. Despite the smeared makeup and tussled look, Drew looked good in the halting, jumping digital stream. Sybil knew that they would have to have a much worse connection for Drew to say the same thing about her. Sybil felt puffy from too many carbs and not enough exercise. She didn't bother with makeup most days, not that she ever did that much, but fact was, she never had a pair of sweatpants in New York, and now, when not in camo campaign clothes, it was her uniform.

"Move home, Sybil," Drew said. Behind Drew a naked man passed, trim firm butt walking away.

Explains the makeup, Sybil thought.

After she visited Dan at Good Shepherd, she made a stop at Walmart. She didn't like going in there, given all it had done to main streets and all the trash she talked about it, and she hoped no one would see her, which she realized was silly. It was a classic deadlock: if someone found her in Walmart, the person finding her was in Walmart as well, so there. Not unlike being spotted in a sex toy store in the Village. She wondered if other shoppers were embarrassed to be there. She looked around at her fellow customers. No, she decided.

It was morning and she felt off duty and didn't have her camo costume on, instead she had opted for a North-Face black jacket and sweats. That's how she saw her camo brand − as a costume, like Halloween. That idea was safer than thinking it could actually be her. She went to electronics and looked over the workout videos. "Bahamas Butt Buster," "Hawaiian Hot," "Cleveland Crunch Crushes," and other absurdities confronted her, all with crazy tan young women with mogul mid-sections and big hair on the cover. Which one? All the same promises, all the same high likelihood of landing in a garage sale in about a year. She picked up the Cleveland thing. Why Cleveland of all places? Wait − why not stream a workout? These videos were antiques. Peloton is where it's at.

"I hear Cleveland Crunch crushes it," a voice said behind Sybil, making her jump.

"Good morning, Mayor," Sybil said over her shoulder to Jon Fjord, standing too close behind her. It occurred to her that this guy had a way of popping up out of nowhere. He asked what she was up to, and she told him she was visiting her father and needed a few things.

"I heard about Dan. I'm sorry."

She turned toward him, holding her Cleveland Crunches Blu-ray box. She backed up a step to take back some personal space. She thanked him, and said it was going well for Dan.

"You know what else I heard? You're going to debate Balzac?"

"How did you hear that so fast?"

He ignored her question. "Debating Balzac will be like trading punches with Jell-O. Everyone is going to end up covered in goo, but only one of you is going to care."

She wasn't sure exactly what that meant, but the imagery was solid.

"Would you like some help preparing?"

"Yes, I sure do." And then she realized too late that he meant from him.

"When…"

"Or, no, that's okay." She backed up even further.

"Really, I'm happy to."

She knew she couldn't get out of this gracefully. "No, thanks anyway, Fjord."

"Seriously, I can help." He flashed a beguiling smile.

She felt backed in a corner, so, not unlike a mouse lashing out at a cat when all other options are gone, she said, "Why? Why would you help me, Fjord?"

"Like I said before: I want Ahnwee to stay right where it is."

"Seriously." She crossed her arms, stepping even further back, and bumping into a round woman looking at toner. Sybil said sorry.

"I know our towns have had something of a rivalry, but seriously, who cares? It's the twenty-first century; small towns are in this together. Plus, I'm sick of Balzac giving religion a bad name. Plus-plus, I like you."

At nearly atomic speed, she sorted and analyzed what she just heard, mainly the last part, and considered that perhaps he was joking. "You like me?" she said with the maximum amount of incredulity she could inflect.

"Well, yeah." His smile became even more beguiling.

Jon Fjord. Self-absorbed, self-important Fjord. Mr. Despar Jon Fjord. In Sybil's estimation, Jon Fjord was far more likely to die of autoerotic asphyxiation while looking in the mirror than expressing a genuine attraction to anyone but himself. Yes, Sybil decided he was full of it and working some angle.

"Bye, Fjord," she said, walking away.

Sybil decided it was a good time to go home. Feeling a bit rattled by the encounter with Fjord, she drove through Despar, nearly running a stoplight, slamming on her brakes at the last minute. I didn't see that coming, she thought. Not the light, Fjord. What was his plan? Was he working for Balzac? He seemed authentically to not like Balzac, but how authentic was Fjord? She had to admit, his being attracted to her – if for real – would not be all bad. He was hot. Yes, he was. He was eligible, which was rare around these parts. What if she had him wrong all this time? What if he was sincere? But she decided, no way; he was working a plan, and that plan wouldn't be good for her or for Ahnwee.

Leaving town toward Ahnwee, the car rolled along the empty highway, fields all around, lake off in the distance to the left. She saw the patch of trees before she saw the sign for South Pacific Jerky and decided to stop. She needed some sanity after a strange morning. No cars were in the lot except Sig's Cadillac, and she went in. He wasn't there, so she called his name.

"Hey," he said, coming in the back door. "I didn't hear you in that stealthy Prius."

He said for her to join him out back, and they sat in the sun in old lawn chairs facing the now harvested cornfields that bordered his property. All of Sig's flowers were dead and gone, but it was a beautiful Indian summer day, and they both knew this would be their last chance for this until spring. A book was open on the plastic table next to Sig's chair: *The Metamorphosis*. "The pastor loaned it to me," he said. "What a downer."

Sybil had not read it, but she was sure his assessment was accurate, given what she did know. "How's business?"

"Can't complain. Crush?" He said, and she thought about Jon Fjord. Sig held up an orange bottle, and she understood.

She took it and took a sip. Tasted like a time machine to a different decade, whatever that tastes like.

He asked about her business, and she said she could complain. She didn't mention the fact that she was barely making money, putting all her time into the campaign.

"You've sacrificed a lot," Sig said.

That made her flush – no one had said that since this all began, not even Sybil to herself. She told him how she appreciated his help and his skills, how he should run for office someday himself.

"A little person for congress? That'd be the day. No, I'm a freak show. I know it."

"You are not a freak show."

"I know that too, but to a lot of people I am. I hear them talking. 'Midget Jerky' is what most people seem to call my business, sometimes even when they are in the store. I was at the grocery Sunday in Despar, and a skinny teenager called me Tyrion Lannister."

"Who?"

"I punched him in the balls. Punk. But the point is…ah, I don't know what the point is."

Sybil thought he looked both sad and angry. She never considered what it was like for him. *She* thought she was an outsider? "Seems like it could be lonely out here by yourself, Sig."

He didn't answer directly, instead, "You have no idea how much I appreciate working with you and Ruby and everyone on this."

Sybil almost said, why wouldn't they work with him, but realized he had already answered that question. Instead, "Of course. You've been a tremendous amount of help. It means a lot to me." And it did – even though she hadn't considered it until right then. But yes – where would she be without Sig and Ruby and the campaign? Dan in a home and her all alone every day. She barely knew them before this all started, one more person in the area, someone to say hi to. But now she looked forward to seeing them at the campaign headquarters, at Flump's Café, on the campaign trail.

They drank the Crushes and looked out over the fields of corn.

"Yeah, it gets pretty lonely," Sig said.

Sybil thought, there is a lot of that going around these days.

"So," Sig started, a bit too loud, "enough about me. How are you hanging in there?"

"Good. I guess. I'm worried that I'm fooling myself." County Commissioner? What made her think she could be a County Commissioner?

"No, you're not fooling yourself." He took a sip of the bright orange drink. "Well, maybe."

"Hey – "

"But in a good way. Seriously. There's nothing wrong with believing in yourself. And you want to do it for your community, your town. Both the kind of traits anyone should look up to."

She felt a blush coming on.

"Do you think Balzac is running because he cares, or because he cares about himself?

"Himself, for sure."

"There you go."

Sybil thought about it. She realized that she wasn't doing it for her town, either. No, she was doing it for her friends. For Ruby and Pastor Farber, Augie and G, even Jackson and the girls. And even though his place wouldn't be torn down, Sig as well.

"How can you lose?" he said, speaking with his hands.

"Pretty easily."

He laughed. "Well, yes, but as long as you're doing it for the right reasons, as long as you're being true to yourself, you may lose, but you'll never be beaten. You'll be like Obi-wan Kenobi, you can be struck down, but you'll never be defeated."

She was buying all of it until the *Star Wars* reference.

Chapter 24: You Can't Go Wrong With Ann Taylor

True to yourself.

That's what Sig said. Be true to yourself, and while you may lose, you can't be beaten.

Sybil stood in front of the mirror looking at what she had become: a nearly middle-aged woman in all camouflage clothes, pandering to the lowest, the absolute lowest common dominator.

What's so funny about a campaign of ideas? Isn't protecting small towns an idea worth campaigning for? All her life, like all Americans, she saw politicians say and do anything to get and stay in power. She never wanted that for herself. All she wanted was her friends to be happy, her dad to live out his life in his home, and for herself to belong, to feel useful. Looked like a fail all-round.

The debate would begin in one hour, and part of her didn't want to leave the house. The other part wanted to leave the house and keep going until she hit the ocean. She wished she would become sick, just like in civics class, but her body was letting her down by not heaving.

The debate would be at Third Lutheran. When they had negotiated terms of the debate, Balzac got to pick the moderator and Sybil the venue. That seemed like a win, picking

Third Lutheran, until too late she remembered that many of the good people of Ahnwee thought she was some pervert from New York. Ruby and Sig reassured her that no one still thought that, given a well-earned distrust of the media, people's short memories, and her camo outfit. Plus, Sig said, people were listening. People did care about the town. Sybil thought that a nice idea, but optimistic: Ahnweeians seemed as passive as ever.

Then, when she had heard who the moderator was, it brought back memories, or, more accurately, nightmares. "Cara Carrington? Seriously? She's the moderator?" she said to Ruby.

"Don't worry, Sybil. It simply can't go as poorly as it did this summer," Ruby replied, knitting away on what appeared to be a third arm on a sweater.

Flashbacks of the press conference on the steps, the miserable news story, the whole mess. "Really? You don't think so? It can't go as bad?"

Ruby stopped knitting and looked over her glasses at Sybil for a beat too long. "Ya, sure."

"This will be different," Sig said. "No evil editing. Straight to cable access. Live to tape."

That conversation was two days before the debate at the campaign headquarters.

Now it was the moment of truth.

Sybil did not drive to the ocean. Instead, she walked alone from her house toward Broadway and the church. She generally liked this time of year, mid-October, the sound of leaves crunching under her feet, the cool, dry air. She noted the lack of pig manure smell and considered it a good omen. The strobe began, and she knew that the sun had fallen behind the wind turbine. The effect on Broadway was like a slow movie projector.

The debate was to start at seven, and she arrived at six-fifteen. Ruby and Sig were there already, as was Pastor Farber since it was his place. The cable access people were there, dragging around cords and black boxes of something, one pimply-faced kid setting up microphones at the two pulpits. Pastor Farber said he had a spare podium, a second pulpit was what he must have meant, Sybil thought.

"Sybil, you've got to get ready," Sig said at the front of the nave, looking nervous.

"I am ready. Ready as I'll ever be."

"But Sybil…" Ruby said.

"No buts."

They both looked surprised, and Sybil felt powerful, more powerful than she'd felt for a good while. She smiled. She looked comfortable in her smart red Ann Taylor power suit. A power suit that, after all the work of the campaign, all the walking door to door, after long days and skipping meals and daily Cleveland Crunches, now fit perfectly.

Sig and Ruby looked at each other and shrugged. "Well, good for you," Ruby said.

"Is this because of the 'true to yourself' crap I spouted?" Sig said.

Sybil didn't say anything, but it was true. Ruby looked at Sig and backhanded his shoulder.

"Ow!"

Sybil didn't care; she knew this was the right decision, or at least the right decision for her. They gathered by the front pew and went through the details. Ruby ticked off the list:

- Jackson and his colleagues agreed to stay away.
- Nothing was ordered from Let's Go Crazy Printz.
- Dan was safe and sound at Good Shepherd in Despar.
- No one invited Björkman or anyone from Wind Energy Now or the Big Moose Casino.

"Well, I'd say we have a green light. Knock them dead," she said to Sybil, squeezing her forearm, before sitting in the front pew with her knitting.

Pastor Farber stood by the door greeting people as they began to filter in. The faithful first, with Augie and G. Then the yard butt people from ten miles out of town, he in his rainbow suspenders and her in her sweatshirt with a picture of a grandchild. More people came, people Sybil knew as townies. She didn't see anyone looking suspicious, but couldn't help but worry that the busload of ringers was on its way.

There was a commotion as someone pushed their way past Pastor Farber and the old people entering the church. "Hey! Hey you!" that someone yelled from the back. "You up front!"

Sybil looked around, confirming that she was the only person standing up front. She pointed at herself.

"Yeah, you! I'm looking for a debate. It's in some church in a town called Amway. What is this, an AA meeting?" Cara Carrington yelled.

"That's 'Ahnwee,' not 'Amway,' and you found it," Sig yelled back. Sybil had not seen him next to her and now she felt guilty.

Cara Carrington pushed her way to the front. She wore a red pantsuit and carried a bag the size of a steamer trunk. "You're kidding me! I thought this was a serious gig. Why would an AA meeting host a debate? What part of 'anonymous' don't you people understand?"

"This isn't…" Sybil tried.

"Not for me to judge. County commissioner debate, right?"

Sybil said yes.

"Whatever. What does a county commissioner do, anyway?"

Sybil realized she really didn't know, other than they seem to tear down towns, but Cara Carrington didn't wait for an answer.

"Where's that zeppelin, Balzac? And who's his opponent?"

Sybil held her hand up as if in sixth grade.

"You?" Cara Carrington let out a little laugh. "He eats goodie two-shoes like you for breakfast. This is going to be like Mike Tyson boxing Stephen Hawking. Suggestion?"

Sybil didn't move a muscle.

"Go for pity. The best you can hope for is that the audience pities you," she said and then turned to Sig. "That counts for something, right shorty?"

"Why are you asking me about 'pity'?" Sig said. "Tulip!"

"Yeah, 'tulip' to you too, Keebler."

"Petunia!" Sig yelled, turned, and stormed off, out the heavy backdoor with a bang.

The much heavier hardwood front door opened again, and in came Jon Fjord. He gave Sybil a little wave. Cara Carrington saw him and pushed her way back down the aisle. Sybil watched as Cara Carrington tattooed herself to his side, saying something Sybil couldn't begin to hear from so far away. Fjord smiled at Sybil and shrugged.

And then it was seven. The pews were full, the wires strung, cameras set, mics checked. Sybil hovered, removed from the pulpit/podium, not wanting to look alone. Cara Carrington stood in the back too close to Fjord. Still no Harry Balzac.

Seven-o-five.

Seven ten.

And just as Sybil started privately celebrating Harry Balzac's no-show, the big front door swung open once more with a bang. A man in a dark suit came in, one hand on his bluetooth earpiece. He was followed by his twin if not by birth, and yet another, that one carrying an eighties-style boom box, all three marching up the aisle, before forming a line in front. The one guy clicked the play button on the boom box and out came the *Rocky* theme. In came Harry Balzac.

Sybil realized her mouth was hanging open like *The Scream*. Seriously? Three guys in suits for an entourage? And why do they look like Secret Service? And *Rocky*?

Harry Balzac wore a white suit even though it was after Labor Day. He began working the crowd, smiling and waving and pointing and calling people by name (some of the time accurately). He bent over to shake hands with the person in the back pew on the aisle, a corn farmer Sybil knew as a man who chewed tobacco and farted often. The man seemed reluctant but shook Balzac's hand. And so it went, moving up the aisle, shaking hands with the old lady retired schoolteacher who lived next to the lake, and the bald guy who lived next door to the church who looked like a wrestler from the sixties, and the nice old guy who always wore a fishing hat whose wife was housebound, right, left, right, left. Sybil felt her blood pressure rising. These were her people. How dare he walk in like a triumphant something or another? The music blared, tinny, a bit flat. The song ended, and the boom box guy hit rewind. The scene was weird enough with the music, now it was plain creepy without. The box clicked, the guy hit play again, and the stupid song returned. I mean, really, Sybil thought, *Rocky*? A boom box?

Then she noticed that it wasn't really working for him. No one seemed pumped up, more annoyed. Some people even refused to shake his hand.

Sybil felt proud of Ahnwee.

After what seemed like forever – Sybil even saw Cara Carrington check her watch – Harry Balzac took the podium to Sybil's left. The music continued, and Balzac made a cutting motion on his neck. The boom box man in the dark suit hit the button but the music didn't stop. He struggled with the boom box, shaking it, slapping it twice. Balzac looked mad, face smashed like a frog. The frustrated Secret Service-type guy flipped the old device over and ripped at the battery compartment, finally liberating a D cell and stopping the stupid tune.

"Hey, Harry," Sybil said.

"My dear," he replied with his best frog smile. "Where's your costume?"

She ignored him.

Cara Carrington walked to the front. "*Rocky*, Harry? What year is this? Jesus H. Christ − sorry father," she said as she passed Pastor Farber.

"Whatever."

Cara Carrington stepped up to the mic stand to one side of the stage and fanned though a small stack of note cards. "Well, the sooner we get started, the sooner we can go somewhere else."

Harry Balzac put one hand on his hip and held the other one out like an opera singer. "God-fearing people of Ahnwee…"

"Shut up, Balzac," Cara Carrington said. "This is a debate, not a speech. And I'm in charge, remember?"

"But of course," he said and nodded.

Sybil thought no way this was going as planned for Balzac. Wasn't Cara Carrington his choice? She seemed more pissed at him than anything. Sybil looked over the sanctuary. The cable access people were doing their thing. The three guys in suits were lined up on one wall, and it occurred to her that they were college aged at best. Ruby sat in the front row, knitting what looked like an octopus, while Sig had come back in when she wasn't looking, and G faded into a corner as if trying to be invisible. Fjord stood in back, arms crossed, and he nodded to her when she looked at him. And the pews were filled with the citizens of Ahnwee.

Cara Carrington explained the rules: she would ask the questions, and Sybil and Harry Balzac would answer them. The audience was free to do whatever it wanted to, come, go, whatever, but she encouraged them to think Maury Povich.

The first question was predictable: introduce yourself and tell the people why they should waste a vote on you. Sybil was ready, and recited her prepared comments, just as Drew coached her to do via Zoom. Time for new leadership, we've lost our way; our communities come first, big business is trying to take our homes, that sort of thing. Balzac countered by talking about the new bike path coming thanks to him, keeping taxes down thanks to him, corn prices up thanks to him, new businesses in Despar thanks to him.

"Reply, Ms. Voss?" Cara Carrington said.

"Those businesses in Despar that Mr. Balzac is so proud of have driven Broadway out of businesses."

Augie yelled from the back, "I'm still here!"

"Except for Augie's. Oh, and me and Ruby. Regardless, the big boxes on the highway are but a symptom of how big business is in charge."

"You bet they are, my dear," Harry interrupted. "They employ people. They sell good things we need at a good price."

"No interrupting, you big turtle!" Cara Carrington yelled. No doubt about it, she had a beef with Balzac.

"Big businesses such as Wind Energy Now," Sybil continued. "They give money to Harry Balzac's campaign so they can take our town. Harry does what they say, not what we, the people say."

To her surprise, the audience cheered and clapped. They were on my side? She thought. She kept going, "We need leadership on all levels of government – including the county – who put the people first."

"Dump Harry Balzac!" someone yelled from a pew, and people clapped.

They ARE on my side! she thought. She couldn't believe that the campaigning actually worked; people had been listening through those screen doors and as they walked by going into Target.

"Good!" Cara Carrington said. "That's the spirit!" she said. "Now, you, Mr. Harry too-drunk-to-get-it-up and calls-me-twenty-times-a-day-ever-since Balzac, question: are you too old and infirm to represent this district?"

He started stumbling through some answer Sybil didn't pay attention to, distracted by Cara Carrington's hyphenated attack. "…Youth is no qualification for County Board. You need Jesus. You need cunning. And most of all: experience. Now, my worthy opponent might have had some experience in leadership when she lived in New York all those years, but we don't know in leading what. Rumor has it that Ms. Voss is in witness protection, but that's just a rumor, so I don't pay any attention to that silliness." Balzac took a drink of water. He seemed to be back on his game after the rough start.

"Your turn, Mayor Voss. Is Harry Balzac too old to be a commissioner or even get it up?"

Sybil looked at Balzac, and he had his ever-present smile. But then she saw it: sweat. He was sweating. He was in trouble. She had no idea what to say; all her talking points were either used or forgotten by the strange scene. "I don't know about that. He's not that old." Utter silence from the pews. She shook her head. "That's not the point."

"It was the point to me," Cara Carrington said.

"The point is, we are a community. Look at you all. I've known some of you my entire life. Pastor Farber, God or no

God, you are the godliest man I've ever met, keeping the faith, never quitting. Augie, you ARE main street. Sig, you have friends. We are your friends. Ruby, you are my best friend and surrogate mother rolled into one. I hope I can be half the woman you are, and I'm sorry you miss your husband so much; no one can replace him, but I hope we, your friends, can make it a little less lonely. G, you need treatment like now, but you are one of us. And all of you. Sure, some of you are pretty eccentric, but I lived in New York, and I can assure you that there are eccentric people everywhere. That's not about small towns, that's just a community. No matter what, you all belong.

"And that's why I'm up here. I moved away and lost my community. New York was fun for a while, but I have to admit to myself that even if my mother didn't pass away leaving me to take care of my father – with no help from my worthless brothers I might add – I probably would have come home sooner or later, anyway. Can't take the small town out of the girl, and all that.

"Bottom line: we've had a rough time as a town. But we can change that. Together, we can fix things. We have a lot to be proud of. We can clean the lake. We can get rid of the manure smell. We can get a tower for the wind turbine that is tall enough so as not to destroy unsuspecting cars. We can get our own freeway exit. And most of all, we can keep others from taking our land.

"I love all of you, and I don't want to be anywhere else but Ahnwee."

The crowd jumped to their feet and cheered.

She looked at Balzac. He looked like he had acid reflux. She looked back at the applauding Ahnweeians. In the back, Fjord gave her a thumbs up. I'm going to win! She thought. I'm actually going to win!

Chapter 25: Vote Manchester United

Sybil lost in a landslide.

"I thought I was doing okay," she said through sobs.

Election night at the Dump Balzac headquarters was not a happy affair.

The polls had closed at eight and statewide returns began coming in via television. Everyone was there – the faithful and the less so. Sybil had on her now good luck red power suit. They got balloons. They got a Jell-O mold in the shape of a fish. Sybil had a banner made at Let's Go Crazy Printz: "We Saved Arnie!" Sybil had read it to the Let's Go Crazy Printz stoners over the phone, and she didn't care a bit. Spirits were high, and some spirits were consumed as well. The three old townies with big stomachs hanging over too-small belts started the night quietly before getting increasingly vociferous.

The first reports on county commissioner races scrolled across the bottom of the screen by eight fifteen: one percent of the vote in, Balzac: 298, Voss 3.

The three men with the stomachs cheered, clearly not getting the idea. The rest observed the men while still ignoring them.

"What polling place was that do you suppose?" Sig asked.

"Got to be in Despar," Ruby replied.

"We'll pick up momentum when we get to Sybil's base."

"What base is that?" an anonymous voice said.

"You know, her base."

"New York lesbians," someone else said from the back, inciting spiked-punch fueled hilarity.

Sybil considered the advantages of going home, parking the car in the garage, and running the engine.

"Don't worry, Sybil," Pastor Farber said. "It's just three hundred votes; meaningless."

The thirty or so hopeful party attendees stood around the workbenches and electronic parts with their punch in hand mostly facing the old analog TV with its back off, wires hanging, parts glowing. They had found the old set under a table in the campaign headquarters and Sig got it working with a converter box and tinfoil. On the screen, Cara Carrington went on about some neo-Nazi elected to the school board of some town in some southern state. They had to wait until eight forty-five for the next county commissioner scroll, since, as Augie pointed out, county commissioner races are generally of less interest than legislative races or even mayoral races, even in an off-year election. Who really knows who their county commissioner is?

Four percent of the vote in, Balzac: 666, Voss 3.

"I didn't pick up one vote in the last half-hour?"

People had theories and made excuses.

The three men with the stomachs did the wave.

The crawl said that Jon Fjord was re-elected. No shock, given that he ran unopposed. Still, Cara Carrington made a point of saying how this was a bright man with a future in state politics and that if he was out there to call her so she could "interview" him. The quotation marks were actual air quotes from Cara Carrington.

At twenty past nine, county commissioner races were

again announced. Twelve percent of the vote in, Balzac: 2072, Voss 655.

"Good!" Ruby said.

"Good?" Sybil said.

The party was down to about twenty people. The three men with stomachs sat on folding chairs, pumping their fist in the air, chanting "We believe!" "We believe we!" "We believe we are going to win!" Sybil wondered how these men of the prairie knew football chants as if they were watching Manchester United.

At ten, the station put a star next to Balzac's name. Seventy-five percent of the vote, Balzac: 22,191, Voss: 656.

"You picked up another one," Sig said.

"Sig, the star means it's over. They declared victory for Balzac," Ruby said.

And then, as if on cue, Cara Carrington said, "And in an interesting race, Harry Balzac, fourteen-term county commissioner and type-two diabetic, has been declared the winner over newcomer Sybil Voss, an Iraq war vet and New York dominatrix."

Instantly, as if they were never there, the only people left at the We Saved Arnie! party were Sybil, Ruby and Sig; Pastor Farber, Augie, G, Jackson, the too-thin girl, the newly ex-teen redhead, and the tall raven-haired bombshell.

Cara Carrington continued, "Voss is the mayor of little Ahnwee, population two hundred souls, and was cursed in her effort to move to a higher office by a crime wave of car vandalism sweeping the tiny town."

"Car vandalism? Sybil said.

Everyone looked at Sig.

He smiled.

"So that's where you went during the debate," Ruby said.

Sig shrugged. "So I carved a drawing of a tulip on her

hood. Sue me."

Sybil couldn't believe it. She was sure she would win after the debate. But the debate was held in Ahnwee, and she probably did win that. But it was broadcast as well – didn't people watch the debate on cable access? Didn't they see how brilliantly she did? But she knew the answer. No one watches cable access. She felt all eyes on her, even if they weren't. She felt naked. She felt like *Carrie*, only with pig poop, not pig blood. Was everyone laughing? No. they weren't. They looked as sad as she was. "Oh, gad darn it. I thought maybe…" they sat, looking at their shoes. "Now what?"

"Time to learn how to swear," Ruby said.

"I guess I should concede."

"To whom?" Ruby said.

"I could call Balzac."

"Why bother?" Ruby replied.

That's when Sybil began to sob. Sig knocked back a shot of punch. Pastor Farber scooped green Jell-O up with a fork. Ruby was not knitting.

No one said anything. Then, G said, "I'll go blow the shit dike."

"Oh, shut up about blowing the dike," Ruby replied while rubbing Sybil's back.

Pastor Farber said, "I guess go home and regroup tomorrow. What else is there?"

"Start packing?" Augie replied.

And, like that, everyone was gone, leaving Sybil and Ruby with a giant mess of old Jell-O and nearly-flat balloons hovering at half-mast.

After a good forty-five minutes of picking up and throwing away, Ruby and Sybil sat down at the old worktable once more. Ruby put a quart of Old Granddad on the table. There was about a third left.

"Where did you find that?" Sybil asked.

Ruby pointed to the far corner. "Fat old football hooligan fuel." She unscrewed the cap and took a drink from the bottle. "Sweet mercy!" She shook her head side to side and handed it to Sybil.

Sybil took a sip. It hit the spot.

"Well, there you go." Ruby said.

Sybil took another sip and put the bottle down. "I really thought…oh, heck."

"Can't say we didn't try." Ruby took a turn with the bottle.

"Yup, we tried. You know what? It was actually kinda fun." Sybil wiped her cheeks.

"It was, wasn't it?" Ruby took a second pass. "Even the camo?"

"Especially the camo." She laughed. "I know where we went wrong."

Ruby asked where.

"We should have had Jackson's girls campaign for me."

They both laughed as if they were on ether at Def Comedy Jam, before Ruby said in a serious tone, "Yeah, maybe."

They each took a turn with the bottle, Sybil's posture deteriorating while Ruby showed no signs of impairment.

"I did have fun," Ruby said. "Ahnwee can be so god-awful boring. Always has been. I don't want to lose my home and business, but it won't be the worst thing to happen. A new start, a new town. Maybe Minneapolis. Time to move forward and start living. I forgot how to do that after my husband died. Maybe, win or lose, getting involved in Save Arnie was just the kick in the pants I needed. Got the blood flowing."

They sat. And sat. And sat, staring at nothing. Then, Sybil asked, "Do you miss him?"

"Sybil, every minute of every day."

Sybil took one last sip. "I miss my dad." She thought that maybe she said something wrong, comparing her dad, who was still alive, to losing a husband, but then she lost her train of thought as a solid buzz took over.

"I know you do. I know," Ruby replied.

"Hey there, pussy cats," Jon Fjord said from the doorway.

Sybil and Ruby looked up, neither seeming surprised by the sudden appearance of Jon Fjord, a reaction driven mostly by the Old Granddad and a little by shell shock. "Come on in, Fjord. I'd offer you a drink, but it's almost gone and Ruby and I aren't interested in sharing."

He looked about as he came over to where they were sitting, but rather than parking it himself, he opted for leaning on the workbench. "I'm sorry you lost, Sybil."

"Are you here to gloat, Fjord?" Sybil said.

"No. I thought you might need some support. Looks like you found it," he said, pointing at the bottle.

Ruby started to get up. "Well, I'm going to leave you two kids alone now, and find my house."

Sybil asked if she needed help getting home, half-hoping she would say yes so she didn't have to be left alone with Fjord. Not that she was scared of him as a feral man, especially given her state, more she had a tingling feeling of the awkward variety.

But Ruby said don't worry about it, and walked with no visible impairment to the door, letting lose a thunderous hiccup on the way out as her only clue to the Old Granddad.

Fjord sat in the vacated chair. "How you holding up?"

"I don't want to talk about it, Fjord. What do you care, anyway?"

"I told you – I wanted you to win. In part so you'd succeed, and in part so Harry Balzac wouldn't."

She tilted the bottle up one more time, hunting for the last sip. She straightened back out, contemplated throwing the bottle across the room, before setting it down next to her. She noted he had on a waist length leather jacket and jeans, looking more like he was going uptown rather than to a victory party. "How come you're not celebrating your win?"

"I was, but after six terms and running unopposed, the party wasn't much of a party. I thanked my supporters at the bar, shook some hands, slapped some backs, and got the hell out of there."

"I thought you liked that sort of thing!"

"Sometimes."

They sat. Sybil considered what a lightweight she was since she was all goofy from about two fingers of booze.

Fjord looked around. "Nice campaign headquarters." They sat some more, staring off into nothing. Then, "Now what?"

She turned her head rather jerkily, as only a tipsy person can do. "Now what, what?"

"What's next for Ahnwee?"

She didn't answer.

Chapter 26: All Is Lost – or Is It?

Sybil drank coffee, holding the mug with both hands, while looking at the laptop on the kitchen table.

"Now you can move home," Drew said.

It was early, and Sybil could see Drew was again in her bathrobe with her makeup suspiciously smeared about. Sybil saw in her little thumbnail that she looked even worse. She held the cup with both hands because her hands were shaking. She didn't have that much to drink, but Sybil didn't drink often, and she thought how that was probably for the best.

"Maybe, Drew. Probably. I'll have to go somewhere."

"What are we, a consolation prize?"

"I didn't mean it like that, Drew. Maybe I did, I don't know. I miss you, you know? But I was hoping…I don't know what I was hoping anymore."

"Come home. Everyone says you need to come home." Drew's pleading smile turned to eyes wide, mouth slack.

Sybil looked behind her as Fjord's tight naked butt walked in the kitchen. "Is there more coffee?" he said, assumedly unaware of the Zoom session underway.

She turned back to Drew who smiled, and Sybil was glad.

After an understandably late start, Sybil spent the afternoon at the store. There was a lot to do. Delayed business, for sure – she'd barely been on eBay during the run up to the election. What orders she had gotten had not been shipped in a couple weeks. Plus, she needed to order boxes to pack everything up, both at the store and at home.

She was strangely at peace. She had tried. In fact, she had given it everything. Now reality: time to think about what's next. New York, "home" as Drew called it? Maybe. Probably. But it would be so far from her dad it was hard to imagine making that work. If her good–for–nothing brothers would help out…but she wouldn't ask them to water a house plant, much less look after and make decisions for their father. Most likely outcome: on about day two or three, one of them would take him fishing, and he'd fall overboard and drown after a boisterous rendition of the *Gilligan's Island* theme.

She could move to Minneapolis. What Minneapolis lacked in the way of subways, it made up for in art galleries and trendy restaurants. She already had the right clothes; all she'd need is a bicycle and a Co-op membership. You could do worse.

Now add Jon Fjord into the equation. Was that just a hookup, fueled by Old Granddad and the need to change the subject? Maybe she had Jon Fjord all wrong. Maybe he wasn't a completely self-centered, passive aggressive egomaniac. In fact, she had ample proof that he was anything but self-centered in one important aspect.

It was just a hookup, she decided. That's all. There was no equation to consider. Still, no regrets there, no matter what else happens. It had been a lonely few years, and having a bubble-butted man in her bed definitely hit the spot.

On the Thursday after the election, Sybil ventured once more to Flump's Café. She considered lying low one more day but decided to thank everyone again for their hard work.

On the way by Knotty Knits, Ruby walked out the door. "Pie?" she said, locking the door behind her.

In the diner, they picked stools in the middle, while Augie fiddled with a vintage Gameboy.

He put it down and poured them both coffee. "Well, there you go."

"Indeed," Sybil said, looking into her coffee as if reading tea leaves.

"What now, Mayor?" Augie asked.

"Nothing. There's nothing left to try. In a week there'll be the county board meeting."

"The one that will seal the deal on the bulldozers," Ruby added.

Sybil couldn't bring herself to say that aloud. "I suppose they'll give us a few months to move."

Ruby asked if Sybil would move back to New York, and Sybil shrugged. "You know. Dad."

"How is your father?" Pastor Farber asked.

Sybil jumped. She hadn't noticed him sitting three stools away. She said he was doing about the same. "I'm sad he'll live to see the town go. You know we are descended from those original German settlers? He is third generation Ahnweeian. I guess that makes me fourth."

"I don't have any idea what I'm going to do," Ruby said. "There's not much to do. First I outlived my husband, and now I outlived my town." A tear traced down her cheek.

Sybil was shocked; Ruby was a rock. She thought she should say something, but what wasn't clear, so she opted for asking Augie, "What about you? What do you think you'll do?"

He put a foot up behind the counter and leaned one elbow on it. "Hard to say. I don't have a lot of options. I could move to Despar, but only over my dead body. Maybe Granite Falls; I have a cousin there. I'm only sixty, so I'd have to find work. I doubt I could open another diner, but maybe someone would hire me as a cook. Again, hard to say. I might just kill myself."

Sybil couldn't believe what he just said, both his age and the suicidal ideation.

"Augie, I understand," Pastor Farber said.

Sybil wondered what on earth he meant by that, but Augie continued.

"Oh, don't look at me like that. I don't have any kids, no wife. I'd have no diner, no home. Not even a town. Don't worry; that's the least of my options, I'd say. No, I think Granite Falls."

Saturday she packed up some Steubenville for UPS to take away on Monday, and in the late afternoon she drove into Despar to visit her dad. Her every-other-day visit plan took a hit with the campaign, but she was determined to make up for it, at least in the time remaining. She went right to his room, but he wasn't there. Back in the hall, she called, "Dad?" looking right and left. She heard noise down the hall and followed it. Music played. A waltz. Strauss, to be exact. In the rec room, Sybil found several nurses and most of the residents – some unassisted, some with walkers, and some in chairs – dancing. And in the middle was her father, cutting a rug in perfect timing, alone, arms out, as if dancing with someone. Sybil watched. This was something. He looked happy. The music ended and he stepped back and bowed, as if the Good Shepherd was Windsor Castle.

"He's doing great," came a voice from behind. She turned to see the usual young nurse who took care of her dad. "Moving around seems to help."

Sybil thanked her, and went to where her father now stood, frozen, as if waiting to be activated by the next song.

"Hi, Dad."

He didn't say anything. He didn't look at her.

"Who were you dancing with?"

He looked ahead, and then he looked down, right into her eyes, making Sybil jump.

"Your mother. Isn't she beautiful?"

Her eyes swelled. She touched his arm lightly. "Yes, Dad. Yes, she is."

"Like I said," the voice said, having followed Sybil without her realizing it, "doing better."

Sybil spent another hour and a half there, an hour longer than typical, but there were no more moments like that. Jingles, yes. Commercials, certainly. Still, it had happened. He had looked happy out on the dance floor. If he could only imagine dancing with his bride, well, so be it. He was happy, and that's what matters.

Sybil drove back toward Ahnwee. Cresting the hill between the towns, she came across South Pacific Jerky, parking lot empty. She hadn't talked to Sig since the election Tuesday. On a whim, she decided to stop. Maybe to thank him one-on-one for all his work on the campaign. Maybe to talk about her dad. Maybe to hint about Jon Fjord spending the night. She didn't know. Maybe all three.

Inside, he was on the phone. He slammed the receiver down. "There you are! We've been looking for you!"

She asked why.

"You won't believe it!"

She wanted to know what was going on, but he said he didn't have time to explain and insisted she follow him into Ahnwee. He led in his 1975 Cadillac Fleetwood, going way too fast for her tastes. As he descended the hill into town – speed limit turning to twenty-five – Sig blasted away at over fifty, timing the wind turbine perfectly like the old pro he was. Sybil obeyed the law, falling way behind Sig, but the town was small, and she'd find him again soon enough. She, too, timed the high-tech windmill spot on, and just like that, she was on Broadway.

She soon found Sig's car, parked in front of Dirty Girls. She parked next to it, even though she had second thoughts about having her car seen there. She did have the only Prius in the county, after all.

As she got out, she finally saw Sig by his Cadillac; he wasn't tall enough to be seen over it. He waved and said come on, hurry. Next to his car, she saw a shiny black Lincoln Navigator, a car unusual for its value in these parts.

"Why are we going in here?" she said, amping up the disdain for the sake of her self-assessed feminist principles.

Sig didn't answer; they walked in, "Send Me in Coach" by John Fogerty blasting. No customers were in the main room. In fact, no dancers, either. Sig seemed to know where to go, walking across the back as if an expert. At a curtain, he pulled it back, and there stood Fjord and Jackson and the newly ex-teen redhead, the tall raven-haired dish, and the too-thin girl with the perfect Minnesota accent, backs turned looking down at something. Then Sybil heard it. Was it cats fighting? No. Maybe a wounded hippo? No, but looking over Sig's head, she could see she was close.

County Commissioner Harry Balzac.

He sat on the floor in the corner, crying like no one ever cried before. Thunderous. The wail of a thousand baritone babies wet and bottleless to boot. He looked up. "Sybil! Praise Jesus you are here!" he held his arms out without getting up. She didn't move.

"Ol' Harry here has got himself in a bit of trouble," Fjord said to Sybil.

"They are threatening me, my dear! Blackmail!"

"Blackmail?" Sybil said.

"Blackmail is such as dirty word," Jackson said.

"It's more on the order of wanting to make a trade," the redhead in a black bustier said.

"Yah, for sure, then," the too-thin girl in a Japanese school-girl outfit said. "You leave our town alone…"

"And we won't post these pics on Snapfish," said the raven-haired model in a bikini.

Pictures? Sybil wondered. And if on cue, the too-thin girl held out her iPhone. She scrolled through a series of pictures of Harry Balzac with his pants off dancing on stage with the two girls, pants off with a girl under each arm, pants off drinking out a large bottle of Jack, and finally Balzac passed out with both girls snuggled up to him doing selfies. Sybil was stunned by what Balzac was doing in the pictures, by the whole scene in front of her, and by the enormous size of Balzac's penis. "Dang," she said.

"I know my dear. How could I suffer such an indiscretion?"

She was referring to his penis. She wasn't surprised at all by his indiscretion, but she thought it better to jump on his train of thought.

"Harry called me this afternoon," Fjord said. "Seems he came in late last night and hasn't left."

"Thank you for helping me, my boy," Balzac said to Fjord.

"I got here, and Harry was on stage, pole dancing."

"He's a pretty good dancer, considering his bulk," the too-thin girl said.

"Luckily no one else was in to see it, being so early. But I suppose that doesn't help, given there are pictures."

"Wait until I tell my friends that you blackmail your customers!" Balzac bellowed.

"Now, Harry, let's get a couple things straight," Jackson replied." One, I'm not blackmailing you, the girls are."

"Here's a tip, Balzac," The raven-haired one said, leaning over, poking him in the chest. "Always tip your dancer. How many times have you been here, and the most I've gotten from you was a Canadian Loonie."

"Second," Jackson continued, "You're not going to tell anybody anything. Why? Because there's no need for anyone to find out, because, third, you're going to stop trying to condemn Ahnwee."

"Sybil, can you help me? Please help me." He held his hands out as if a blind beggar.

This is wrong, Sybil thought. Stooping to blackmail. How unseemly. All along, she had tried to do the right thing. To help people understand that small towns like Ahnwee were valuable and worth protecting. To run an honest campaign, fatigues notwithstanding. It wasn't right to be like them. It wasn't right to win by all means. She looked at the girls. She looked at Jackson and Sig. She looked at Fjord, who really seemed to be enjoying himself. She looked at Harry Balzac, sobbing. She thought: frack the right thing.

"I'd do what these nice women are asking, Harry. Otherwise, I think you're in deep doo."

Chapter 27: It's Not Over Until It's Over

The following week, Sybil, Ruby, Sig, and Fjord – yes, Fjord – plus Jackson and the girls went straight to Flump's Café after the county board meeting. They told Augie and Pastor Farber all about it.

"Nicely done, Mayor," Augie said.

Sybil tried to hold back a huge smile, but it hurt her face, so she quit trying.

"Harry Balzac was masterful," Ruby said knitting away on the octopus sweater.

"What did Balzac say?" Sig said, filling his own coffee from behind the counter. "'Small town life is endangered from all sides, blah blah blah. All they are asking is to be allowed to have their town, yadda yadda. Sounded rather familiar."

It worked. Ahnwee would not be condemned. Ms. Abbie Hoffman had been there to see it, and she had the strangest expression as she congratulated Sybil for their victory. Gas? Stoned? Sybil couldn't quite place it. For sure, sincere was not in the running. Balzac, on the other hand, said nothing to Sybil. He focused on Jackson, the raven-haired beauty, and the too-thin girl in the back. At one point, Sybil saw Raven point to her eyes with her peace fingers and then at Balzac, and Sybil could have sworn she heard him sigh.

"Did you see him talking to the reporter for the Hutchinson paper? It seems saving Ahnwee was all his idea from the start," Fjord said to the group.

It felt weird to Sybil having Fjord there. She had never thought for a minute that Fjord was on their side, no matter what he said. But then that day at Dirty Girls proved otherwise. Sybil never imagined that hooking up with Fjord was anything more than that. Yet a little over a week later, here he was. Not only was he there, they had gotten together twice more since election night. She struggled to sort it all out in her mind: in fact, she couldn't believe it yet. Why not? Was it that she was insecure, and she couldn't believe that Fjord was interested in her? Or could it be that it had been too long since she had first-rate, scream-and-scratch sex?

No matter. Strange or not, she was totally into him. Yes, she liked him a lot.

Still, she kept it quiet, not telling Ruby or Sig anything yet. Why? Could it be that after all the bad things she said in the past, she was embarrassed to be wrong about him? She had a lot to think through. Meanwhile, she was happy that Fjord seemed to go along with staying closeted, without a word spoken between them.

I'll figure out Fjord later, Sybil thought. Now it's time to celebrate. They had won. She had won. They had, she had, saved Ahnwee.

"We have a long way to go to save Ahnwee," Ruby said. "We are safe from Wind Energy Now, but we still have the lawsuits by the Big Moose Casino and Björn Björkman to contend with."

Sybil didn't care. She won. She never won, but that day she won. To have success snatched out of the jaws of failure was...well, it just was. It was the Super Bowl, and Sybil was the MVP. It was the Nobel Peace Prize, and she was flying to

The Hague first class. It was the Oscars, and she had won best actress. It was none of those things, but it felt like it to Sybil.

It was only five but it was already dark. But inside the café, it was light and getting noisy and starting to feel like a real party. More and more people filed in, having heard the news. The usual three old fat men in overalls came in, hooting and hollering. Mouthpiece Alfonse Schreiber came, wearing no coat and still in flip-flops. Fjord and Sig were having their own conversation Sybil couldn't hear. They laughed. Next to Sybil, Jackson yucked it up with Raven, Redhead, and Too-Thin, who were dressed quite normally, in jeans and leather jackets.

"The thing I don't understand is," Sybil asked Raven, Redhead, and Too-Thin, "obviously you took most of the pictures, but who took the pictures of Balzac dancing with all three of you?"

"We are sworn to secrecy," Raven said, Too-Thin making a zipper motion across her mouth. But Sybil knew, mostly because she already guessed, but also because they didn't have much of a poker face, looking right at Fjord.

Augie poured coffee and served pie at a frantic pace. The strippers talked to the three fat guys. Alfonse Schreiber joined Sig and Fjord. Sybil helped Augie serve the pie. Looking around the small diner, she almost cried, thinking about all the support she had gotten from her friends in the room.

Her friends. Great to have a sort of boyfriend, especially with winter coming, but that was nothing compared to what having real friends meant to her. Sybil, Ruby, and Sig looked at each other as if sharing the same thought, and Sybil bent down and hugged Ruby, and bent way over and hugged Sig. Now she had real friends in Ruby and Sig. Not to mention Augie, Jackson, and Pastor Farber.

She looked around. "Where'd Pastor Farber go?" Sybil

asked no one in particular. Several people shrugged. Sybil thought it strange that he would leave, and stranger still that no one seemed to notice, least of all her.

Pastor Farber had returned earlier to Third Lutheran but no one had noticed. Now he was slowly, deliberately putting on his finest vestments once again. Ahnwee was saved, or at least on the way to being saved. Therefore, the church stays, and so does its minister. After months of secretly hoping Ahnwee would be bulldozed, he was once again stuck in Ahnwee.

Therefore, after getting dressed in his best clerical finery, he went to work trying to throw a rope over a rafter in the church. He had ordered a climbing rope from Amazon just for this purpose after his failed overdose. He didn't know from climbing ropes, but it had gotten four-and-a-half stars and the price was right. He stood in full vestments in the center of the church, spun the rope around and heave-hoed it in the air. It went about one-tenth the distance it needed to travel to even touch a rafter. He tried again, and again not even close. He thought, Charlton Heston wouldn't have this much trouble with a rope. He tied the end in a noose first, so there would be some weight to get some momentum. He gave it a twirl, and it fell short by half. He thought, who knew hanging yourself would be so hard? Explains the big market for guns. He needed something heavier, so he cinched the noose tight around a hymnal. The red one. That worked, the hymnal going over the rafter on the first try, then hitting him in the head on the way down. He tied the loose end around a pillar. He put a chair under the rope and put his head through the noose. He thought about how he looked. How long would he hang there until someone found him? He hoped it would be a long time. He didn't know why.

He leaped, kicking the chair at the same time, chair falling with a bang. He dropped, rope stretched tight, until once again he stood on the floor. It hurt his neck, and he thought he would need a chiropractor for sure, but he was definitely not dead. He considered what went wrong. Everything went according to plan, the rope still tied off.

It must be a miracle, he thought.

Months later, he still considered it a miracle, even after discovering that some climbing ropes are made to be stretchy, so that you don't break your back when you fall. Miracles come in lots of forms, after all. Perhaps it was divine intervention that drove him to buy the wrong rope for the job, a rope that was long enough to stretch the one foot it needed to save his life.

Back at Flump's Café, someone had spiked the coffee. The three old men with big stomachs seemed to particularly benefit, and they were greatly enjoying conversation with Raven, Redhead, and Too-Thin. Sig was offering to arm-wrestle all comers at the end of the counter. Ruby and Augie snickered about something. And Fjord was standing a little close to Sybil.

"The next Ahnwee Days is going to be particularly sweet," Fjord said.

Ahnwee Days seemed like a hundred years ago to Sybil. She thought about how that's where she found out about Björn Björkman, the starting point of all this. She thought about Let's Go Crazy Printz, and how they owed her more banners. Speaking of banners, "Where's G?" Sybil asked, noting his absence. Again, people shrugged. Who knew when G would come or go?

In fact, G was quite busy on the hill over Ahnwee at the shit pond. After Sybil lost the election, he had his marching orders, or so he thought: blow the shit dike.

After the election and before the hearing, G had done nothing else but work on how to do it. He didn't want to let anyone down, so he spent all week sitting in the back room at Flump's Café using Augie's laptop, trying to figure out just the right mixture of fertilizer and gasoline and other stuff in order to make a massive explosion. (Augie assumed he was looking at porn.) He had not heard about Balzac's predicament. When he was satisfied with the formula and the plan, he set out to get a U-Haul. Why a U-Haul? Because the white supremacist website he found for making bombs recommended it. Which was too bad, because he could have walked to Despar to rent from Little Moose's Truck Rental, but to get a U-Haul meant hitchhiking to Hutchinson, and nobody picks up a twitchy hitchhiker. It took him over a day to walk it, night and day, mostly because he got lost a couple times. And when he got there, he didn't have a credit card so he couldn't rent anything. Finally, a bit of luck: standing outside the office, a man in just the right sized truck pulled up and left the motor running. G had his U-Haul.

After loading up the U-Haul with the bomb stuff, G drove to a spot where the road was the closest to shit dike and rolled the truck slowly into the field. He worried about driving across the bumpy crop rows, that he wouldn't get his deposit back, a nagging worry that made no sense given he had swiped the truck. He stopped at a pre-selected spot next to some scrubby trees, right alongside the earthen berm. G thought it perfect, as out of sight as he could find. It smelled vile, even G knew that, despite his destroyed sense of smell; it was more that he could feel it on his skin and in his mouth. He went to work. The flashlight in his mouth, he monkeyed around with a cell phone, just as the website said. It was hard to do, and his hands got cold, making it harder. Finally, he got it all set, walked fifteen minutes to a great vantage point to see the whole show, called the number on the cell-phone timer, and…nothing happened.

Then G remembered: there wasn't any cell phone reception in Ahnwee.

He left the truck and walked back to his grain elevator and considered his options. He wished he could search the web, but he had to use Augie's computer to do that, and it was by then the middle of the night.

G sat at his workbench and thought through the problem the rest of the night before exclaiming, "Eureka!" A clock! He could rig a timer! He had a clock. Several timers to be exact, sitting in arm's reach, being necessary to be precise when cooking crank. He learned that from *Breaking Bad*: details count. In fact, he liked that show so much, that he added blue food coloring to his cook, not to deceive as much as in honor of.

He went to sleep. He awoke the next afternoon, the same afternoon as the county board hearing he knew nothing about, and off he went back to the U-Haul with a timer in hand.

And that's where he was when the party at Flump's Café was in full force: hooking up the timer. It took him no time at all. He set it for twenty minutes and off he went back to his special vantage point to watch.

No one asked where Björn Björkman was. Björn Björkman had not heard about the town's victory at the county board meeting, not that he would have cared.

After he finished the chores for the day, he decided to investigate the U-Haul truck he saw parked on his property that morning. He had passed by on the highway and there it was in the field, plain as day, not well hidden at all. He didn't worry at the time. He figured it was just some hippies traveling across the country. He could relate. When he was young, he did the Kerouac thing for a summer, dropping acid on Haight Street, tuned in, turned off – or was it tuned out and turned on? – sleeping in a Peugeot in Gateway Park, going to Seattle and panhandling in Pioneer Square. The whole deal. So if a couple kids driving cross-country needed to crash on his property for the night, that was just Jim-dandy.

If they stayed two nights, however, Björn Björkman would get his gun.

Sure enough, the truck was still there. Björn Björkman parked on the side of the highway and walked across the field, shotgun in hand. He kept quiet, hoping to catch whoever was in the truck by surprise. He thought it would be fun to scare the shit out of the hippies and – who knows? – maybe catch them having sex or something. He got to the passenger window and was disappointed to see no one inside. He opened the door, and found nothing of interest, other than a bag of White Castle trash, which wasn't that interesting. He slammed the door, stepped back, and ran his fingers through his hair. He looked around but didn't see anything out of the ordinary, so he walked back to his truck, started it up, and backed out onto the highway.

The party finally winding down, Ruby and Sybil left Flump's Café. Standing out front, they said their goodbyes but didn't move right away, enjoying the cold, fresh air and lights of Broadway.

A fireball erupted on the horizon. The light from a half-mile away hit first, giving Ruby two seconds to say, "What the hell is that?!" before they were hit by the sound of five thousand pounds of ammonium nitrate and gasoline blowing a U-Haul – and one side of the shit dike – to smithereens. A mushroom cloud reminiscent of Bikini Atoll grew in the sky. A blow-you-backwards wind followed, a pig shit wind.

Björn Björkman was only a few hundred yards away downhill from the blast behind the wheel of his truck. He put his elbow over his eyes, blinded by the explosion. The roar was louder than anything he had ever heard. Louder than Mother Björkman's hog call. Louder than M-80s in a metal garbage can. Louder than Led Zeppelin in 1977. When he finally lowered his arm from his eyes, he saw a cloud ascending from the top of the hill and a tsunami of thick, brown muck descending toward him.

He floored the pickup, squealing it in a circle and speeding away from impending doom, toward Ahnwee below. There was no place else to go, lest he get swept away by the brown pudding. Faster and faster went the pickup truck with the brown slurry close behind. Driving like a maniac, Björn Björkman stayed ahead of the deluge – hog sludge apparently is not as fast as a real tsunami – his lead beginning to grow as he entered Ahnwee. He was going to make it, he thought, and felt relief. This feeling was soon replaced by a sense that that he had forgotten something.

That something was the wind turbine. The huge blade hit the side of the pickup square on, like a wedge in a sand trap, golfing him and his truck a good fifty feet in the air, landing upside down in someone's backyard.

He laid on the roof of the truck, not having worn his seatbelt, long believing seatbelts to be a U.N. conspiracy. He was dazed. He might have blacked out for a moment, but he was unsure. For sure, he was sore as all heck but didn't feel anything broken. Gingerly he crawled out of the broken passenger window. He got himself up on his elbows and finally to standing by pulling himself up on a rusty swing set, looking toward a house in front of him, downhill. In the window, an elderly man stared at the truck and him, mouth agape. He heard and felt a rumbling but wasn't sure if it was his head or for real. The man in the window appeared to move his gaze, now looking past him. Björn Björkman turned to look, right as a Diamond Head-worthy wave of pig shit hit him.

When Pastor Farber, rubbing his sore neck, heard the explosion, he ran outside the church and saw the mushroom cloud. The pig shit wind nearly knocked him over, but he braced himself and shielded his eyes. The swirling cloud darkened the sky. Disoriented, he walked down the steps in front of the church, wind pushing back. What had happened? In the distance the Ahnwee water tower, fresh with "Despar High Rules" graffiti, twisted and fell with a crash. A new sound grew, a low rumbling muck sound, plus the occasional crash and car alarm. Bud came running down the street faster than he probably had in years. Behind him, from up Broadway, the tsunami of pig shit moved as fast as a car driven by an old lady on Sunday, flowing around and enveloping buildings and sweeping away anything not nailed down. The dog ran to him and stopped. Standing by the pastor's side, he proceeded to bark, since what else was a dog to do.

Pastor Farber, frozen in place, witnessed a four-foot wave of pig poo race toward him, boiling with assorted lawn butts and campaign signs. And then, defying all logic, Pastor Farber defended the church. Perhaps it was instinct; perhaps it was his true feelings coming out, that he did in fact want to save the church. He stood, as if braced for a tug of war, holding out and up one hand in the universal sign of "Stop." Eyes of steel, teeth clenched, he had nothing to lose. He yelled in pure seminarian mission zeal into the din, "Behold His mighty hands!"

The pastor's best line ever – taken right from *The Ten Commandments* – was wasted with only the dog to hear it. But his effort was not. Just as the shit flood got to Third Lutheran, it split into two streams right at the steps to the church, at the feet of Pastor Farber, arms outstretched. The shit flowed past on both sides, the dog barking at each.

Pastor Farber stood his ground, determination fueled by success. Then, as if an apparition, Björn Björkman flowed by, nearly submerged in the brown syrup with only his face exposed, arms thrashing in the air. Just as quickly as he had come, he was gone, swept downhill in a flood of irony.

Later people would speculate as to how it could be that the church was the only building to survive – the nuances of topography, curbs, and steps protecting the largest building in town – but Pastor Farber knew: he had parted the shit sea.

The explosion knocked G on his back. He got up, and jumped for joy at his success, until the shit-wind knocked him again off his feet. He got back up. He could still see the lights of Ahnwee below, the tsunami boiling downhill. He saw Björn Björkman's truck get some serious hang time, landing out of sight. The shit hit the wind turbine. Being much newer and stronger, it did not topple like the water tower, but instead the blades threw brown goo into the air as the blade stirred the manure. G watched as the shit-wave hit the first house and the next and the next, until all the houses on the south side of town were surrounded in gunk. The brown slurry flowed down Broadway. G couldn't see the good Pastor on the steps, but he did see it break into two branches at the church before rejoining on the other side. It slowed, viscosity not lending itself to the now almost flat terrain.

A sea of brown covering the town.

Maybe blowing the shit dike wasn't such a great idea after all, G thought. He couldn't imagine why they wanted him to do it. He considered that for a good long time, before deciding that maybe this would be a great time to see what California was like.

It took Sybil and Ruby mere seconds to realize what was going on. Sybil ran in the café and yelled, "Run for your life!" The people inside had heard the explosion and didn't need to be told twice. Sybil, Fjord, Ruby, and Sig ran down Broadway with Augie, Jackson, Raven and Too-Thin, Alfonse Schreiber and all the rest trailing. Sybil looked back to see the shit-flow sliding down the street. It was like a tidal wave except in slow motion, making disturbing slurping sounds. Sybil and Fjord each grabbed Ruby's hands and together they ran faster. The group ran to the end of Broadway, though a vacant lot, and finally to the drainage ditch the separated Ahnwee from the casino parking lot and loading dock. Ahead a handful of people gathered, looking up at the mushroom cloud and watching the Ahnweeians fleeing like Indonesian vacationers. Sybil, Fjord, and Ruby went in the ditch together, dead cat-tails and mud slowing their progress. Sybil thought that if the brown stuff got to them now, they'd surely drown in the pit soon full of shit. But they got though the cold mud and made it to the other side, the rest of Flump's Café celebrants right behind them. Fjord and Ruby turned to look at the unnatural disaster as Sybil leaned over, hands to knees, huffing and puff-ing, reminded once again that she hadn't worked out in ages.

Coming out of a poorly-lit loading dock door, the big *Downton Abbey*-watching guard with long hair yelled, "Hey, there's a reason why there's no road between Anal-wee and our casino. Drive around through Despar like everyone else." Sybil looked up at him, as he looked past her for the first time. "Holy shit!" he said, pointing, before retreating though his door with a slam.

Sybil and company watched as the rolling brown dough approached the ditch, everything it had found riding along – a mailbox, lawn furniture, small trees, patio umbrellas, a formerly pink flamingo. Out of the loading dock door came the guard again, this time with Malcolm Moose followed by a stream of casino employees. Together, the handful of Ahnwee refugees and the casino spectators watched as the smelly slurry, with one last drop of momentum, made it to the drainage ditch, the flood stopping not twenty feet from the casino. No one said anything, not even Malcolm Moose, mouth looking something like a goldfish's, opening and closing wordlessly. The shit slowly flowed down the drainage ditch and into Lake Ahnwee, turning the water from its usual unnatural Day-Glo yellow into a light brown, a strange steam rising.

Finally, all was quiet, except calls for help from multiple houses. Just minutes after it had all begun, the scene of brown devastation was complete.

Ruby turned to Sybil and said, "Did anyone ever explicitly tell G *not* to blow the shit dike?"

Chapter 28: Hitting the Trifecta

A sweet, Minnesota prairie breeze blew from the north, bringing nothing but fresh clean air to the occupants of Broadway. "Here's your soy latte," said Sybil Voss, former Mayor of Ahnwee, handing the cup over to a waif in formfitting running gear. The old yellow lab lay next to Sybil, dog drowsing in the shade of the coffee cart, as Sybil toiled.

"I'd like an iced mocha, please," said the next person in line, a large woman with a fanny pack.

"You betcha." Sybil hated saying "you betcha," but she found the tourists expected it and liked it.

The banner hanging over the street said, "Second Annual Founder's Day" spelled correctly. The "second annual" part dated it and was inaccurate, but Sybil didn't care. What Sybil knew was that a year and a half after the flood, the line to Sybil's coffee cart grew to six impatient type As. She and her helper tried to step it up. She could see weather might be a problem, so better to make some money while the sun literally shines. They predicted thunderstorms for midday, and it looked to be coming true – with any luck the parade would come off before that happened, but after that, to Sybil, let it rain.

At Ahnwee Days two years before, she could never have

conceived the sight in front of her: actual tourists walking back and forth, every parking spot on Broadway taken by Subarus with bike racks and Priuses other than hers. A cacophony of click-clack on the pavement from those special shoes that snap on bike pedals. A good half of the tourists in bright spandex covered with logos as if they are racing in the Tour de France, the other half with cameras and wearing Patagonia hiking shorts and Smartwool socks, even though walking a two-block main street was as close to hiking as they were going to get.

Whatever. Annoying tourists or not, even on an average day she made more money selling coffee confections than she used to do in a month of retail at New York 'Tique. Now with a successful Second Annual Ahnwee Days, she figured she could open a 401K. The fact that her sign on the side of the cart said, "Coughy" didn't do a thing to depress her or keep away business.

Looking up from her espresso machine, Sybil could see she wasn't the only one making money. Augie and a couple of kids from Despar he hired were selling Flump Burgers as fast and they could get them in the buns. Up and down Broadway new vendors plied their wares: stained glass, painted rocks, candles, string "art," driftwood "art," barn wood frames, tie-dye, and quilts. A Peruvian guy selling CDs played the pan flute over a recording. Sybil made eye contact with Ruby, selling her yarn a few doors down. Ruby smiled.

It was all hard to believe any of it happened.

The day after G blew up the shit dike, Sybil toured the remains of her town with the governor and a reporter in a National Guard helicopter. The slurry of pig waste covered yards, enveloped houses, and buried roads. The wind turbine continued to turn, churning the brown goop, still throwing the occasional clot up in the air (it would make for the best video on the evening news). A florescent brown cloud drifting skyward from the lake, a phenomenon that would never be fully explained, other than to note that there was something about the chemistry of the pig poo combined with the cocktail of lake pollution that caused a chemical reaction. For the next few days, the glowing steam could be seen from as far away as Despar.

Sybil and the governor saw that, in fact, the town had not been completely destroyed; the church remained high and dry. As they hovered, out the front door ran Pastor Farber, white sheet around his face like a Tuareg of the Sahara, waving his hands in the air in the universal signal of please save me from this ocean of pig shit. Bud stood next to him as if he were Lassie. The governor and Sybil watched as another helicopter arrived and pulled the reverend up and away, and the old dog, too.

The next day's *New York Times* story exclaimed, "You-Know-What Hits the Fan in Minnesota Town." It continued, "The two hundred mostly elderly in the town of Ahnwee, Minnesota, received a lesson in gravity and fluid dynamics when a dike holding back millions of gallons of pig waste was bombed by terrorists." The article went on to describe the scene, and then, "Some who lived in higher and more fortunate spots walked out of it to smell-less safety; however, most got trapped in their houses and, after the worst night of their lives, were rescued off their roofs by helicopters in a scene resembling a brown Hurricane Katrina."

The terrorist angle was never fully explored, and the rest of the country seemed to accept that. That ISIS or whomever would stoop to blowing up a shit dam and flooding a Minnesota prairie town with brown soft serve was beyond question. Where would they strike next? More fences were added to the Canadian border, people's hand lotion didn't make it through

TSA, and billions were added to the defense budget. There was one copycat, a teen, first identified as Middle Eastern but later corrected to Ojibwe, who blew up a porta potty in Duluth with an M-80, to nowhere near the same affect.

The good news was that no one died except Björn Björkman, which to a jaded nation played more humorous than sad. It definitely kept the late-night talks in materials for a week. Said one: "In Minnesota, a man died when his vehicle was hit by wind turbine blade, tossing him into a giant flood of pig waste. The man's name? Lucky Björkman." In fact, it took two days to find Lucky Björkman's badly boil-covered body near the north end of the crap field. The experts said he likely had survived for a while and was trying to backstroke out of the sea of waste, before becoming fatigued and eventually sinking.

The town enjoyed a good deal of fame, to say the least. The reporters on the scene couldn't get enough of describing the smell. "It is like you are in a porta potty that fell off a truck and rolled over and over." "Imagine a gang of Hell's Angels eating six plates of jalapeno poppers and all passing gas at once in an elevator." "It's like falling into an outhouse last used by a sumo wrestler after eating fatty salmon with lots of miso." Those were some of Sybil's favorites. She never mentioned that it usually smelled like that even before the dam break.

Sybil appeared on morning network shows, talking about the fight to save Ahnwee and how small towns were an endangered species. It was a message that resonated with the American public. But fame is fleeting, and eventually Kanye West did something or another and Ahnwee was no longer the shiny object de jour. But the national media attention did its job. Disaster funds were secured. Clean up began with bulldozers, hoses, and straw. Buildings were rebuilt, better than they ever were. They even cleaned up the lake, the Army Corp of Engineers replacing all the soil in and around it, planting native grasses, and giving it a fresh start of reasonably clean water from Björkman's own well. Remarkably, birds nested and eagles soared, and fish swam. Finally, a bike path between Willmar and Despar, which as originally planned was to go nowhere near Ahnwee, was rerouted right through town.

At the same time, a curious, more durable narrative developed, not about a town destroyed but a church saved. Pastor Farber became the story. He did all the morning talks, discussing the nature of miracles and opening hearts to hope. Donations poured into the church, and he was able to restore it better than new, complete with a new gym for teenagers to get off the street...should teenagers return to Ahnwee. Perhaps more important than the church was how Pastor Farber changed himself. He saw what happened as truly a miracle. He was there. He parted the sea like Charlton Heston, a thick brown sea at that. There was in fact a God with a capital G! Those stupid existentialists were wrong. God had a purpose for him. He was sure of it. He poured his heart into his church once again and, importantly, set up a website talking about what it meant to believe. He wrote a book that landed on the bestseller list, *The Power of Faith: How I Parted the Brown Sea and How You Can, Too.* Krista Tippett interviewed him. And while no additional people from town went to Third Lutheran, thousands from all over the world did, to see where the miracle had happened. They attended his services. They prayed for their own miracles. They tithed. And at a table in front of the miracle church at Ahnwee Days two years later, they bought little Ziplocs of genuine Ahnwee Miracle Pig Poop from the minister.

Ahnwee, destroyed by shit, had in fact scored a trifecta: bicyclists, pilgrims, and shit tourists.

Standing on the busy sidewalk slinging coffee drinks, Sybil thought about all that and more. On Broadway there was a new ice cream parlor, a bike repair and rental business, a card shop and scrapbooking emporium, a bistro/wine bar with a chef from Minneapolis. There was a new bank. Ruby's Knotty Knits yarn store was bigger than before and full of stock and happy customers. And, next to the new playhouse presenting an Equity production of *Waiting for Godot*, was Sybil's coffee shop: New York Brew. Every morning she opened at ten. Late for a coffeehouse, but no one in Ahnwee commuted anywhere, and the place was for tourists driving two hours from the Twin Cities. Every morning she wore camo. A brand is a brand.

Sybil could see Ruby look across the street at Augie and his humming food stand. He waved at her. It was more than solidarity. Ruby and Augie were an item as well. After the shit storm, Augie crashed with his relatives in Granite Falls, but they turned out to be too annoying to deal with, both having fallen under the spell of Amway. Meanwhile, Ruby rented a flat above Norm's Hardware that wasn't much, but it was a roof. Soon, Augie, hearing from Ruby about her good luck for Amway-free accommodations, moved in across the hall. Nothing makes the heart grow fonder than proximity, and soon they were the Luke and Laura of Despar. They had known each other since they could crawl; "Better late than never," Augie told Sybil once.

Down the block, Sig has a line to his jerky tent, his canvas sign saying "Genuine Ahnwee Jerky!" Even from a good distance away, Sybil heard him say, "Petunia!" in regard to something. Mrs. Björn Björkman rubbed his neck and he smiled. He looked embarrassed. After the explosion, no more was heard about Björn Björkman – or his estate – owning Ahnwee. The missus didn't know about such things, and the

Björkman operation went bankrupt from lack of insurance, since Björn believed insurance was a ruse of the Trilateral Commission. After a very short period of mourning, Mother Björkman could be seen more and more frequently at South Pacific Jerky/Ahnwee Jerky, until there was no denying it – they were an item. An odd-looking couple, to be sure, since she must have outweighed him by a factor of four, but good for Sig, Sybil thought. Yet another romance to come out of this.

One person she sort of missed was G. No one had heard from him since his job well done. Sybil guessed that a meth cook, already living underground, would probably have no trouble not being found.

Across the street, Jon Fjord stood in line for a Flump Burger. He looked at her, and she averted her eyes in hope that he didn't see her looking. Her I'm-depressed-that-I-was-thrashed-in-the-election hookup, which at first showed so much promise, had fizzled. After that fateful November shit-flood, she went home with him, and there she stayed until she couldn't deal with it any longer. After all, who gets spray tans in the prairie of Minnesota? Hell, who gets them anywhere? she thought. No hard feelings: they had some fun. The sexual chemistry was there, but Sybil wanted a relationship built more on being comfortable on the couch and a bit less on going out every night and glad-handing townspeople.

"One iced mocha," said Raven, handing the customer with the fanny pack the cup.

Sybil smiled at Raven. Raven, AKA Shelby – now there's a comfortable relationship, Sybil thought. Here's a person I can lie on the couch with, legs tangled up, and watch *Orange is the New Black*. Who would have guessed? Certainly not Sybil. One day, not long after the flood and shortly after Sybil moved into a temporary FEMA trailer court, she ran into Shelby at Fleet

Farm. She was out of a job until Dirty Girls could be rebuilt. Shelby, much to Sybil's surprise, looked like a normal person; it just never occurred to Sybil that Raven/Shelby would ever wear sweatpants. They chatted about all that happened and what they were doing these days, and before she knew it, they were having coffee and then dinner and then breakfast, and then etcetera, etcetera. Now they lived in Sybil's newly rebuilt house, and Shelby went back to college online while driving a forklift at Wind Energy Now and helping Sybil out with the coffee biz once in a while. A bit May-December, granted, but they were happy with it. While anyone with eyes would agree Shelby was an attractive young woman, no one would guess she was once a stripper. Not that Sybil cared if people knew; eat your heart out – those washboard abs were only for Sybil now.

The sun disappeared behind ominous clouds. The kind that look like grey buns. Maybe the parade would be okay, she thought; she could hear the band beginning to play. Fjord had arranged for the Despar High marching band to lead the way. The crowd parted and lined the sidewalk as the pimply-faced young people marched proudly and earnestly in the green and white despar high colors. Sybil knew the song but couldn't put her finger on it. Then she figured it out: "Fight the Power." Behind the band followed a white convertible with Mayor Jackson, Redhead, and Too-Thin sitting on the top of the bench seat, waving. He wore a suit and they wore cut-offs and tight t-shirts with "Dirty" and "Girls" stretched over each boob. They saw Sybil and especially Shelby, and waved emphatically.

Mayor Jackson. Sybil hadn't run for re-election. No, enough was enough. But when Jackson got elected, she said to Ruby, "WTF?"

Ruby replied, "Well, it was his turn."

The next car passed with Miss Despar High in an evening gown, with a magnet on the door saying "Savories Bistro." Next was a float dedicated to the flood, all in brown crêpe paper, with Boy Scouts throwing out fun-sized Tootsie Rolls. More cars and more floats, including one by a group of pilgrims who made a giant papier-mâché hand to resemble how Pastor Farber held out his hand stopping the shit tsunami. Next was a float from the Minneapolis Aquatennial parade, which wasn't clear as to what it was supposed to be since the heavy metal guy who towed it a hundred and thirty miles did it at seventy, and most of it blew apart. It was either a float to encourage child restraint seats or a sailboat. Finally, the float she was waiting for: a tractor pulling a flatbed with elderly people in lawn chairs, each holding a small American flag. The sign on the door said, "Good Shepherd Nursing Home," and there was Dan holding his flag. Sybil jumped up and down waving and yelling his name, but he didn't move, staring off catatonically.

She leaned over and scratched the dog behind the ear. He groaned. While he may now belong to the minister, she knew he would always be the town's dog. He had been a metaphor for Ahnwee: old, beat up, seen better days, but still there. Now he was out of place, no longer able to sleep in the middle of Broadway, not fitting in with the brightly colored spandex city people on composite bikes, or the Lexus crowd getting in touch with America, or the pilgrims trying to believe in something, even if it's the resilience of a church in the face of shit. No, to Sybil, the dog was a remnant of the old, disaster-prone Ahnwee.

When the band got to where the road now went around rather than through the wind turbine, they did a perfect two right angles and came back down Broadway for another pass. The car with Miss Despar passed again, magnet on the side now saying, "Big Moose Casino and Trailer Park." She looked at Fjord across the street. He shrugged and smiled back.

After the shit storm, Malcolm Moose no longer wanted anything to do with Ahnwee, and no more was heard on that score. Instead, they bought land on the other side of the highway, and they had their trailer park. But the worst was yet to come for Malcolm Moose and the casino. Because of the bike path and all the publicity about small town plight, the state added an exit off the freeway for Ahnwee, cutting across Big Moose land, which the state annexed by – wait for it – breaking a treaty. Court cases were expected to last for years on that, but either way, there was now an exit for Ahnwee.

The clouds looked even worse, but the parade was just about over. Finally, the Good Shepherd flatbed went by again, and Sybil looked for her father. He wasn't there. Had he fallen off? Then she saw him, behind the last float. For the second time in the history of little Ahnwee, Dan marched proudly down Broadway buck naked, this time in what appeared to be an Egyptian military high step. She waved at him as he went by. He looked at her and waved back. She half-laughed, half-coughed, half-cried with joy.

Sybil still couldn't believe it. All's well that ends well.

Sirens went off, making all the good Midwestern prairie people stop where they were and look at the sky. Shelby pulled out her iPhone, cell phone service now available from all major carriers with the new towers on the edge of town. "Tornado warning," Shelby said.

Then, like a mob of meerkats, all eyes looked west, over the lake, where a huge tornado suctioned up water, cattails, and bird nests.

"#$%@#," Sybil said.

Author's Note

Small towns aren't dead.

Forgotten, maybe. Ignored, certainly. Under-resourced? You bet. But far from dead.

In the past 25 years, I have had two jobs that took me to Greater Minnesota. First, with Rural AIDS Action Network, where I traveled around the state meeting and working with the most incredible, caring, and loving people you could ever imagine. Second, with the state health department, where I had the opportunity to work with local public health in every county in Minnesota. What all these folks had in common was that they were overworked, underpaid, and bringing their A-game every day to the people of their community. Truly inspiring.

So, by writing about small town life, I want to present a different narrative than hopelessness; one that, while completely incomplete, is one that is a bit more supportive of the challenges they face. And if not that, then one that is at least a little funny.

On another topic, the big question in this book is: Who's land is it, anyway?

And of course, we all know the answer to that. As I write this, I am sitting on Dakota land, as is all of fictional Ahnwee, about half of Minnesota, and a big chunk of the United States. Taking this land, and all Indigenous lands, is one of two original sins of the United States that define and curse us to today, sins that need to somehow be addressed through reparations or something, Heck, maybe we can start with honoring existing treaty rights.

This is why I include members of the Dakota nation in this book: because it would be impossible – or even ridiculous – not to. I also include a paragraph or two on the 1862 Dakota War. I do this for two reasons. First, I think it would be impossible to ignore it – that war defined the place where my fictional town sits and continues to define the real Minnesota to today. Second, I can't help but notice not many of my fellow white people seem to know that there was a war. Who can blame them? When I went to school in Minnesota, there was not one mention of this incredibly important and formative event. History class seemed mostly focused on Europeans, like a certain Genoese asshole with a funny hat.

If you want to learn more, here's a homework assignment: read *Bury My Heart at Wounded Knee: An Indian History of the American West* by American writer Dee Brown. Then go read actual American Indian authors, not white guys wring about American Indians, such as Louise Erdrich, Sherman Alexie, Linda LeGarde Grover, Tommy Orange, Stephen Graham Jones, Diane Wison, etc., etc. You'll thank me later.

Acknowledgments

Books are hard to write. First, there are a lot of words, and I can't type worth a damn. Second, you have to know stuff, which actually is the least of my problems since I'm a guy and therefore I'm sure I know pretty much everything. Third, you have to make up a lot of stuff, which, while a great deal of fun, can also give you a headache.

All that is one reason writing a book is not the act of an individual but of a village of supporters and yes-men-and-women and non-binary people who help you put all those words into some semblance of order.

Nah, I'm kidding. It was all me. I can't blame it on anyone else.

A giant pig shit pond high over a town? That'd be me. A meth addict dressed as a cowboy? Me. An existential minister? Me again. For better or worse, I have no one to blame but myself for creating a small town founded by a German doomsday cult.

That said, I still have a long list of people to thank, because throughout this they have not blocked my calls, ghosted me on social media, or called the puzzle house and told them to send a wagon.

Thank you to all the fellow writers who have offered me

advice and support in writing group after writing group having to read early versions of this when it was even more drivel than it is now: Steve W., Megan, Steven P., Don, Ed, Vince, Marcela, Teresa, Ross, Drew, Barry, Mo, Adam, Mary, Flo, Kate, Abdul, Brian D, Eimile, Paul, Jake, James, Lauren, Kindi, Amit, Brian M, and many, many more I'm sorry to forget at the moment.

Thank you to John Anderson – not the 1980 presidential candidate (well, him too) – the incredibly talented photographer who took my candid author photo during a meeting where, from the looks of it, I was saying something inappropriate to my colleague.

Thank you to the Loft Literary Center, where I learned how to write, sort of.

Thank you to Elizabeth Ford, publisher extraordinaire, for your talent and belief in this project, and most of all, for having the same warped sense of humor as me.

Thank you to all the literary agents and publishers I queried and rejected me. Who's sorry now?

Thank you to my fantastic book cover artist, Eilidh Muldoon, for her inspired work and for only communicating through emails so I don't have to figure out how to pronounce her name.

Thank you to Luca Guariento, for the fabulous job on the book layout and dealing with all the last-minute changes.

And most importantly, thank you to my incredible wife, Mariann, who always believed in me, and if she didn't, kept it to herself.

About the Author

Hi there; it's me, the author. Did you know authors write these, even though they are in third person? "William E Burleson is the author of blah blah blah." Not me, nope. Instead, I thought I'd dispose of the fourth wall that I'd been bumping up against all story long and just tell you what's the what:

I live, work, and play in Minneapolis, Minnesota, where I have spent virtually my entire life.

I am married to a wonderful woman who never rolls her eyes at me. Not once. Amazing. We have two loving little dogs and a perfect-sized little house a stone's throw from the Mississippi, where said dogs get two walks a day.

I am the proud owner of possibly the most random curriculum vitae ever. Here it is, in order: I've been a movie theater usher (best job ever). I went to the U of M (as in Minnesota – follow along) for architecture (which I really sucked at and dropped out). I sold cigarettes at Woolworth (which I was good at, and I got to see Prince once). I was a corporate retail manager (hated) and a glass artist (loved). I finally got around to getting a bachelor's degree in my forties (cobbling together a degree in non-profit management and human services). I parlayed that into a job in HIV services and prevention (yes, including handing out condoms in bars), then at the state health department ("Syphilis Elimination Coordinator" – it was right there on my business card), and, for my last few years of gainful employment, as a government communications lackey.

Since then I've sworn off making money by starting a little boutique literary publishing house: Flexible Press, LLC. I think I have finally found my calling. (Maybe. We'll see.) Best part of this project is getting to know so many cool authors and giving money away (every book benefits a non-profit).

Finally, maybe you want to know about writing credits: over the last twenty years my short stories have appeared in over two dozen literary journals and anthologies, including *The New Guard*, *American Fiction* 14 and 16, and *The Prague Review*. I've been nominated for a *Pushcart*, won an award (for humor!), and have placed in many other contests.

I have also been published extensively in non-fiction, most notably my book, *Bi America* (Haworth Press, 2005), as well as for the *Hennepin History Magazine* and a bunch of other stuff that you can look up yourself at williamburleson.com.

Cheers!

– Bill

For more about *Ahnwee Days*, a map of Ahnwee, and other extras, visit williamburleson.com/extras.